I0623165

SHE'S THE ONE
WHO THINKS TOO MUCH

S. R. CRONIN

To June, with deep thanks for listening to my stories when we were little, for all the creative help with my writing once we were grown, and most of all for giving me the chance to know how wonderful it is to have, and to be, a sister.

And to Akira Kurosawa, a famous Japanese filmmaker I rediscovered after creating these seven stories. Two of his most famous films must have slipped into my unconscious decades ago. I thank him for the insights that came with them.

Warning: You Are About to Enter Ilari

Welcome to the thirteenth century in a universe almost identical to your own. The one major difference here is the existence of *Ilari*.

Ilari (el ARE ee) is a small hidden coalition of principalities in far eastern Europe. It has never been conquered thanks to its natural protection and the magic of its people. The lack of outside influence means that much will be new to you. But fear not, you have tools to help.

A map of *Ilari* is located at the front and back of this book. The back also has a description of the twelve nichnas (tiny principalities) that comprise *Ilari*.

Ilarians do not use any variation of the Roman calendar, as Rome never invaded their realm. Each chapter starts with a picture of the Ilarian calendar. The darkened area shows when that chapter takes place.

Ilarians use nine-day anks and forty-five-day eighths of the year. Each eighth begins with one of their eight seasonal holidays. Details are at the back of the book.

They have some unique words with no English translation. Those words are also given to you at the back of the book.

On the last page, you will find a list of the characters you are about to meet.

All of this information is also on the website *Seven Troublesome Sisters* at https://troublesome7sisters.xyz/ and can be downloaded and printed.

Ilarians of the 1200s have contact with the outside even though legend says interaction with others used to be rare. Ilarian scholars know facts about world history and have some idea of current events beyond their borders. What they know matches what you know because the world outside of *Ilari* is like ours.

However, the world inside is filled with surprises.

Enjoy your visit!

The Map of Ilari

The Year of Immense Concern

~ 1 ~

The Worries Begin

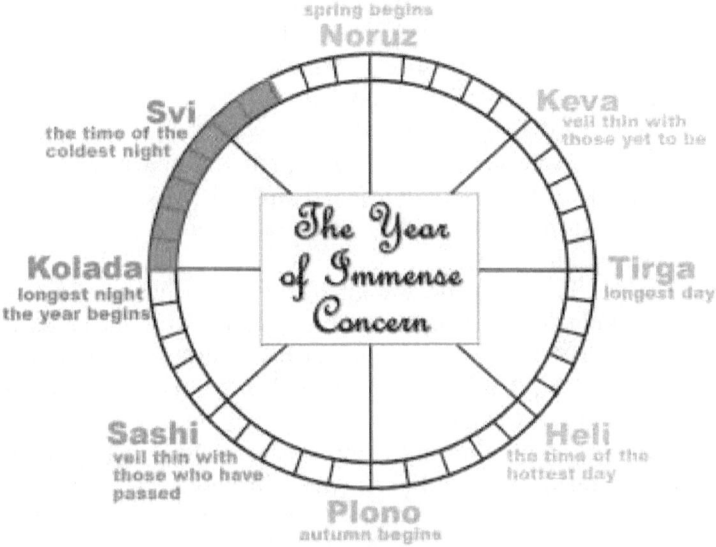

spring begins
Noruz

Svi
the time of the
coldest night

Keva
veil thin with
those yet to be

Kolada
longest night
the year begins

*The Year
of Immense
Concern*

Tirga
longest day

Sashi
veil thin with
those who have
passed

Heli
the time of the
hottest day

Plono
autumn begins

"What's your name?"

His smile as he asked was everything it was supposed to be. Playful, inviting, even a bit sensuous. I knew his name, of course. He was a prince of Pilk, the richest nichna in Ilari. He ran his eyes over my modest farm girl's clothing, and his appreciative nod told me I'd been picked for the size of my breasts.

Perhaps my mother was right. Seducing a prince could be as easy as seducing a farmer. It certainly had been easy enough to attract this one.

"Ryalgar," I answered him.

"Like the rock? Your family has studied science?" His gaze moved up to my eyes, and he seemed satisfied.

"Yes, Your Highness. My father is a soil expert."

"Please. My name is Nevik. We're just two young people here, two tidzys, looking for another with whom to celebrate the winter solstice, right?"

He picked up my hand and brushed my knuckles with a whisper of a kiss. The gesture melted away my apprehension as I reminded myself this was exactly why I came here.

After that, we ate, drank, and danced amid the wild burning torches and countless candles that signaled a proper Kolada celebration. As we flirted and talked, this prince became more than eligible royalty; he was someone I enjoyed. When the night waned, I accepted his invitation to wander off and have sex in one of the many private rooms in the palace.

It wasn't my first time, but the truth was that for one my age, I was relatively inexperienced. Many of my younger sisters had embraced the promiscuity permitted around holidays with far more enthusiasm. I was kind of embarrassed to be that intimate with a person I hardly knew.

Yet, Nevik was gentle and kind as we did what people do to celebrate Kolada. His fingers lingered on the soft fabric as he removed the rich red dress my mother had insisted be tailored for me for this night. Then he held me and he stroked my hair. He even told me I was beautiful.

Me, beautiful? With my common brown hair and eyes, and my strong-boned farmer's build? Me, still unmarried at my age, with six younger sisters all hoping I would get on with it so they need not embarrass me by marrying first? Me, the somewhat awkward oldest daughter who frustrated her parents by preferring her studies to the company of men?

I demurred and told him he was handsome, too, but I told the truth. He had curly brown hair and his eyes crinkled when he smiled in a way that made me want to smile too.

He held me closer and said, "You mean it, and you've no idea how seldom I get a sincere compliment."

I had to laugh. "That's true for everyone, not just a prince, you know."

After his surprise faded, he looked at me with respect.

2

"You're right. I never thought about it before, but those who flatter to get their way are in everyone's lives, aren't they?"

Odd as it seems, I think that's what did it. That moment. We looked at each other and both felt we'd just spent the longest night of the year with someone interesting.

"I'd like to see you again," he said.

"That would be nice."

****

To be honest, my mother *hadn't* told me it was just as easy to seduce a prince. She'd told me it was just as easy to *fall in love* with a prince. She'd said it over and over, since I was a little girl. I knew she had ambitions for me and my sisters, and I suppose she wanted to make sure I got the point.

I did but, despite her plans, I never imagined a prince in my future. I knew I wasn't the sparkly type, the sort to attract the eye of a Royal who could have any woman he chose.

Now, I worried her oft-repeated proclamation was right. I found Nevik attractive, sweet, and capable of carrying on an intelligent conversation. How rare was that? The truth was I liked him. I *could* be in the process of falling in love with a prince.

I realized Mom had *never* claimed it would be equally easy to get him to fall in love with me.

I decided to go to the Velka.

There were one or two of them at any farmer's market, selling herbs and potions. These women of the forest were reputed to be helpful in all sorts of matters, not just the medical and women's issues us farm folk consulted them for. Perhaps they had something to keep me from falling in love, so I wouldn't humiliate myself and my family by becoming enamored with a prince who didn't want me.

It couldn't hurt to ask.

I'd never spoken to a Velka before, which was unusual as most mothers took their daughters to the Velka at puberty, so the young woman could learn how to remain childfree until she was ready to marry. But my mother broke with tradition and taught me about such issues herself, after she got the herbs and supplies from the Velka for me.

Even when I'd been intrigued by the Velka as a little girl, my mother always grabbed my arm and pulled me away.

"I just want to look," I'd complain, pointing to the pretty jars on display, but the hardness in her face told me I'd better not push the issue.

I often asked my dad why my mother disliked the Velka and wouldn't let me near them. Each time he brushed me off saying it was a complicated matter.

Whatever her reason, I knew she wouldn't like what I was about to do now. So, I told her I was going to ride my horse over to the market to buy some ribbons and buttons to make my clothes more attractive. She knew of my interaction with Nevik, of course, and knew he'd invited me to join him in the mountains for a few days. She'd been acting particularly affectionate to me since his invitation came, and she didn't question my need for new ornamentation. She even pressed a few extra coins into my hand.

"Don't skimp." She smiled.

Of course, if I *did* marry a prince, the dowry to my parents would pay for those ribbons and buttons a thousand times over. Not that I was being cynical about this.

****

A warm winter sun melted the snow on the ground, and I stepped with care to avoid the mud and slush as I made my way into the noise of the crowded stalls. Although tools, clothes, drinks, and food of all types were sold, the smell of winter cider filled the air today.

The Velka woman was older than most; her gray hair turned nearly white in the long braids she wore wrapped around her head. Like my father, she had a slighter build than most in Vinx, and she looked at me as though she was pleased to see me.

"Ryalgar. It's a pleasure to finally meet you." She reached out her hands to me in a gesture of warmth and even familiarity.

"Do I know you?"

"No. Of course not. Forgive my forwardness. I know *of* you. You're Markita's daughter. We'd hoped to meet you when your menses began."

"Uh, yes. My mother chose to handle things differently."

An odd expression passed over the older woman's face but she only said "How can I help you today?"

Out came the story of my handsome prince and my fear that my growing affections wouldn't be returned, leaving me as an even more pronounced failure for my family. The Velka woman listened with kindness, so I told her everything, more than I'd told my sisters or the few girlfriends I'd stayed in touch with and certainly more than I'd told my parents. I saw out of the corner of my eye that another had arrived and taken over handling the customers.

"It's to your credit that you don't ask me for a potion to make sure he falls in love with you instead."

"You have such a thing?"

"Of course not. Would you buy it if we did?"

"Of course not. Who wants a man who's obtained like that?"

"No sensible woman." The Velka laughed. "The best I can do for you is to offer something to dull your own emotions, making you less receptive to his allure. I don't recommend it, though, because it will dull all your feelings. Grief, joy, fear. You need these to experience life."

"Maybe I could purchase a bit of it? For emergencies?"

She laughed again and her laugh was warm. "Unfortunately, it's slow to act and slow to leave, so it's not something you pop into your mouth when you're in a predicament. I can give it to you as a powder. Perhaps having a little of it tucked in your pocket will make you feel stronger when you go to the mountains with your prince."

I thanked her and made the purchase, checking to see how many coins I had left to buy the items my mother was expecting me to bring home.

"Don't be so quick to use this potion," she cautioned. "You don't yet know this prince's mind, do you?"

As I was leaving, she added "Ryalgar, come back here any time to talk. Especially as things get more complicated, the way they always do. I think you'll find we Velka are quite good at listening."

****

"You don't recognize your own beauty, do you?"

We were snowed in, cozy inside a little mountain cabin he'd arranged. We'd arrived in a horse-drawn sleigh and now a fire he'd built crackled and lit the walls. Two glasses of full-bodied red dinner wine sat on the dresser, barely touched. I wondered if he realized the entire setting was a fantasy come true for a country girl like me.

"Your hair isn't 'just brown.' It's the color of a fine stout. As are your eyes. Your body is fit and confident. I don't care for tiny women. Look at the size of your breasts!"

I'm sure I blushed at this, and he laughed.

"I'm becoming quite taken with you," he said and I could tell he meant it. I touched the Velka's tiny pouch of powder in my pocket and considered throwing it into the fire when he wasn't looking.

Then he ran his fingertips along the side of my face, and his other hand found the small of my back. He pulled me closer to him with enough force to make me feel wanted and enough gentleness to make me feel safe. By the time his lips were on mine I'd forgotten all about the potion I'd tucked away.

We had lots of sex over the next two days. I'd never had a partner more than once, and it fascinated me to discover how two people could learn to please each other more with repetition. Oh, so he liked that. My goodness, he could tell I liked this. No wonder married couples stuck together. It became more fun each time we did it.

I was sad the morning we had to leave, but knew it was time to go. We'd gone through all our provisions, and the cold, clear day would make for easy travel.

"Each back to our chores," he said as he finished the last of the hard bread and cheese for breakfast.

"What chores does a prince have?" I regretted it as soon as I said it. Of course, he did something other than play all day.

"Surely you're not that naïve."

"I'm not. But you *are* a second son. What specific responsibilities are given to you?" I was trying to cover up my stupid comment with a legitimate question. He knew it, and he let it pass. I supposed that was what people who cared for each other did.

"Believe it or not, I'm working with our generals to develop a battle plan."

6

"What for? We've lived in peace with our neighboring kingdoms for generations. Why would they attack us now?"

"I doubt they will. Our biggest problems come from marauding thieves or minor quarrels between the nichnas. But we've good reason to think that's about to change."

I must have looked puzzled because he kept on explaining.

"You do know travelers and traders from beyond our kingdom visit us, don't you?"

I nodded. Outsiders mostly went to Pilk and seldom bothered with farming nichnas like mine. Pilk not only had most of Ilari's money and goods, but it also sat on the confluence of The Wide River that formed our boundary on two sides and The Little River that ran out of our mountains and through the realm. Pilk was our center of trade, so of course foreign merchants went there.

"Well, they all bring news along with their spices and silks. For years, many have spoken of horsemen from far to the east, horsemen who have become fierce in recent times. They say their land is so cold and barren they can grow nothing, and they live only on the meat and milk of their yaks and horses."

"It's hard to imagine what sort of people could call such desolation home," I said. I wrapped up the remaining apples as I spoke. "Imagine life without fruits like these."

"Word is they've developed a taste for farmed goods and have been making their way outward, raiding farms."

"That's horrible. Do they take all the farmers' food?"

"Most of it. But if the farmers fight back, then they kill them all and burn everything to the ground."

"I'm glad they're far away."

Nevik reached towards me and brushed the hair out of my eyes. It was a gentle gesture, but one that invited me to see more clearly.

"People like that are *never* far enough away. We've tracked the reports and these Mongols, as they're called, are getting closer. We think they'll be in Ilari in a year or two."

I'd never heard something so frightening before. "What can we do? Why don't my people in Vinx know about this? Given our location, we'd be the first to be attacked!"

Again, he gave me a look of surprise.

"We all realize that. The rulers from every nichna, including Vinx, are working hard to develop the best defense plan for Ilari.

My father has given me the important task of overseeing this effort."

He stood a little taller as he spoke, as if this assignment made him proud.

"I recognize how the lives of people will depend on our plan. I promise you, Ryalgar, I will do my best."

There was nothing more to say. He gathered up his things, to return to the task of preparing to save my world and everything in it. I gathered up my things to return to the task of feeding the chickens and waiting for the winter wheat to sprout in the spring.

****

As the oldest girl with no brothers, my father sometimes asked me to help with farming tasks normally done by males. Lucky for me, his expertise on rocks and soil brought in extra income, enabling us to hire seasonal laborers. When they were gone for the winter, though, Dad needed another person to hold up ends of things and hand him tools.

My father was more slightly built than many men, but years of farming had kept him strong, so my part was seldom strenuous. Today, he repaired farm equipment in the large barn, and I could see his thinning gray hair as he bent over a bin of metal pieces. At his direction, I picked up the end of a wagon axle so he could pound a joining cuff on it with a large wooden mallet.

"Your mother is quite excited about this prince who's taken an interest in you," he said.

My first thought was that the prince's interest in me mostly involved sex, but that seemed an awkward response to give my father.

"I'm not sure anything will come of it."

He turned his attention away to remove a small clamp from a piece of metal and said nothing.

"Why does mom hate the Velka so much?"

"Why won't you quit asking me that question?" he replied.

"It's been a year since I last asked you. My life is changing. I want to know."

He sighed. "I guess I've always known I'd have to tell you sooner or later."

"Did she get in a fight with them?"

"No." He put down his tools and leaned against the wagon. "It's nothing like what you think."

"So tell me." I stood closer to him, unwilling to let him turn away and go back to work without answering me. Not this time.

He took a deep breath and swallowed, then he looked right at me.

"My mother isn't dead." His voice was almost a whisper.

"What? Grandma died right after Grandpa. When I was only four. I remember it."

"No, you remember me telling you she'd died. She didn't. She ran away, Ryalgar. To do something she wanted to do and couldn't while she was married."

It wasn't hard to guess. "*Grandma* became a Velka?" Now this was interesting.

"She did."

"I, I think that's great. Why would mother care?"

"Think about it. She'd just given birth to your twin sisters. She already had three little girls aged four and younger. That was a lot to care for. Her own mom had died years ago, and she had no sisters to help her. She wanted your grandmother to come live with us and give her a hand. Instead …"

Well, I guess a certain amount of resentment made sense. "How did *you* feel about this?"

He ran his tongue around his teeth, considering his answer. "I saw your mother's point. If ever a mother-in-law could be helpful, this was the time. And, I saw *my* mother's point. If she didn't go then, she probably never would. She'd already raised three children of her own; she'd earned the right to her happiness."

"So why not tell me this years ago? Why pretend she'd died?"

"Your mother insisted. Under the circumstances, it seemed wise to humor her."

I didn't know what else to say. My mother's reaction seemed extreme, but she could be that way sometimes. It must have hurt dad something awful.

Then I thought of the one remaining question that mattered. "Do you ever see Grandma?"

"Once in a while. She comes to the farmer's market in Vinx, hoping to get a glimpse of one of you girls. I try to get over there sometimes without your mom and when I do, we talk. She … she

9

still cares about all of us." He wiped at his eyes. "Now, enough of this. I want you to promise me you won't mention this conversation to your mother, okay?"

"Believe me, I won't." I gave a nervous laugh.

He pointed to a small nail he wanted me to hand him. I stretched my left arm out as far as I could, but the nail sat barely beyond my reach. I stretched harder with my mind, so the feeling inside of my hand went beyond the tips of my fingers. My sense of my hand grasped the nail in a way my real hand couldn't, and it rolled towards me until I could pick it up.

"That thing you just did?"

"What thing?"

"You know what. Moving that nail. Don't you ever let your mother see you do that."

"She probably has. I do it a lot."

Dad shook his head. "Try not to, okay? Your grandma used to do that and they say it's why the Velka wanted her. Don't you know they seek out women with such skills?"

"No. I didn't know."

I didn't say anything more, but for the rest of the day I wondered if the older woman who'd given me the potion was my grandmother.

~ 2 ~

More Truths

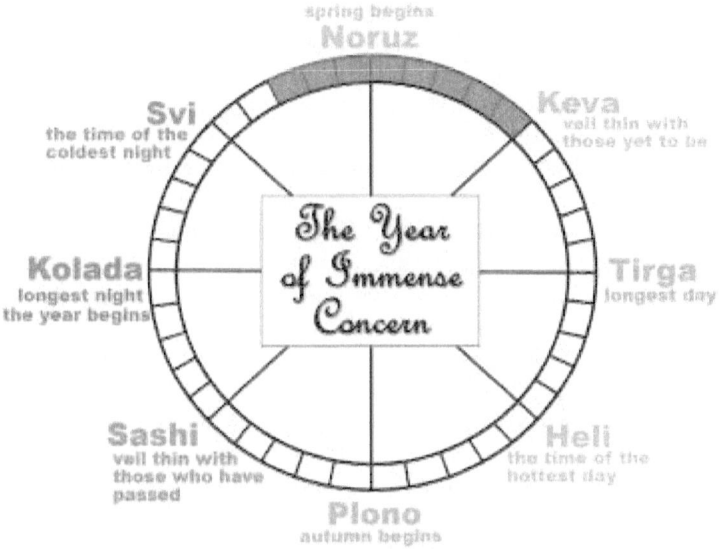

"I didn't want to make up another excuse to go to the market, so I waited for an afternoon with good weather when my mother was elsewhere.

"I'm going for a ride," I told Coral, the sister who was less than a year younger than I.

"I'll come too." She caught my expression. "Or not. Are you and your prince meeting somewhere?"

I smiled and let her think what she wanted.

The woman I suspected was my grandmother stood waiting for me in the market. I struggled to remember her given name. Aliza? Aliz? Did the Velka keep their names? I had no idea. Yet it didn't seem right to call her "Grandma." What if I was wrong? Or what if she wanted nothing to do with me now that I knew her secret?

"Aliz?" It came out as a question as I walked up to her. She smiled when I said it.

"I'm so glad you've finally talked to Yasen. Does your father agree this nonsense has gone on long enough?" She reached her arms out towards me to take my hands in hers.

I stopped where I stood, fidgeting instead with the coin purse in my hands. Her eagerness made me nervous.

"Aliz will do for now," she said, accepting my reticence. "I'm glad you came back."

"I only came to tell you I knew who you were. It seems I've been misled, and I prefer truths."

"Don't we all? This ridiculous charade of being dead was hardly my idea."

"Then what do you want from me?" The question came out harsher than I intended, but she kept matching my defensiveness with warmth.

"I'm offering you a chance to get to know me," she said. "If you want. If you don't, I'll go back to being dead, at least as far as you're concerned."

"Don't do that." I finally managed a smile to soften my words. "This is a lot to sort through."

"Of course it is, and there is about to be more. But I think you already suspect that, too, don't you?"

She was right. After my father's comment about moving the nail, I did wonder if she wanted to recruit me. I didn't want to say so. In case I was right? Or in case I was wrong?

"If you've guessed you'll be offered a chance to join us, you're correct. Not many are asked, you know."

"I couldn't possibly."

"You couldn't possibly *at this time*. I'm only planting a seed. Letting you know you'd be welcome. More than welcome. The Velka do have ways of discovering a woman's true talents and training her to grow well beyond anything she once expected.

There is great satisfaction in learning to be powerful. Don't say no. Think about it."

I told her I'd consider it, then I told myself I'd do no such a thing. After all, I had a lover. I had a family. I had a potentially wonderful future ahead. Yet …. her claims intrigued me.

Powerful? Why would I want to be powerful?

Then I remembered Nevik's chilling words about the wild horsemen from the east who swept into farmers' lands taking all they wanted and leaving a trail of destruction behind.

Perhaps Ilari was going to need all the powerful people it could find.

Perhaps I should learn to be one of them.

****

Noruz was only days away.

When Nevik sent a message inviting me to meet him at the market in Gruen, I felt sure he wanted to make holiday plans. We'd met a half dozen times since our celebration of the winter solstice ten anks ago, and our affection for each other had grown with each encounter. I assumed we were no longer unattached tidzys but would celebrate the spring equinox together the way lovers did. I couldn't have been more surprised when he told me it wouldn't be possible.

"I called you here to make sure you understood. To tell you in person. I'm sorry Ryalgar, but I have an obligation to be at the palace participating in the usual festivities. You know."

Yes, I did know.

"So, your family hasn't heard about me?" I couldn't imagine why not. With twelve nichnas in Ilari and often several princes from each ruling family, it wasn't unusual for a prince to court and marry a commoner. My mother's ambitions for her daughters weren't completely unrealistic.

"No, they know I'm seeing you." Then he added "Please understand. Mine is a complicated situation."

It sounded like the way my father described Grandma and the Velka. I was getting to hate complicated situations.

"Fine. Perhaps I'll enjoy a little variety myself," I said.

"Don't be that way. Come on. Forget about this silly holiday. Tell me what you've been up to."

I guess I wanted to impress him. With all my studies finally finished, my life had settled into farm chores, time with friends and family, and time with him. There wasn't much to share. So ....

"The Velka invited me to join them." I said it with a defiant glare. Of course, I expected him to respond with "you couldn't possibly" or "that's ridiculous."

Instead, he said, "That's terrific."

When I stared at him, probably with my mouth open, he added, "It's an honor. I've heard they don't ask many. You'd be great at it, whatever it is they do, exactly. Because you'd be great at anything. And you do need something to do now that you've gone through all the schooling in Ilari. That knowledge of yours ought to be used for something."

It was the moment I knew he'd never marry me.

For all the false rumors and silly superstitions people believe about the Velka, the one thing everyone does know is the Velka are not allowed to marry. They cannot even live with a man. Theories vary about what they can and can't do for sexual relief, but a permanent partnership with a male is out of the question.

"Are you thinking about it?" he asked.

"Yes. I am." And, as of that moment, I was.

****

I feigned an illness as Noruz approached, though I knew no one in my family was fooled. My mother brought food and drink to my room, making her way through my door with the same large-boned and shapely frame she'd passed on to me. She'd pulled her long dark hair, streaked with grey, behind her head, and the harshness served to accentuate the sadness in her face. She understood my solitude through the holiday to be the bad news it was.

All my younger sisters were home from school, and each one made her way alone to my room to offer consolation. By the time the holiday was over, I'd told each sister about my dilemma and gotten six different perspectives. It was clear each had talked to the others and my mother as well. Such was life in a household with eight women.

An ank later, when Nevik invited me to join him in Ilari's wine region, I made up a conflict. I knew it was childish and I'd see him sooner or later, but I wasn't ready.

The ank after that I took my horse and rode to Vinx's market. No one asked where I was going.

Aliz worked at the market that day, and she invited me back behind the curtain where the extra inventory was kept. She gestured for me to sit in a chair. I did and she surprised me when she lit a stick of incense, placing it so the smoke blew directly in my face. For a moment anyway. Then it didn't.

"Can you keep flies away from your body, too?" she asked.

"Sometimes. Definitely those small gnats that come out in early summer."

She nodded. "We call it oomrush. Mind motion. We can help you develop it."

"Why?" I could see no reason for the Velka to recruit women with unusual abilities. What did a bunch of ladies living safely in the forest need with that?

"*Why?*" My question surprised her, and amused her, too. "Do you really think we'd be allowed to live in peace in the open forest, with our independent lives and the bit of wealth we've amassed from our work, if the citizens of Ilari weren't a little afraid of us?"

She had a point.

"Ryalgar, I've followed your path through all our institutes of higher learning. You attended classes at nearly all of them, yet you never settled on any subject. Yasen told me you simply liked to study."

"I do. It seemed to me we educate women mostly to make them better mates and mothers; so why not learn about everything? I had fun doing it and my father's enthusiastic support of education helped."

She nodded. "You like knowing. You like making things go the way you think they should. You organize, you plan, you analyze. You even strategize. You know what you are?"

I shook my head. I had no idea what I was.

She laughed. "You're a leader, one born to run things. You could have an important place with us, for along with everything else we do, we need leaders. Are you ready to join us?"

Given the way she asked, I reconsidered. Me, the oldest of seven, had grown up running a small band of girls. Now she offered the chance to learn to run a much larger one. It had more appeal than I expected.

"I'd like to think about it. If I say yes, can I take a few anks to finish things up and to say my goodbyes?"

She nodded. "Take your time. You let us know when you're ready. Here." She handed me a handwritten page, done in neat script. "You obviously read and write well. Take this home and look it over. It lists several truths about us you should know. The biggest one is that unless you have relatives who insist on pretending you're dead," and she paused "you'll find those goodbyes aren't going to be as emotional as you're thinking. The Velka have plenty of contact with those they love. And, they can have as much or as little sex as they want with whomever they chose."

"I didn't know that."

"Most people don't. One of the few requirements we have is that our women live together in the forest. We gain our strength from it, but it's resulted in a lot of silly rumors. In truth, what our women do with their free time is their own business."

"Oh. That's nice to know."

I wasn't sure how that last bit of flexibility would affect me, but an ank later I found out.

****

"I owe you the full truth," Nevik said. "I owed it to you well before this, and I'm sorry I hesitated. I honestly never thought I'd come to care for you so much."

Nevik looked like our separation had been harder on him than it had been on me, and I was getting some satisfaction from that. This time, he'd invited me to a second home his family owned. That meant they *had* to know of our relationship, and the message wasn't lost on me.

"I missed you, too," I said. And I had. Along with the obvious things, I missed the crinkles around his eyes that made me smile.

"I'm glad. Ryalgar. Look. I have something quite difficult to tell you."

"Okay." I sat up, hands folded in my lap as if I was about to listen to an important lecture.

"I'm already engaged."

"You're what?

"Engaged."

"To be married? When? Why didn't you tell me?"

"I can't tell anyone."

"But--I don't understand. Why keep such a thing secret?"

"There's nothing to understand. It's an arranged marriage. One of convenience for my family and hers."

"That's ridiculous. No one does something so barbaric anymore."

"Exactly. Yet our parents did. Thus, the secrecy until she and I meet publicly and fake a believable courtship."

"Who is this woman?"

"She's not from Ilari, but from a neighboring kingdom from which we need some access rights regarding the river. Her people need ... never mind, it doesn't matter. It's important to both of our families that this appears to be a marriage of choice."

"Have you met her?"

"Once. She made it quite clear she was in love with another, a boy she'd grown up with, and she had every intention of discretely continuing her romance after our inconvenient marriage. I was not to touch her except for two brief periods when we will try to conceive a child. She laid down the ground rules."

"I see." And I did. Nevik wasn't looking for a wife, and he didn't need a girlfriend, either. What he needed was a mistress. A discrete woman with a life of her own and no jealous husband. What he needed was a Velka. And what he *wanted* was a Velka who he found to be attractive and interesting. One who cared for him and whom he cared for too.

What he wanted was me.

****

As Keva got closer, the weather improved. Spring blossoms appeared and the wind became soft and warm. I liked getting out of the house and walking around the farm because it gave me time to think.

Keva was the most sensuous of the eight holidays, the one when even the most reticent sought a partner for the pleasures of the body. Ilarians blamed this seasonal lust on the Goddess and the yearnings of those yet to be. Children conceived while celebrating Keva were called "merry-begots" and thought to be blessed.

I knew I'd celebrate Keva alone this year, while Nevik performed his princely duties at the palace. Although I was sad, Nevik's situation hadn't left me as angry as it probably should have. It explained his not celebrating Noruz with me, and it explained why he wanted me to join the Velka. I liked things that made sense, even if they grew from painful truths.

As I walked by a mother duck with nine tiny, adorable ducklings following her, I came to a similar conclusion about my mother. The little chicks splashed in a puddle, with the exuberance only shown by the young, and I understood my mother's frustration at not getting the help she needed. I thought of how desperate she must have felt. Some women are designed to raise a brood, like this mother duck, but not my mom. She was more of a well-bred horse, designed for a single child at a time. She'd likely been sinking under the weight of so many uncontrollable toddlers.

When her oldest showed the same bizarre affinity as the hated mother-in-law for moving small objects with her mind, my mother must have been terrified of losing me to what she saw as the other side. No wonder she'd grabbed my arm and pulled me away with a vehemence that sometimes hurt.

It made sense, and once it did, I wasn't angry with her anymore. At least, not as much.

And I knew what my decision was, too. I didn't have to celebrate Keva alone. I had another option. Women typically joined the Velka on a holiday, and Keva would be as good a time as any.

Mom must have done some similar soul searching of her own, for when I told her about Nevik's engagement, and my plan to join the Velka, she handled it better than I expected.

"If you're going to do this," she said. "I won't make it any harder on you. Why would I? You've suffered enough from this prince's rebuke."

"I know about my grandmother." Somehow, after she was so kind about my decision, I thought she had a right to know.

"Your father told me. It's to your credit you tried to spare my feelings by not bringing it up. Don't think because I send *you* off with my love, I've in any way forgiven her."

"Mom, she ...."

"Don't judge me. Your dad told you only a small piece of the story. Let's leave it at that."

Oh dear. I said no more but wondered if I'd ever learn the rest.

I saw my father's sadness when I told him I was leaving, but I could also tell he was proud of me and glad to see me forge a relationship with his kin. He may also have been relieved he no longer had to worry about a spinster daughter. Actually, everyone was probably relieved about that.

He added one more reason he was glad to see me go. One I hadn't thought of.

"Surely your prince mentioned the preparations for war being made in Pilk?"

"He did."

"Scary business, these thieving horsemen," he said. "I take comfort knowing one of my children will be hidden in the forest, far from harm. Stay safe in your new home."

"I promise I will." When I said it to him, I meant it. I never planned to do otherwise.

I sent messages to my four sisters away at school, asking them to please come home for Keva so they could join Coral and Sulphur in escorting me to the forest's edge. They all arrived a day or two early, each with mixed emotions about my decision, though for every one the mix was different.

Then on a beautiful sky-blue day, halfway between the first day of spring and the first day of summer, I said goodbye to my mother, who didn't wish to come, and I set off for the forest's edge with my father and sisters. I'd been told the Velka had seven entry places where the overgrowth was contained well enough for an adult to make their way through. We'd been asked to ride to Vinx's central entry point, the one near the market.

All seven of us girls dressed in our finest clothes, with flowers woven into our hair as if we were on our way to a wedding. The extra pomp seemed silly to me, but the others insisted I do this properly. I knew some people referred to this occasion as a woman's marriage to the forest.

I'd been told the Velka would meet me inside and to bring little with me. After handing the reigns of my mare over to my father so he could lead her back home, I donned the rucksack holding my few things, waved goodbye to my family, and stepped in between the trees to see what would happen next.

~ 3 ~

Entering the Forest

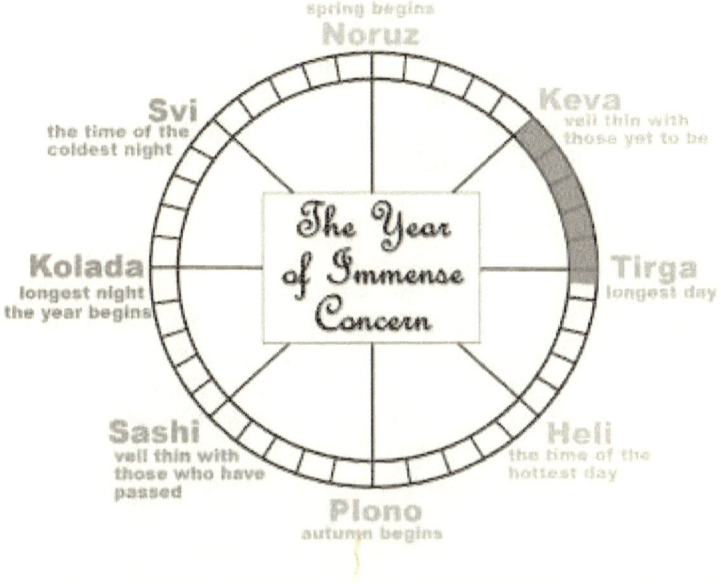

spring begins
Noruz

Svi
the time of the
coldest night

Keva
veil thin with
those yet to be

Kolada
longest night
the year begins

*The Year
of Immense
Concern*

Tirga
longest day

Sashi
veil thin with
those who have
passed

Heli
the time of the
hottest day

Plono
autumn begins

I wasn't sure what to expect as I pushed my way through several feet of dense underbrush complicated by tangled vines with tiny sharp thorns. It got so hard to move forward I considered giving up. Had I misunderstood Aliz's instruction on where to enter? Then, I saw a person waiting for me on the far side of a group of bushes. I scrambled towards her.

"Sorry this is so difficult, but because Ilari considers this all open forest, we're forbidden from putting up fences or gates. We need to discourage intruders somehow."

The woman was at least ten years older but slender and fit, and she wore men's clothing -- trousers and boots. "I'm a guide," she explained. She handed me the reins to an animal hidden by the shrubbery. "Hop on. Small, slow animals do better in here."

I looked at what I was about to mount. "A donkey?"

"We use them exclusively. I know you'll miss your horse, but trust me, she wouldn't be happy in the forest."

As I got on, I noticed a narrow path barely visible through the overgrown shrubbery.

I felt fine until the animal began to move. Then the dense vegetation and thick overhanging trees grew closer. Soon the branches seemed to reach for me and I shivered and drew myself in tighter. Out of nowhere, I couldn't breathe.

"I'm sorry. I have to stop." I felt silly as I dismounted and squatted on the ground in my best clothes, gasping for air. "I don't know what's wrong with me."

"Take your time. It happens to a lot of women at first, but you ladies from the open fields of Vinx seem to have the worst of it."

I looked around at the cloying green tendrils everywhere and closed my eyes, doing my best to imagine the sky.

"There are places in the forest that are more open," she assured me. "Only the edges are this bad. Come on. You'll see."

After riding for a while, I saw what she meant. Deep in the forest, the trees grew larger and their branches were higher off the ground. The heavy shade made for fewer shrubs and less thorny vines. The sky peeked through the pine needles and the leaves, and I could see several feet ahead. It helped.

We rounded a corner into a large open space, cleared to hold a massive stone building larger than any barn in Vinx. Unfortunately, the branches of the giant trees reached over its roof, touching each other in the middle of the clearing and covering the open sky even here.

"What's this place?" I asked.

"Our main lodge and your new home. Welcome."

My grandmother greeted me with a hug. Her steps seemed lighter here, and her face younger, and I sensed her excitement at my arrival. She showed me to my room, the way she might have if I'd come to visit her as a granddaughter years ago.

My bedroom was large and in a corner with windows on two sides.

"I knew you'd have trouble adjusting," she said. "This room is more than most newcomers get, but I want you to feel at home with little delay. You'll find clothes and things in the armoire. Everything in this room is for you. Rest a bit and join us in the main hall for dinner. You'll hear the chimes a short time before it is served."

With that, she left me to stare through the windows at the trees.

Would I get used to this place? What if I didn't? I supposed women left the Velka, but I knew already how disappointed Aliz would be if I did. Perhaps my sisters would be disappointed too, having the unmarried sister return. Nevik would be sad; I'd no longer be his perfect mate.

I'd made a lot of people happy with my decision to come here. Now I needed to discover if the decision made me happy, too.

Over the next few days, I learned much. The Velka numbered over a thousand, not the mere few hundred others guessed. This was their largest building, and it was centuries old, as were the trees around it. It housed over eighty women and was home to the Conclave, the Velka's governing body.

Most novices entered the Velka with a great deal of freedom when it came to choosing their path, their housemates, and their living situation. Other lodges, smaller houses, and even one-woman cabins and tents scattered throughout the forest were options for them, but not me. Aliz told me I was being groomed to be a part of the Conclave. It seemed the Velka already had my life planned.

Novices didn't leave the forest until at least two eighths of a year had passed. Common wisdom held that much of our power came from the trees, and a woman needed to be one with them before she stepped out of the forest for the first time. I exhaled slowly when I got this news. Two eighths seemed like a long time to wait until I saw the open sky.

From the first night on, the women were mostly friendly to me, and the food was excellent. I learned the Velka had growers, makers, and sellers, as well as cooks, cleaners, and teachers. All Velka had at least two roles and some had many.

An older woman in the main hall took me aside after my first dinner and assigned me a few household chores. I would spend some of my time as a cleaner, polishing and dusting in the main living room. My duties were so few and easy I suspected others must do more but it seemed awkward to ask.

The next morning at breakfast, Aliz sat next to me to go over my training.

"All our novices attend a class that meets most mornings. In it, you'll learn about the history and ways of the Velka. You'll get tours of the lodge and the surrounding grounds. We've discovered it's the best way to get those questions answered, and to get the new people to know each other, too. You start today and keep attending until the instructor decides you've finished."

That was fine. I'd always liked classes.

Then Aliz told me to join a small group of women with an affinity for oomrush. They met right after lunch in the main living room. A few of the women within earshot looked at me with more interest when they overheard this.

I was delighted. You couldn't give me too many classes to take, and I'd come hoping to learn more about this talent that had baffled me all of my life.

Finally, she told me I'd spend some evenings with her and other Velka to learn more about the Conclave.

"This will be an informal class, conducted on a situationally-dependent basis." Her description confused me, but I didn't ask questions. I'd noticed a couple of less-than-warm glances exchanged when this last edict was conveyed. The looks said *Why does the new girl get to do this? Is it her grandmother's influence?*

Was it? Probably, but I wasn't sure what I could do about it one way or another.

After a couple of anks, I decided to ask about seeing Nevik. I'd noticed other women came and went, missing classes and chores on occasion, and it didn't seem to bother anyone.

We were in the kitchen and our instructor, a chubby and friendly woman from Gruen, was going over how the Velka traded our skills and products for food and drinks, as few edible items grew in the shade of the forest despite our considerable abilities with plants.

"Uh, I know I can't, shouldn't, leave the forest yet, but I was told … well … that I could … um …"

The other four girls in my morning session giggled and our instructor slapped the table with mirth. "Spit it out, Ryalgar. You're getting horny? What's your pleasure?"

"Um. There's a man. We were lovers before I came here. I'd like to get word to him. To find a way to see him."

"To *see* him. Right. Well, orientation instructors like me assist the new girls with all such requests for *seeing*. So, we've got Velka going out to markets in each nichna in the realm. Where would this man of yours be found?"

"He's in Pilk."

"Plenty going that direction. Must be a dozen markets there. Can you be more specific?"

"Uh, I think you'd find him at the palace."

"Ah. You're hooking up with a Svadlu, are you? Those military types can be sexy. I've had a few myself."

I looked down at my hands.

"Not to worry," she added, trying to guess why I hesitated to say more. "When I said we Velka value discretion, I meant it. Word of your soldier friend will not leave the forest. You can count on it."

"Actually, he's a prince."

"You're sleeping with a member of the Pilk royal family? Seriously?"

I had everyone's full attention now.

"His name is Nevik."

She slammed her hand down a second time and laughed out loud. "You're telling me the golden granddaughter we recruited is also secretly sleeping with the guy who just got betrothed to some fancy princess from another realm?"

I nodded. "That sounds like Nevik."

"Well, you do know how to make things difficult, don't you?"

I'd never considered myself someone prone to cause trouble, but I saw her point.

"This one will take some discretion. But, okay. We have small cottages barely inside the forest over towards Pilk. They're a good place for people to *see* each other. I'll look into it for you."

The other girls now eyed me with a combination of respect and envy. It was one of those irritating things about women. We couldn't help judging our sisters by the caliber of the men they slept with. What a stupid habit.

****

Time ran together in the forest. Without markets and schools, there was little difference between the six workdays of the ank and the three-day ank-break at the end. My classes met most days, on whichever of the nine the instructor decided. My favorite part was always the afternoon.

A dozen of us gathered in a large living room to learn about the art of moving objects with our minds. The glass in the windows of this room could be raised to let the fresh spring air rush in. I always sat by a window.

Two of the older women were our informal teachers, but we all contributed. Most of us could only nudge small items or move smoke and dust in the air, though a couple of the younger women were more advanced.

We practiced and exchanged tips and sometimes we speculated about how oomrush worked or when it could be useful. I suppose I got a little better with each session, but mostly I enjoyed visiting with others who could also do something odd I'd always done.

One of the two more skilled women took a liking to me, and we sat together at dinner. Her name was Joli, and she was the only other woman I'd ever met who cut her hair the way my sister Sulphur did. Joli's dark, thick locks were longer, though; they ended just above her shoulders. She had what I guessed most people would consider a pretty face, and somehow the shorter hair looked right on her.

She invited me to come have a drink in her room after dinner, and I accepted. Her place was smaller, but as I settled into her chair and she offered me after-dinner wine, we began exchanging confidences the way women do.

I learned she was from Zur, the only nichna in Ilari's large central forest. The Zurians had been trying to drive the Velka out of the open forest for centuries, hoping to incorporate it into Zur. The Svadlu had stepped in many times because the rest of Ilaria wanted unincorporated space in the middle of the realm, and most wanted the Velka to survive.

Zur and the Velka had such a history of animosity that it surprised me any Zurian would join us. Then Joli told me she'd been here five years, ever since her oomrush abilities became so strong she had to concentrate on not using them.

"It was no way to live. You should have seen the fear in my boyfriend's eyes the first time I slipped up and moved something big enough for him to notice."

I understood. It had been hard enough trying to hide my nascent talents from my mother.

When I told her about my ongoing dalliance with the otherwise-engaged Nevik, her reaction surprised me.

"Could you have been luckier?"

"You think falling in love with an already-betrothed man was lucky?"

"What if he hadn't been? Can you imagine you, a smart lady, primping and preening around the royalty of Pilk for the rest of your life? Think about it, Ryalgar. You'd be miserable. Probably make him miserable too. Instead, every so often you get to sneak off and have your fun with him. Best of all worlds. I think the princess that got stuck with him has done you a huge favor."

I hadn't quite looked at it that way, but it made me feel better about my situation.

Later, after I'd returned to my room, I realized I'd made a friend.

****

My orientation instructor kept her word. She told me Nevik had been contacted and while he had to celebrate the upcoming summer solstice with his betrothed, of course, he would make arrangements to see me soon after Tirga. My heart clenched at the thought of his eagerness to celebrate with *her* when he'd spurned me on a previous holiday, but I focused on how it was all a sad charade for him. There would no enjoyment in their celebration. I had to remember that.

A few days after Tirga, a guide offered to take me to a cottage along the perimeter of the forest, and then to fetch Nevik. He came through the door with a huge grin on his face and hugged me longer than he had before.

The guide cleared her throat.

"Help yourselves to the provisions. I'll be back tomorrow afternoon." We barely heard her leave.

The hugging turned to kissing which turned to undressing and I understood my body had missed him more than I realized. That day, spent sharing pleasure, became the most enjoyable day I'd ever had. I think Nevik felt freer now that he didn't have to pretend anything about our future. Maybe I felt freer, too. At any rate, we knew exactly what we were there for, and we both took full advantage of our opportunity.

The next morning he started to complain about *her*, and how cold she was, but I asked him to stop. I may not have been this princess's greatest fan, but if I'd been forced into a marriage, I'd be cold too.

"Let's keep her out of our bed," I said. He agreed and suggested we go back to being in it.

Once the sun was overhead, the outside world intruded again.

"Do you want news of your family?" he asked.

"Of course I do."

My grandmother Aliz, and the others who went to the market in Vinx, sometimes brought back tidbits, but I always wanted to know more.

"Do you know your sister Coral is pregnant?"

"That can't be. She isn't seeing anyone, and she'd never be so careless. And how would you know?"

He held up the palms of his hands to stop my questions.

"It seems she is seeing one of the Svadlu. I don't know him personally, but we move in similar circles and men talk, too, you know. His name is Davor, he's older than us by at least eight years, and he's high in rank. From Lev. Was made a Mozdol a few years back after that nasty business with the band of thieves who crossed the river into Lev."

"I remember hearing about that. So he's technically a prince?" Well, my mother would be delighted.

Nevik shrugged. He seemed to share the average Royal's lower opinion of the honorary princes known as Mozdols. "He's kind of a womanizer, I've heard, but he seems to have taken a genuine shine to your sister. Word is they were discussing marriage when nature surprised them."

"And now?"

"I think a wedding is being planned soon. I don't know more."

The conversation cooled me off. Good thing, as my nether regions needed a rest.

"I've got to contact her. Get her some herbs to help. I wonder how my folks took the news?"

He shrugged again, realizing the mood between us had passed.

"You Velka seem to have an excellent communication network going between the nichnas. Perhaps better than our Svadlu do. Finding out more and getting messages to her should be no problem."

"Then it should also be easy to get messages to you." I let my hand wander to the parts of him that must have been every bit as worn out as mine. "How do you feel about getting more invitations from me to visit?"

"I'd love that, but my ability to sneak away, even overnight, is going to get more limited as, uh, my wedding nears. And, of course, as our training to fend off these invaders becomes more intensive. How would you feel about me letting your women in the market know when I'm available?"

"That works too. Discretion is highly valued here. I've already learned how important it is to keep each other's secrets. It would be safe."

"Then you'll hear from me soon. And often."

As he put his arm around me and I laid my head on his shoulder, I realized two things. One. Somewhere amid all the wonderful sex, I'd fallen in love with this prince. Two. I could tell he'd fallen in love with me. And yes, it had all been every bit as easy as my mother had claimed.

~ 4 ~

The Mysterious Conclave

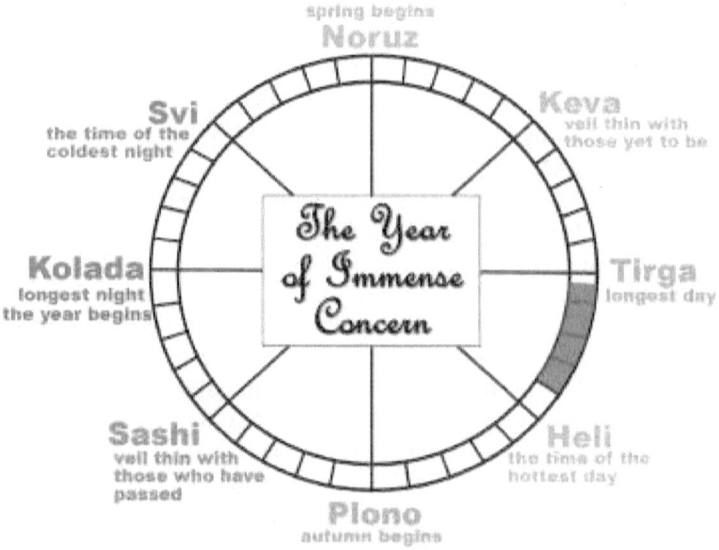

My evenings were unpredictable. Often, I had the time to myself; occasionally Aliz had me observe conversations between her and others in charge of various aspects of Velka life. In these cases, she offered little explanation and discouraged questions.

"Just listen," she'd say.

Sometimes the two of us would visit in her room or mine, the way we might have if she'd never joined the Velka. I felt her desire for my allegiance or at least my understanding. She had the latter, but I wasn't going to give up an understanding of my mother's point of view, too.

Finally one night I broached the taboo topic we'd been avoiding.

"Why didn't you wait a year? Help my mother through those first tough eighths with the twins and then join the Velka? Would that have been so hard?"

She took a sip of her sweet late-evening amber wine as she gathered her composure. I guessed she'd been expecting the question and had her answer ready.

"There were two obvious reasons not to do that, dear. One, I was afraid I'd become too attached to all of you girls, and I wouldn't be able to leave. Two, I was afraid that what did happen would. Your mother got pregnant *again*, only eighths after the twins were born. Our methods don't always work, you know, and she seems uncommonly fertile."

"She could have used your help with the next child, too."

My grandmother stood and walked toward the door. She didn't turn to face me until she got there.

"We shouldn't need to discuss this again. Ever."

She left before I could respond.

We didn't meet for several nights after that awkward conversation and the next time we got together, many more women were present. Most were older than I, and I deduced this was an actual gathering of the Conclave. I was being allowed to sit in.

To my surprise, much of the talk centered around the Mongols and the coming winter. The Velka had few contacts outside of Ilari, but they had plenty of dealings with those inside the realm. Bringing information back into the forest seemed common and even expected.

It appeared the Conclave had already decided we'd hide ourselves when this invasion occurred. We now debated how to go about it.

"If we're lucky, they'll never even try to enter the forest because they won't know we exist," one woman said.

"We can't count on that," another replied.

"Word is they get their power from their horses. They're weak without them."

Another laughed. "Horses can't charge through the perimeter we've got."

"No perimeter matters if they set fire to the forest," a woman older than my grandmother said.

"Our perimeter won't burn. We tell you that at every single meeting."

"Well, we need to improve it anyway," she replied. "If we can make it more impermeable, we should."

"Don't forget some of us want to leave occasionally. And let others in." I'd met this woman before. Boyanne lived down the hall from me, and always greeted me with warmth. I'd had no idea she was in the Conclave.

"Coming and going may be a luxury we can't afford until this threat passes," said another woman who'd yet to speak.

I could tell one group wanted to cut all ties with Ilari until the Mongols were long gone. The other not only wished to maintain contact but also felt an obligation to help the rest of Ilari in what little ways we could.

"You've joined us at a difficult time," one of the kinder women said to me, acknowledging my presence for the first time that evening. "What do you think?"

They all turned to me, and I understood the importance of my answer.

"At this stage, I think it's crucial we don't decide."

Recommending no decision doesn't usually win admiration, but I knew it was our best choice, so I tried to say it better.

"I mean, it would be foolish to isolate now, when this invasion could be over a year away or never happen at all. Right? Yet, however unpleasant it seems, drawing a thick curtain around the Velka could be how we survive when the time comes. So it'd also be foolish not to have plans in place for such an extreme strategy. What I'm trying to say is I don't think we gain anything by arguing about what is best until we know more."

"Out of the mouth of babes," laughed one of the women. "Well said. Let's spend no more time trying to convince our sisters of our beliefs. We need a permeable boundary now and a kick-in-the-arse plan to close it fast if we must."

My grandmother smiled. One of the less friendly women turned to her.

"Yes, Aliz. She'll do."

I saw my grandmother look into other several faces with one of her eyebrows raised in question, and I saw nods in response from around the room. The women had taken a silent vote and made a decision. I'd be allowed in the Conclave.

Part of my happiness at passing their subtle test came from the new confidence I gained with my grandmother. I felt bolder, and more entitled to ask her questions. Growing up I'd heard plenty of strange things about the Velka, many of which I already knew to be completely false. But one rumor haunted me.

"Can I ask you a question?" I said the next time she and I spent an evening together.

"Of course."

"Is it true that long ago the Velka were more powerful than they are now?"

My grandmother shrugged. "It's a persistent rumor. The women who trained me, women no longer with us, they mostly found that idea offensive. They insisted we were as strong as ever but had fallen victim to one of those ideas that appeal to people. You know .... things used to be so much better."

I had to laugh. "It's true. People do love to think that about everything. I don't know why..."

She could have left it there, with my curiosity satisfied, but she didn't.

"And yet ... there are things in our history, things you don't know of yet but maybe someday will learn ... let's just say they do make me wonder."

Interesting. I should have let it drop there, realizing she'd shared more she should, but I seldom could resist asking one more question.

"If so, what do you think happened to us?"

"Nothing. I mean I'm fairly certain nothing particular happened. I think we were more powerful once only because we needed to be."

"And now?"

She smiled, following my reasoning. "Now? I hope we're still capable of being as powerful as we need to be."

****

33

Coral and I had been close growing up, as two sisters less than a year apart often are. Yet, ours was a closeness of convenience. Our next sister, Sulphur, was a year and a half younger than Coral, and we both had less in common with her than with each other. Don't get me wrong. Sulphur was easy to love, despite the unfortunate name my father saddled her with. But she was different from the rest of us, pretty much from the day she was born.

Coral and I grew up more like partners in crime than friends. We were two girls working together to keep five little sisters out of trouble and two parents out of our hair. It was the way kids in a family usually worked together, whether they realized it or not. Family dynamics is everyone's first and most basic lesson in social skills.

As Coral's visit approached, I looked forward to seeing her more than I expected. I ran down the steps of the lodge to greet her, and I hugged her before she got her second leg completely off the little donkey.

"Careful." She laughed at my uncharacteristic burst of affection but I knew she appreciated it. She'd missed me, too.

"Tell me about this man Davor!" I said as soon as she and I settled into my room.

As she praised the soldier and Mozdol she planned to marry, I couldn't shut out Nevik's words about him being a womanizer.

"He has so much more flair than anyone from Vinx ever would."

Was that good or not? Rather than comment, I offered her the packet of things I'd assembled to keep her and her baby healthy through the pregnancy. She took my gift, but I detected some envy when she responded by asking me if I thought she had magical tendencies too.

"Do you know what a luski is?" she asked.

I thought back to the words my instructors made me memorize for the various talents considered to be magic. This was one of them, but it wasn't practiced by the Velka. Many people thought luskies were imaginary, and most thought they were dangerous. Odd, because being a luski related to mothers and small children.

"Kind of. Why?"

She took a deep breath and I could see how nervous the subject made her.

"I know this sounds ridiculous, so don't laugh. A friend at school thinks I could be one."

"You?? Coral, I don't think it's possible. You don't have a child yet." Too bad some well-meaning friend put *this* crazy idea into my sister's head.

"Yes, but I am having one and, well, I did play mother to my younger sisters. Never mind. It's stupid. I don't know what she was thinking."

Bat scump. I'd offended her by dismissing her question too quickly. I tried to recover. "Wait. There may be some truth to it. I'll learn more."

But Coral didn't want to talk about it any further, so she turned the topic to Nevik. Given his well-publicized engagement, I'd decided to keep quiet about my affair, but when I saw the pity in her eyes, I reconsidered. She wasn't a gossip, and I hated having her feel sorry for me.

"He's visited me twice now," I confessed, "and our time together is more precious than ever."

"That makes no sense. Everyone in Ilari knows he met a princess from outside the realm during the Tirga celebrations and now the two of them are madly in love. A wedding is expected."

"I know. Things are not always what they seem, Coral. Nevik is playing a role he must play. Please understand. My happiness depends on your discretion."

My situation appeared to sink in. "Oh. I see. You have my silence, of course," she said. Then she added a comment she didn't even know was hurtful. "Is *that* why you joined the Velka? So you could be the mistress of a prince?"

"No. It is not. I joined the Velka because they can teach me to develop powers I have. The occasional night with Nevik is a bonus."

She backed off. Even if she didn't understand why she'd offended me, she knew she had. Well, at least now we were even.

"Nights with him are likely to become less frequent," I said, trying to return to the air of shared confidences. "Aside from the appearances he'll need to keep up with his new wife, I'm told there is this group of marauders moving westward every winter, stealing crops. Soon they'll threaten our realm."

"I've heard of them, too. Davor spoke of frightening horsemen from the east."

"That's them. Nevik, as the second prince of Pilk, has been put in charge of training the Svadlu to repel them. It's a big responsibility. He says they could attack as soon as this winter."

This time I seemed to have struck a sensitive chord with her.

"I know. Davor says that's why he'll need to keep a second home in Pilk. Most of his time will be spent on this training, too."

Now it was my turn to say "Oh. I see." Davor, the known womanizer, was going to keep a second home? That couldn't be good. I searched for something else, something positive to say.

"Would you like me to come to your wedding? I'll be there if you want me to."

"I'd like nothing better!"

And with that we were back where we'd started, happy to see each other.

The women I lived with gave Coral and I plenty of time and space to visit, and no one expected me at my classes while she was there. Later, I'd realize each of them had a similar memory, a recollection of their first visit by a loved one from the old life.

They knew how hard the few days after she left would be, too. I received more sympathetic glances and occasional hugs than I had since I'd arrived. Then, a few days after that, everything returned to normal.

****

Most days I managed to keep my feeling of being suffocated by the trees tucked into a corner of my mind where it couldn't take over. I watched it the way I'd watch a wild animal looking for a way into my home. As long as I stayed alert, it couldn't get in.

But the panicky feeling would come upon me when I forgot about it. It happened at night, as I fell asleep, or when I was concentrating hard on something like adding numbers in my head or searching for something in my room. When it overtook me by surprise, I'd have to sit still, breathe slowly, and remind myself I was okay. I had everything I needed. Nothing could hurt me. In one more ank, my two eighths of a year would be up and I'd be free to leave the forest. Or so I thought.

"That two eighths thing is more of a guideline, really," my orientation instructor said when I asked her about going to my sister's wedding. "I've already been told you'll be expected to wait longer than most before your first trip out."

"But that's not fair. Her marriage is anks after my two-eighths occurs *and* going to her wedding is a reasonable request!"

It already annoyed me I was being required to attend this class after two new girls who'd started after me were told they were done. Was I a slow learner? I'd never been one before.

"You must have noticed you're getting choice treatment," she said. "Nice room. Fewer chores. These things come at a cost. They own a bigger piece of you. I happen to know they want you to learn more from me because I've been told to keep you in my class indefinitely."

Really?

"Heli, they probably expect you to help me teach this class eventually. So don't be annoyed with me. We're going to be spending too much time together for that."

I responded with equal honesty. "I like your class. I don't want to quit it. I just don't like the idea of people thinking I'm stupid."

She laughed. "No one does. Better get used to the idea of people thinking you're special, though, and not everyone liking you for it."

"Is that why they won't let me go to my sister's wedding? Am I being punished by someone who doesn't want me to be treated so well?"

"I don't think so. My guess is someone here has pinned a lot of hopes on you and wants to make sure you come back after you leave for the first time."

"Of course I'll come back."

She gave me a funny look. "Don't be so sure. There are a lot of firsts you haven't had yet, like the first time you see the open sky again. Nothing can prepare you for how that feels and someone probably fears you're not ready to handle it yet."

I didn't care what anyone thought. I wasn't willing to disappoint Coral, not on her big day. Not when I feared so much about her marriage would turn out to be a disappointment.

~ 5 ~

Seeing the Sky

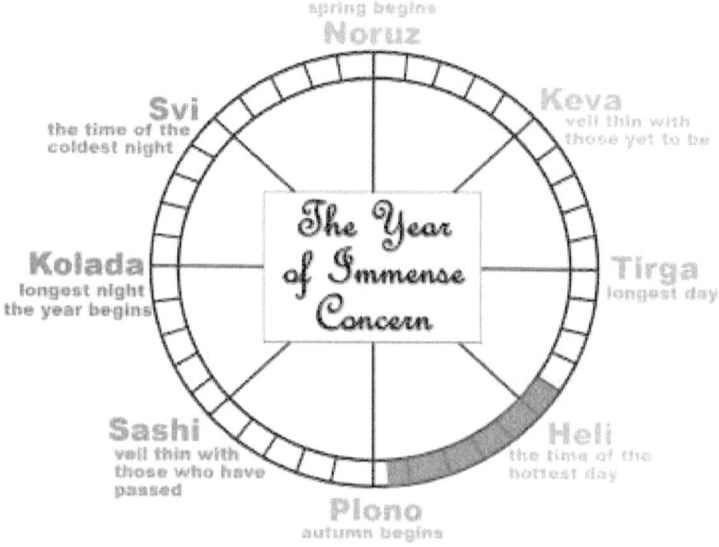

Desperate to get permission to leave, I did the one thing I wanted to do the least. I begged my grandmother. I figured if she wasn't the one directly responsible for holding me here, she at least had some sway with whoever was.

"It means this much to you?" she asked. I wondered if she understood how little I wanted to have this conversation with her.

"It means that and more. I wouldn't be living here if I'd suspected you'd deny me this. *Especially* after that entire handwritten sheet you gave me about all the freedoms I'd have."

Yes, I was willing to use every technique of persuasion available to me. She held up her hand.

"Spare me the next part, where you tell me how much *you* value your connection to your family," she said. "I'll sign off on this, Ryalgar, if you give me your word you will return."

So my instructor had been right. I gave her my word.

The day after we celebrated Heli, I learned Coral's wedding would occur on the autumn equinox. Sulphur would come to the lodge two anks before and spend several days with me. Then she and I would be taken to the edge of the forest where someone in my family would meet us to take me back to my *old* home. To visit.

As the time for Sulphur's arrival grew closer, I worried. Coral never asked people inconsiderate questions, and she responded politely to any that were asked of her. It was her way to be kindhearted. Sulphur, on the other hand, tended to say what was on her mind, to Heli with the emotions of others.

Back in Vinx, I'd usually preferred Sulphur's honesty to Coral's unending niceness. But now, I had no way to predict what Sulphur might criticize or take offense at, and I didn't need my new family at odds with my sister.

So her wide, admiring eyes surprised me as she and her little donkey came into the clearing around our main lodge. She slipped off her mount and gave a low whistle.

"Now *this* is impressive." I'd forgotten Sulphur was as blunt with her approval as she was with her criticism. "Pruck. How did you manage to get a deal like this?"

I laughed. "It's a long story." This sister and I had some catching up to do.

Sulphur was the sort of woman everyone stared at. She was half a head taller than most and long ago she'd defied tradition and cut her hair into a short mane of bright gold. She had a robust woman's figure, a man's strong muscles, and her directness served to make others try to please her. The Velka were no more immune to her allure than most, and I had to smile at the number of women who'd never approached me before, but now were anxious to sit at my table for dinner.

The first night, I brushed away invitations for the two of us to join others in various common areas. I wanted to talk to my sister. By myself. However, when it became obvious Joli wanted to come back to my room with us, I couldn't say no. Joli was the best friend I had here; the least I could do was let her be part of this visit.

So, the three of us poured ourselves sweet late-evening amber wine to sip and settled into the chairs in my room. Joli was courteous enough to let Sulphur and I cover the basic family news without interrupting but she leaned forward with an impish smile once the conversation turned to my life with the Velka.

"So many women learning to be strong. I had no idea," Sulphur said. "But what is it you people do all day?"

Joli squirmed in her chair and I had a rather good idea of what would happen next. A wisp of Sulphur's blonde hair flew into her eyes. Sulphur brushed it out. It came back. Sulphur looked puzzled, then brushed it out again. It came back more forcefully. Sulphur glared at me.

"Don't look at me. She's doing it." I nodded towards Joli. "I'm not that good. At least not yet."

"So you don't just sit around making herbal potions?"

"We do a lot of things," I said. "Everyone develops whatever skills they have. Some do make potions. Others have, uh, more unusual talents."

Sulphur drummed her fingers on the table a few times as she came to a decision. "This place is way better than I thought."

The next day, I learned more about Sulphur's ambitions. She'd always been the family protector, scaring away troublemakers with her sheer force of will. It was hard to imagine her leading any life typical for a woman. Yet, I'd never guessed she aspired to join the Svadlu. The military was so incompatible with the refined and intellectual way our parents had raised us. Besides, women weren't allowed in often and, those that were, didn't have an easy life.

"It's like you being here," she said. "I want to be where I belong, too."

"I'm glad *you're* so sure I'm where I'm meant to be." I laughed. "Who else knows about this ambition of yours?"

"Only Dad, so far. He's offered to help me."

"Good for Dad. Do you have a plan to get in?"

"I do, now that our dear sister Coral is about to wed a highly respected member of the Svadlu."

Okay. That made sense. Everyone knew Svadlu hopefuls, especially the female ones, were more likely to get in with a sponsor. Would Davor be willing to help Sulphur? We hadn't talked about Davor yet. I wondered what Sulphur thought about him.

"Davor's such a nice man, I can't imagine him saying no to me," she said.

Hmmm. That was a little different from what Nevik thought.

"I'm going to ask him at Coral's wedding," she added. "I'm hoping he'll feel particularly generous on such a happy day."

For all her astuteness in many arenas, my striking sister was naïve in others. I worried that Davor's alleged happiness about his upcoming marriage could be one of those things that fell into her blind spot.

After my quiet acceptance into the Conclave, my grandmother had begun inviting me to attend every gathering. I went, I listened, I learned. With each invitation, however, I noticed more of the younger Velka resented me. I knew I'd done nothing to offend these new detractors, so I'd decided dislike was as contagious as any emotion. Dislike for me had been spreading and I'd felt powerless to stop it.

Then Sulphur's arrival turned the tide. As she and I dined in the main hall each night, her natural sunshine slowly melted away the ill-will of those who behaved coldly to me only so they'd be better liked themselves.

The core group, the ones who had real issues with me, never joined our table, of course. They sulked at us from across the room. That was fine with me. Sulphur had not only stopped the progress of a growing animosity, but she'd also helped me figure out which women were my real problem.

"Would you be interested in joining us if this thing with the Svadlu doesn't work out?" I felt a sisterly obligation to ask Sulphur. I wasn't sure how I felt about the idea, but I suspected my grandmother could make it happen. She'd already greeted

Sulphur with warmth, and they'd had lunch together. Sulphur said it had gone well.

"No. I'm going to be a Svadlu."

"You know, you could be joining them right before the most dangerous time in our history."

"Yup. The horrible Mongols are coming." She made a face.

"It's not a joke, Sulphur. Nevik thinks it could be this winter. They've defeated many a strong army, based on what traders have told us."

"I know. It's one of the reasons I want to join now. To be there, to help defend Vinx. Surely you can see how the rivers and the mountains keep us safe to the north and west and the south."

My sister's analysis of how our realm would be attacked matched mine.

"I know. Any well-thought-out attack on Ilari has to come in through the east," I said. "Through Vinx." I wondered if the inevitable scared her as much as it did me.

"Horsemen could charge right through the grazing pastures of Bisu. That fence the Bisuites have up is a joke."

"It's only meant to keep cattle in," I said.

"Obviously. And the Mongols will blow right by those cows and into the grain-growing fields of Vinx. It's going to take strength to stop them. I want to be part of this."

"So do I." I didn't realize it until I said it. "I don't want to hide in the forest while my homeland is raided, and my people are killed."

"Hiding is what civilians usually do," she said. Then, as she watched my face. "But you're not a normal civilian, are you?" She looked thoughtful. "Maybe you can get better at that oomer stuff."

"Oomrush."

"Yeah, that. Is there a way it can be used in battle?"

"Not that I know of. The Velka consider it more of a peculiarity than a power. But maybe."

"You want to help? Find a way to use that thing you do. You stop an army with a more skilled army, but having something extra in your back pocket never hurts."

I agreed, wondering if the places already overrun by the Mongols had had anything like the Velka.

****

Nothing could have prepared me for the feeling of leaving the forest. It was like I'd been laying under a thick blanket and someone lifted it off. At its best, the blanket gave warmth and comfort, but it remained heavy and restricting, too. As I stepped into the light, I took big, full, deep breaths reaching from the top of my head to my toes. I looked out to the horizon. Everything was okay.

My sister Olivine met us, leading our horses so we could ride them home. Mine whinnied in joy when she saw me, and I threw my arms around her neck. The Velka who'd accompanied Sulphur and I to the forest's edge gave me a salute and turned to lead our donkeys back to the lodge.

It was a handoff. Of me. From the Velka to the world.

As we approached the farm, I saw Coral hanging up freshly washed bedding in our yard. Perfect timing. I'd done research for her before I left, and I had news for her not meant for the ears of others.

I greeted her with a hug then whispered "I've learned more about luskies."

"Not now," she said as we stood hidden behind sheets billowing in the wind. The smell of fresh soap surrounded us. I supposed she wanted to talk about Davor, or wedding plans, or maybe about the pregnancy instead.

"No, listen. I've discovered that we Velka can't recognize a luski. It takes another luski to tell and to train a new luski, too."

"So?"

"So based on what I've learned, you really could be one. They're not all mothers: it has to do with being a nurturer. And you're certainly one of those, right?"

"Look, Ryalgar, I'm getting married in three days. I don't need this now."

Of course. My timing was awful. "You don't have to do anything about it," I said. "I'm looking for a luski to talk to you. They're hard to find; most go to extraordinary pains to hide what they can do. But I'll find one."

She changed the subject.

"I've heard this invasion could happen this winter," she said. "Davor has found me a house because he'll be gone a lot, training in Pilk. It's close to school, and I'm going to keep teaching after the wedding, all the way until my time gets close."

That was good news. Coral loved her job as a teacher, and I'd always found it odd when pregnant women weren't allowed to keep doing what they did. On a farm, both human and animal mothers carried on with life as they carried their young.

"What will you do when it's time for the baby to be born?"

"I thought I'd stay with Mom and Dad, but Davor wants me to go somewhere safer. Safer than here. Ryalgar, I don't want Vinx *not* to be a safe place."

I thought I understood. "You think you could protect yourself if you were a luski?"

She looked behind me and I turned. My mother came towards us with a tray holding fizzy green afternoon wine and honey cakes.

"There you girls are," she called to us. "Welcome home, Ryalgar! Come, let me look at you. Coral and I are dying to fill you in on the wedding plans, aren't we?"

As the talk moved on to the food and the flowers, the clothes and the guest list, I noticed the worry on Coral's face. I'd find a luski to talk to her soon.

****

As I settled into my old bed that night, after eighths of being away, my thoughts turned to a holiday long ago. I was ten. It was one of the rare times our whole family had gone out. Mom walked with the twins, Dad carried frail Iolite on one hip while holding Gypsum's hand, and I'd been ordered to hang onto Coral and Sulphur.

The marketplace was full of vendors offering us treats. A lone man stumbled into our path, probably drunk. He tripped trying to avoid my mother and sisters and, as he fell, he gave my mother a furious look.

"Get out of my way, you stupid pruska," he said. "And take your little pruskas with you." He waved his hand at me and my sisters. "Pruskas, every prucking one!"

My mother turned to my father, expecting him to defend his family's honor from what must have been a deep insult. But my father was no fighter. He let go of Gypsum, turned to the stranger, and offered him his hand. My mother cried out in indignation.

"Let me help you up, sir. I can tell the day has not gone your way. Get some rest and sober up, and perhaps then the holiday will turn more to your liking."

The man stood, muttered something I couldn't hear, and stumbled off.

My father turned to my mother.

"Be reasonable, Markita. What would I have accomplished arguing with a drunk? Come now. Let's not let him ruin our celebration."

I wanted to know what the man had meant, of course, but I was afraid to ask in front of everyone. Early the next morning, my curiosity overcame my fear. As Mom and I made breakfast for the family, I said "What's a pruska?"

My mother stood up tall and inhaled as if I'd struck her.

"It's a girl who asks too many questions, that's what. A girl who thinks she has to know everything and who cares more about getting information than she does about the feelings of her mother."

She glared at me. I supposed she wanted me to say she was wrong, that of course I cared about her feelings, but I'd turned away and hadn't said a word. She barely spoke to me for days afterward.

~ 6 ~

The Dream Wedding

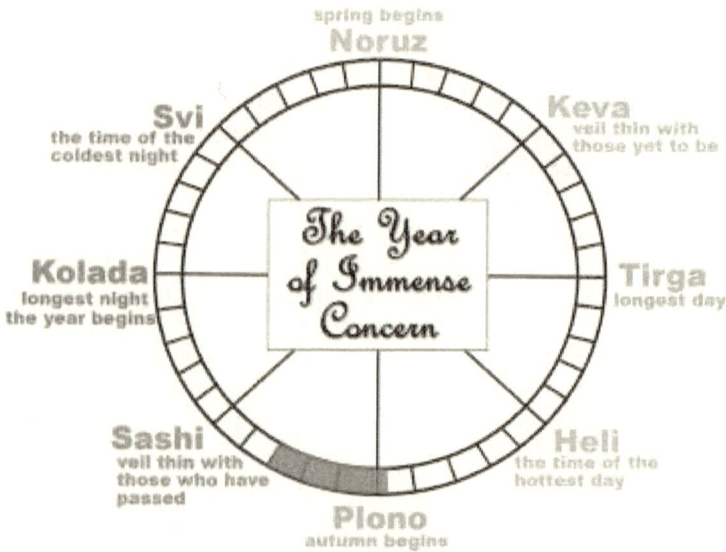

Davor arrived the day before the wedding, with his parents, a younger brother, and two old friends. They were too many for us to house, so they took lodging at a nearby inn, to the relief of everyone in my family.

When Coral learned no more of his relations or friends were coming for the ceremony, I saw the flash of embarrassment cross her face. My family had expected a few dozen from his side, at least.

I tried to make conversation with Davor over a dinner the two families shared that night. Although he was polite, he showed little interest in getting to know me. That annoyed me, so I pushed him for information.

"Do you think this swarm of Mongols will attack us this winter or wait till the next?"

He raised an eyebrow.

"I don't generally discuss military intelligence with civilians. I'm sure you understand."

He downed his last swallow of ale and motioned to a server to bring him another. I tapped him on the arm.

"Do you think the Mongols will enter through the grasslands of Bisu? It's by far the easiest way into Ilaria and word is they have horses they prefer to let graze before they attack."

He gave me a more serious look.

"The Velka have women from all of the nichnas," I added. "We amass our own intelligence, for our own protection. I'm sure you understand."

His tight little smile was one of acquiescence. "Unlike some of my peers, I do respect the Velka's abilities. But surely you women know you couldn't be safer than you are deep in the forest of Ilari."

I nodded as though he'd said something of value. Having started him on a subject he knew well, I hoped he couldn't resist sharing more of his expertise. I was right.

"I'm speaking of you and the Zurians, too, of course, because they live in the forest as well. In fact, if we Svadlu don't handle this invasion well, the Velka and Zur could be all that's left of Ilari once the Mongols are through with us."

"Then we both understand how serious this is." I gave him my brightest smile. "If the Svadlu send the entire army to the obvious entrance to the realm, we're all safe, if they prevail. If they hedge their bets and keep some fighters in reserve, they're more likely to lose the initial battle but could still protect some of the nichnas if the Mongols get through. Just *not* Vinx and Bisu. They'd have to give them up."

A server set another beverage in front of him and he gave the mug an eager glance.

"Look. We'll protect everything we can. Sacrifices may have to be made. Okay?"

47

S. R. Cronin

With that, he downed half the contents of his new mug, turned his full back towards me, and began to talk to one of his friends. I don't think he realized what he'd just shared. I now knew the Svadlu would at least consider sacrificing my homeland.

****

My mother didn't ask me a direct question until the day of the wedding. To be fair, she had her hands full till then. Coral's ardor for Davor appeared lessened, my other sisters weren't around much until the big day, and Dad only helped with the preparations when asked. Mom carried the brunt of the wedding on her shoulders, charging ahead with cheery determination as her second-born prepared to marry an honorary prince. Meanwhile, my life interested her far less now that I could no longer snag a royal husband.

But once the servers cleared the food and the musicians began to play, she turned to me.

"I'm curious. Did your grandmother express any interest in attending your sister's wedding?"

I didn't know what to say. "I'm sure she wouldn't have considered it unless she was invited."

"She didn't ask to be invited?"

"She seems to be under the impression you want her to stay dead. Is that not true?"

My mother sighed. "Under the circumstances, this charade makes no sense anymore. I've told all of your sisters the truth."

"Good. I'll let grandmother know she's come back to life. I think she'll be glad."

As people got up to dance and others began to clap to the music, the room grew noisier and Mom said no more. So I spoke, raising my voice to be heard over the commotion.

"I want you to know I'm content there. It's not perfect, but I *have* found a place to belong." When she still said nothing, I leaned in close to her and added in a loud whisper "and I'm seeing Nevik when he can get away."

She heard me and sucked in her breath. She brought her mouth inches from my ear. "It's a dangerous game, being the mistress of royalty. What are you thinking? The jealous wife of a ruler is no enemy to have."

48

"It's more complicated."

"I don't care what he tells you, dear. Be careful. This often does not end well for the woman in your shoes."

I looked away towards the festivities. My parents had rented a facility used to store barley in the winter and there was a faint earthy smell to the place. No one from Vinx minded; it smelled like home to us. However, I'd overheard a few comments about the odor from the Levish, and noticed most of them stood together near the door.

In the center of the room, Davor put on a good show, despite his small entourage. Coral danced with him, playing her part, while my other five sisters engaged with the guests, most of them dancing and flirting the way young women did.

The guests were full of ale and wine and many complimented my father on the fine celebration he'd hosted. More than one of them cast a pitying glance my way as they spoke.

"Does it bother you that you'll never have a day like this?" There was nothing mean in my mother's tone. She wanted to know.

I gave her an honest answer. "Not nearly as much as you'd think. I suspect I'm having a better day than Coral is, and that tells me something."

Two days later it was time to go back. I'd had precious moments with my family and spent as much time staring at the horizon as I could. I realized how much I loved the nichna of my birth.

Part of me wanted to stay and soak in more of the big wide sky. Another part of me knew I couldn't. If I wanted a Vinx to come home to for as long as I lived, I needed to find a way to defend it. For based on what a half-drunk Davor told me, the Svadlu might be forced to abandon Bisu and Vinx as part of their strategy.

I couldn't imagine how I could do what the entire Svadlu could not. But if there was a way, any way at all, it involved my returning to the forest and learning to do things beyond my wildest dreams.

On the day of my return, Olivine rode to the forest with me. As I gave her my horse's reins and waved her off, I thought I was okay. Then as I stepped into the dense growth around the perimeter, a wave of nausea overtook me with such strength I couldn't move. I clutched my stomach, waiting for it to subside. It didn't.

Why was the part of me that wanted to stay under the open sky putting up this unexpected fight?

Go, I ordered my legs. *I command you to move.* But as I tried to lift one, I knew I was going to vomit.

"You okay out there?" The Velka guide waiting for me must have heard me retch.

"I'm fine." I turned back to my legs.

You have nowhere else to go. Your food, water, and clothing all are in the forest. Your friends are there.

My legs ignored me.

If you don't cut out this nonsense and go into the forest, everyone you love is going to die.

I spat the words out at my own body, and something cold and numb replaced the nausea. Good. I lifted one leg. I lifted the other. My arms engaged and I made my way back in. I was shaking by the time I mounted the small donkey, but I was moving. Moving deeper into the forest.

****

The next time Nevik and I spent a night together in one of the Velka's cozy cabins along the forest's edge, my mother's words came back to haunt me.

"I've heard your wedding is in a few anks." I couldn't help pointing it out.

"I thought we agreed to not waste our precious time together discussing parts of my life over which I have no control. But yes, it is."

"Are you warming to her?" I asked.

His eyes narrowed.

"Is she warming to you?

"Ryalgar. Would you feel more secure if we had a private ceremony of our own? One in which I stated that, beyond a doubt, you are and will always be the only woman I will ever love?"

It was a nice offer, really, but it made me realize I didn't doubt his love. Not now. He meant what he said and, to the extent anyone can predict how they'll feel for the rest of their life, he believed I would be the one who always had his heart.

I *was* worried about her, and his family, and all the things neither of us could predict. No private ceremony would ease those fears. That was what public ceremonies were for, to place constraints on people and force them to try to work through the unpredictable. He and I would never have that.

"No," I said. "It's not necessary."

"Your sister's wedding has you thinking?"

"I suppose. She seems happy about being a mother and a teacher. She and Davor are forging an arrangement of convenience, I think." I took his hand in mine and played with his fingers as I talked. It gave me something to do with my nervous energy. "I wouldn't trade places with her."

"I'm glad. It's a shame someone other than that idiot didn't get her pregnant." Those were harsh words coming from Nevik. "Sorry. I understand he's now your brother-in-law, and you need to make the best of it. How did *you* find him to be?"

"I wasn't impressed one-on-one, but he knows how to charm people. He has a sense of obligation; so I think he'll do his part providing for her and the child. Have you had dealings with him yet?"

Nevik pulled his hand away from mine.

"Oh yes. The man seemed to think *he* was going to be put in charge of our preparations for the Mongols. Managed to stir things up a good bit when it didn't go his way. He and his buddies continue to do a lot of loud grumbling about me, hoping to convince my father he made a mistake."

"It *is* a lot of responsibility, Nevik. Are you sure you want to fight him for this honor?"

He gave me a funny look. "The problem with military leaders is they only think about winning. They're trained to consider the outcome of the battle, not the welfare of the people. The princes of Pilk have always looked out for all of Ilari and will continue doing so. It's why my father didn't put Davor or any other Mozdol in charge of our preparations, and it's why he won't change his mind."

I understood, perhaps better than Nevik realized.

Davor and his Svadlu pals would sacrifice Vinx and Bisu to the Mongols. Even I could see how giving up those two nichnas would make protecting the rest of Ilari easier. Maybe the Svadlu had ideas about relocating the endangered citizens as they gave up the land? I couldn't imagine such a scheme working out well for the Vinxites and Bisuites, but I was willing to assume the Svadlu weren't starting with a plan involving wholesale slaughter in two nichnas.

Nevik had let me know he and his family didn't like the Svadlu's approach. I supposed I should be glad someone argued for the safety of my homeland and the man I loved was on their side. However, my family's safety would depend on who was in charge in the end. Much as I loved Nevik, I recognized Davor was louder, more experienced, and probably more conniving if he wanted to be.

It didn't matter how much lip service the Svadlu paid Nevik now. Once the battle started, his opinion probably wouldn't matter.

~ 7 ~

Becoming an Expert

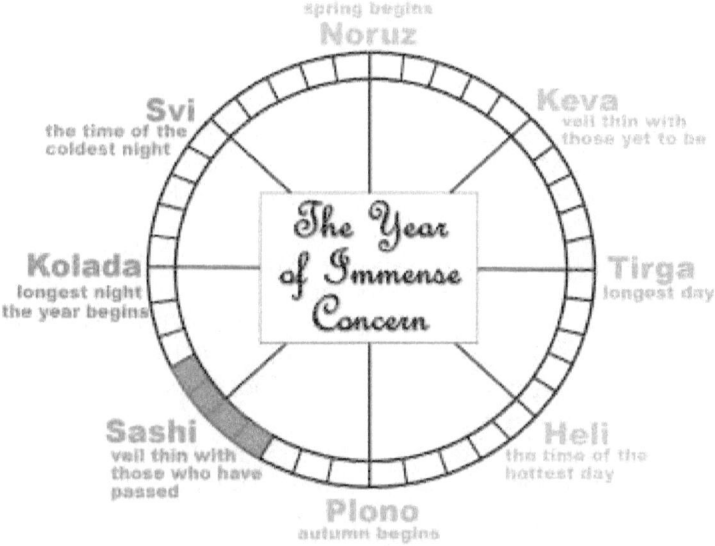

After my exchange with Nevik, I became obsessed with learning everything I could about the Mongols. At first, I interrogated any Velka with information. Then I found and read all the written material we had. After an ank I'd exhausted those avenues, so I asked permission to leave to seek others throughout the realm who knew more.

Now that I'd proven I could and would force myself to return, and now that I had an important reason for going, no one objected.

My years as a student left me with a strong knowledge of history and geography, and with contacts at every place of advanced learning. I headed to Pilk to meet with as many of my former teachers as I could find. My visit surprised most and my career choice intrigued many, but none hesitated to give me information and most helped me more than I expected. This impending attack spooked every thinking person.

My grandmother and the other Velka leaders gave me a lot of freedom during this time, and as I came and went, no one complained when I missed most of my classes and many of their gatherings. Perhaps the new intensity, even desperation, they saw in me helped. I began to hear I'd been put in charge of the Velka response to the invasion. I supposed that was a logical explanation for my actions. Eventually, I began to wonder if it was true.

The main problem with learning more about our expected attackers was that they killed most of the people who challenged them. The few who were left to talk fled in terror, making it hard to separate their fearful exaggeration from the truth. Yet, consistent stories emerged, stories appearing to have come to us from different survivors.

I placed the following facts in my basket of known truths.

The Mongols were arrogant, often attacking with far fewer soldiers than they expected to encounter. This was good. However, they had reason to be so confident. Their smaller army almost always vanquished the larger armies defending their own homes. This was not good.

They were fierce, but not invincible; they lost the occasional battle. More importantly, after such a loss they'd walked away from a handful of potential conquests, deciding some acquisitions weren't worth the trouble in a world filled with others easy to defeat.

That had to be Ilari's goal. We couldn't fight them off forever but perhaps we could make our way onto their not-worth-the-trouble list. I vowed to learn more about those few places.

Much of their ferocity came from their ability to fight on horseback. They wore a sort of thick leather clothing providing them some protection from swords, lances, and arrows. On horseback, they moved with a speed and unpredictability that overwhelmed others.

I tried to think of how this reliance on their horses could be used against them.

Stories varied as to their motives. Some claimed they killed everyone, including the children, and burnt their conquered lands to the ground. These versions portrayed them as a raging evil, with only a desire to destroy.

Others told tales of negotiation and options of servitude and tribute. Perhaps only those who would not serve were destroyed without mercy? This would be a useful technique, likely to yield more surrenders.

Every report said the Mongols came from a perpetually cold land to the east. They attacked in winter because they were uncomfortable when it was warm. Interesting. They also came from wide open plains, like my own in Vinx, but far larger. They disliked fighting in forests, which was understandable given their reliance on horses. They considered the bright blue sky to be holy. Hmm. I agreed.

They had their superstitions. The most interesting one to me was a love of the number ten. They would attack with a hundred, or a thousand, or ten thousand. They avoided fractions of those amounts. What an oddity. Perhaps there was a vulnerability there.

We in Ilari seldom took a census, but the most recent one estimated we were just under fifty thousand people. The Mongol's pride caused them to attack with fewer soldiers than they expected to fight. So, they probably wouldn't bring ten thousand horsemen down upon our tiny realm.

How large an army would they expect us to have? I'd learned our Svadlu numbered only a couple of hundred, but other realms, those not blessed with as many years of peace, maintained an army ten times our size. So, if our attackers expected to meet two or three thousand defenders, we'd probably be attacked by a thousand of them. Knowing the precise size of one's foe had to be helpful.

One last story got repeated consistently. The Mongols strove not to lose a single warrior in their battles. I don't know why that moved me, but it seemed strangely compassionate. Soldiers were considered disposable everywhere, as far as I knew. I suspected these people had more to them than my sources knew.

****

My time in Pilk allowed me to visit with my younger sister Gypsum, a student there. A tall, thin young woman with wispy, almost white-blonde hair, Gypsum had never cared much for school. It surprised me she'd lasted as long in her advanced education as she had. I thought she was smarter than most, but the orderliness of education rubbed her wrong. Her keen mind preferred fewer fences.

When I asked about her plans, she hesitated as if she had something she wanted to share, then she demurred. Whatever it was she almost told me, I'd have to learn about it another day. I felt sure the details of what I was doing would bore her, so I never mentioned I'd come to Pilk for research. Instead, we spent a pleasant afternoon together drinking wine and laughing over old memories. I confess some of my mother's least pleasant behavior supplied the foundation for much of our shared mirth.

My travels also made it easier for me to rendezvous with Nevik, and I took advantage of the opportunity several times. I enjoyed the sex, and our affection for each other remained, but more complicated issues had entered the mix.

He finally spoke up.

"You look at me with pleading in your eyes. I liked it better when you looked at me with longing."

He was right. I desperately wanted him to keep the idea of defending Vinx on the table. Though the relationship between a prince and a farm girl is never balanced, my growing need for Nevik to stand up for the safety of my home skewed our situation even more. I changed the subject. Kind of.

"How is your struggle for command going? Do most of the Svadlu back you, or has Davor turned them against you?"

"I have the backing of my father, the ruling prince of Pilk. That's all I need."

I took his answer to mean it wasn't going as well as he'd have liked. He wasn't finished though.

"Look, I don't discuss military issues, with you or anyone, but it's obvious you've figured out the main disagreement between me and Davor's crowd. So yes, you're right. The Svadlu believe the Mongols are fiercer than the Royals will admit, and they think we need to give up the six easternmost nichnas and concentrate on defending the western six.

What? They'd give away six *of them?*

"Of course you've looked at a map and no doubt realize how much easier it would be to defend western Ilari, thanks to the geography. All except for the border on the east side of Pilk, that is, and I'm sure, with all the questions you've been asking, you've heard about the wall being built there and you've certainly figured out why."

Nevik had to be the first man in my life who had overestimated my knowledge. Under other circumstances, it would be charming.

No, I hadn't looked at a map. Not *that* hard. I hadn't heard about a wall. But then, all my focus had been on the Mongols, not on Ilari's plans for defense. I thought my best bet was to pretend like I knew everything he assumed I did. Then he'd keep talking.

"I don't like it, Ryalgar, not a bit. I promise you, I'll do everything in my power to see their plan is never accepted. Now, can we *please* go back to having fun together?"

I curled into his arms and said no more.

The next morning, I thanked him for his trust in me and his commitment to all of Ilari. I promised him I'd never bring it up again. I wish he hadn't looked so relieved.

I had also wanted to ask him to help keep Davor's *other* worst impulse in check by discouraging him from courting other women publicly and embarrassing my sister. Davor didn't know Nevik had any tie to my family, of course, but I was hoping a little princely disapproval of unseemly behavior could be a factor.

Or not.

The more I thought about it, the more it seemed likely Davor would flirt with other women *more* if he thought Nevik disapproved. I decided not to mention my request.

****

I enjoyed the Sashi festivities in Pilk, despite spending the night alone in a stylish inn. But after Sashi, autumn turns fast towards winter, and I knew it was time to get off the road.

As I entered the forest, I rediscovered one of nature's basic facts. Leaves fall off most trees in the autumn. Because trees weren't all that common on the plains of Vinx, this hadn't affected me much other than to note the seasonal beauty. But now, the overpowering canopy of the forest was reduced by half as only branches, twigs, and pine needles blocked my view of the sky. I sighed a deep, long, happy sigh. Coming and going would be easier for me in the winter.

Once I returned to the lodge, I could tell something had changed. My oomrush group still met and welcomed me back, but my morning class had been disbanded. All the other women graduated, the instructor said, and there were no more novices in my absence. She seemed distant and distracted.

Grandmother gave me a day to settle in, then invited me for afternoon wine in her room. Joli sought me out beforehand, studying me like she was considering how much to tell me.

"Spit it out," I said.

"I think you may have been kicked out of the Conclave."

I had to laugh. "Well, I wasn't in it for long, was I? If traveling around the realm for a few anks seeking information is enough to get me banned, I wasn't going to last anyway."

"It could be worse than that," Joli said. I could tell this unlikely Velka from Zur cared about me, and I felt the stronger for having an ally here.

"I missed you too," I said. She rolled her eyes and we hugged in greeting.

"So, what crime did I commit by leaving?"

"I'm fairly sure some women in the Conclave started it. You know the ones; Hana, Natia, and Indris? The three of them are always hanging out together."

Yes, I knew them. They'd refused to sit at the table with Sulphur and me and had appeared to resent me from the beginning.

"They're kind of the youngest in the group, besides you. I bet they thought they'd be running the Velka someday," Joli said. "Then when the granddaughter of the supreme leader joined up, they saw their ambitions crumble. Just guessing here."

"I wish they knew how little I cared about running the Velka."

"I don't think it matters. Your grandmother has ambitions for you, and that's enough to pruck up their plans."

"I don't think my grandmother is any kind of supreme leader."

Joli laughed. "It's hard to tell around here, isn't it? They do keep that Conclave thing intentionally vague. Anyway, your loyalty to the Velka has come under question and that's not good. You have issues to clear up."

****

My grandmother did say "welcome back" as I walked into the room, but the two other older women said nothing. She gestured me towards a chair.

"You begin, Aliz," one of them said without looking at me.

"These are difficult times." My grandmother seemed to be choosing her words with care. "Rough times for a young woman to join the Velka. She understandably has strong loyalties to her home, and yet we count on her to place her allegiance to us above all else."

The third woman spoke. "Because we recognize this, we've stopped accepting novices until this threat of a Mongol invasion passes. Do you think that's wise?"

"I do." I meant it. They had a valid point.

"We've even asked our two most recent novices to return to their original nichnas, for the time being at least. One was happy to go, the other was upset," the first woman said.

"Which brings us to the problem of you." My grandmother spoke, calling *me* the problem. I felt a little dizzy and my knees were weak. Of all the indignities in the world, was I now going to be kicked out of the Velka, the one place where I'd finally found a home?

"Please, no."

"I'm glad you feel that way," she said. She stood and began pacing as she talked. I guessed she didn't want to look me in the eye. "I have to ask you an important question. For the past few anks, you've scoured the realm for information about this new threat. We've supported you, allowing you time away, and providing you with considerable resources, without asking for justification. But we need to know. Do you seek to protect us? Or Vinx?" She turned and faced me directly. "There are others who insist the safety of Vinx is your priority."

Those "others" had to be Hana, Natia, and Idris.

Luckily, I knew my answer to her question.

59

"There is no difference."

"Oh, goat scump. Don't give us some all-for-one platitude," the first woman said. "Life doesn't work that way."

Her response made me angry enough to say things I wouldn't have and to exaggerate a truth here and there. I sat up straight in my chair, letting a bit of my indignation show.

"It's no platitude. Plenty of Velka know I'm in a relationship with a prince of Pilk, but not as many know he's the one charged with overseeing training the army. Meanwhile, my sister just married a Mozdol who speaks for the soldiers, and I spent time with him, drunk, at her wedding. I have more facts than I should and more than I should tell you."

"Your connections can be verified," my grandmother said. "But if your loyalty lies with us, prove it by telling us what you know."

I knew she'd say that, and I had every intention of doing so. After all, Nevik had only asked I not discuss the defense of Ilari with him. He'd said nothing about my discussing it with others.

"A drastic plan is being considered to surrender no less than six of the easternmost nichnas to the Mongols. Half the realm. They've started building a wall along the eastern border of Pilk as we speak, to facilitate this. Check on it if you like."

Please don't let Nevik have been wrong about the wall.

"It's a strategic plan opposed by many, including my prince. Yet, if our army's recommendations prevail over the wishes of the Royals, this will be their position."

The three women's faces were filled with disbelief.

"Imagine a map in your head," I asked them "Look hard. This plan would leave the open forest, our part of the forest, surrounded on three sides by the Mongols. How long do you think we'll survive once these invaders can spend all day, every day, trying to set our forest on fire? We know our best growers can't withstand that. Not forever. And once the Mongols begin pushing into our territory, our only direction to run will be into the arms of our adversaries, the Zurians."

The women looked at each other. "You've learned much," the third woman acknowledged as she took a sip of her fizzy pale green afternoon wine.

"More than you know. I've also been learning about the people who will be invading us, and I've been hatching a plan to protect us all."

It was a bold claim, but as I said it, I knew it was true. That was exactly what I'd been doing, I just hadn't realized it.

"You? Protect us? How?"

I held up my hands, palms out, to ask for patience. "My plan is in the beginning stages, but it would involve many of the Velka fighting, in their own way, and none of us going into hiding. It will take me two anks to firm it up now that my research is done. I'm asking you for the chance to do so. Then, I'll present it to you, properly thought out." I turned to the first woman. "No goat scump."

"Kolada is but four anks away," she answered. "You better think fast. They could invade at any time."

"I'll be hoping for, at worst, a late-winter attack," I said. "What I'm considering can be done in stages. The more time we have, the more we can do. Doing anything leaves our fate in better hands than nothing at all."

The warmth was back in my grandmother's eyes. Could I have made her happier?

"I propose we put Ryalgar in charge of the Velka's response to the Mongol invasion," she declared.

The other two women looked at each other. One sighed, the other shrugged.

"Formulate your plan," one of them said and the other nodded.

They didn't seem to share my grandmother's enthusiasm for turning this over to me, but I'd convinced them of the need for action, and I suspected they didn't have an alternative to propose.

Or maybe my friend Joli was right. Maybe Grandma was the supreme leader of the Velka. Who knew?

~ 8 ~

Weaponizing Oomrush

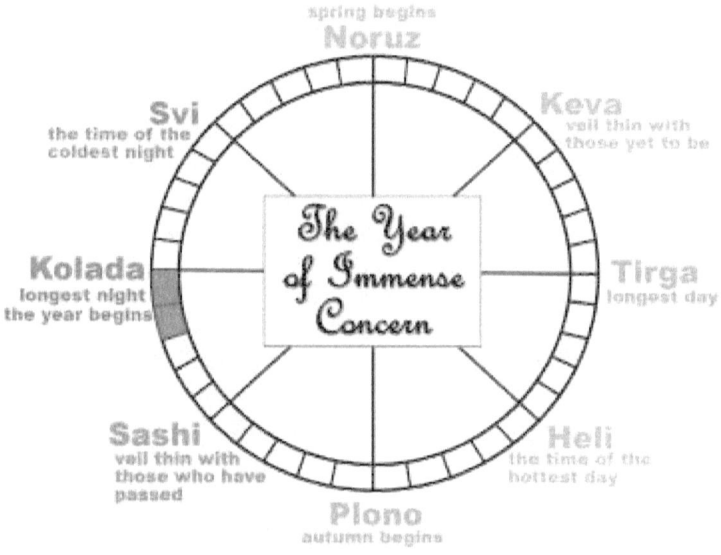

spring begins
Noruz

Svi
the time of the
coldest night

Keva
veil thin with
those yet to be

*The Year
of Immense
Concern*

Kolada
longest night
the year begins

Tirga
longest day

Sashi
veil thin with
those who have
passed

Heli
the time of the
hottest day

Plono
autumn begins

I consulted Joli right away because I trusted her. Besides, she was one of the best oomrushers we had, and I already knew oomrushing would somehow be part of my plan. And, she came from a culture of fighters. Zur continually tried to push its boundaries outward, and the Svadlu spent a good part of their time restraining the Zurians. Joli had grown up amid this. As I hoped, she had no trouble coming up with ideas for weaponizing oomrush.

"Smoke. It's the easiest thing to move. Maybe we can make it heavy enough to blind them."

"That's a good idea. I like it, except a lot of smoke does require a lot of fire. I'm not sure I want to set Ilari on fire to save it."

"Okay then, how about gnats? Most of us can direct small insects. We could breed a scump load of them, and send swarms of them after the Mongols."

"Yeah, but then we'd have a scump load of bugs on our hands. Why not use dust instead? Can we move dust into their eyes?"

"I could, but most can't. Bugs are already up in the air, flying around. Dust is hard because you have to get it off the ground and going."

"You're right." I remembered a science class I particularly enjoyed, one about things. If you threw a thing upwards it always came back down. If you kicked a thing, it kept going for a while. If a thing was sitting still, it took effort to get it going. I'd liked studying how things behaved.

"If we could manage to put the dust in the air and get it moving first, then it would be easier for oomrushers to control it," I said.

"Well, if you're going to bother do that, why use dust? Get something sharper. Those awful stickers you step on out in the field aren't so heavy, and getting one of those in your eyes would have more impact."

"Okay, then, why stop at stickers? If something heavier than a gnat is moving through the air, do you think we can train ourselves to keep it going farther than it normally would?"

"Like what kind of thing?"

"I don't know. A knife? A javelin?"

Joli gave me a grin. "You'd have made a good Zurian. That's an ambitious idea. My first thought is no oomrusher can influence an object so large, but then again, as far as I know, no oomrusher has tried."

We both grinned now.

"Let's get some apple seeds. Flick them and see what we can do once they are up in the air and moving."

Joli and I spent most of the next ank in my room playing with apple seeds, tiny balls of silk thread, and the dried bodies of dead bugs. One by one we brought in others from our afternoon oomrush sessions. Word spread about what we were working on and how it could be vital to the survival of the Velka. So far, every woman we'd asked was eager to help.

Others brought us food and increasingly larger items to throw against the walls. We were working with dried twigs when my grandmother knocked. She entered, looked at the five of us sitting on the floor amidst the mess on my carpet, and winced.

"Watch this," Joli said. She picked up a small twig and threw it like one would throw a tiny knife. It went halfway across the room and fell to the floor. Aliz looked unimpressed.

"And this." Joli picked up a second twig, threw it in the same fashion, but stared at it with intensity as it flew. This time, it drove itself into a pillow across the room. My grandmother raised an eyebrow.

"You're going to attack them with twigs?"

"Possibly. If we can get lots of them to go far enough," I said. "We have an ability here that's never been used for fighting, at least as far as we know. It will be a total surprise to these Mongols. To everyone, actually. We're trying to figure out the best way to use it."

"I see. Do you want me to send word for your sister Olivine not to visit you next ank?"

Pruck. I'd forgotten all about that. Back at Coral's wedding, Olivine and I had made plans for her to come to see me a few days before Kolada, as it would likely get too cold for her to travel afterward. I'd been looking forward to it until I became obsessed with saving the realm. Now, it seemed I didn't have the time for something so frivolous.

"I can't stop this now. Please, let her know I want her to come, but we need to make it after winter."

"Suit yourself." She took a step back towards the door, then turned towards me. "Ryalgar, she was only going to stay for two days. Consider how the break could do you good and your comrades as well." She gestured at the women sitting around me who'd barely left my room except to sleep. "Every one of you could use a bath."

I understood tactfully conveyed instructions when I heard them. I could have ignored Aliz and insisted Olivine not come, but my grandmother's request showed wisdom. I'd bathe, and I'd take the break.

History would show it to be one of my best decisions.

****

Olivine and I had always gotten on well, even though Olivine wasn't close to anyone, except perhaps her twin sister Celestine. She was a loner as a child, preferring to spend time with her paints and pens instead of other humans. By the time she was twelve, she produced beautiful sketches and paintings, some of which the school sold in the market to raise funds for supplies.

I always got the feeling she couldn't wait to finish her conversations with people and return to her art. Yet, I respected her passion for doing something well, and I admired the tiny birds, flowers, and leaves that filled her creations.

She was four years younger than I and had only finished her advanced studies half a year ago. I sensed there was a boyfriend she'd chosen to keep secret, giving Sulphur a chance to make her way, much as Coral had done for me. What a shame this stupid pecking order persisted.

I hoped the boyfriend was a prince or close enough to one. Otherwise my mother was likely to make Olivine's life miserable.

When Olivine arrived, she dismounted from the little donkey with care, reminding me how much smaller she was. At least half a head shorter than me, she had a slight build in contrast to my hardy one.

I watched the other women study her. Shades of bronze glistened in her light brown hair, but it was nothing of note compared to Coral's flaming orange or Sulphur's unusual short gold mane. *She's not as impressive as the other two.* I saw it in their faces.

But Olivine was physically unimpressive from a distance only because her most striking feature, her intense green eyes, could only be seen up close. And she became more impressive when you saw the beauty of what she could do.

This sister received polite greetings from most of the Velka, as all our visitors do, but between my recent absences and her reticent nature, most people left us alone. I noticed that Hana, Natia, and Idris didn't even bother to say hello.

Given all the time we had to talk, I struggled to make conversation. I didn't want to push her to tell me about her possible boyfriend; that story was hers to tell in her own time. I didn't want to tell her about how I was still with Nevik, I'd already decided the group outside the Velka who knew my secret was plenty large. So she gave me news from home, and I told her a little about life in the forest, and then we just sat together, two people with too many things they both thought they shouldn't say.

I finally blinked.

"You know how I can move smoke around? Well, they're teaching me to get better at that here."

"That's great. I've heard the Velka like women who can do that, and they also recruit the ones who are really good with plants. And making potions, of course. Tell me, do they ever teach people who can do other things, even if they *aren't* Velka?"

"Not usually. We call this thing I do oomrush. Do you know an oomrusher who wants to be trained?"

"No. Nothing like that."

I waited. It was her turn to blink.

"I found out there is a name for what I can do, too."

She could do something? How had I missed this?

"Really? What's it called?"

I feared she wouldn't want to discuss it, but Olivine kept talking.

"Some artists have it. It's called a long-eye. You can focus on things far away and see them like they were close up. I mean, everything else goes blurry except for the bird or insect or flower, and it gets really big. Clearer, too, and lighter if it's kind of dark."

She'd done many of her paintings in our yard. This long-eye thing explained how her creations were so varied and so lifelike.

"I've been meeting with other artists since I finished school. We paint together and encourage each other. Mother thinks it's a waste of time, but Dad says it makes sense, and I should try to get as good as I can. Anyway, four of us in the group are long-eyes. I just wondered if there was a way we could get better."

"Is it only artists who can do this?"

"No, I don't think so. I mean, all the ones I know are artists but Bohdan says ...." She froze.

Bohdan? So. There was a boyfriend.

"Do you want to tell me who Bohdan is?" I gave her my best conspiratorial smile.

She could have lied about him, but she didn't. Instead, she shook her head and looked ready to cry.

"No. Not yet. Please. There's a problem."

Okay. If anyone could empathize with a problematic relationship, it was me. I backed off.

"So, you use your long-eye for your art. That's wonderful. Do you, I don't know, use it otherwise?"

"Yeah. Remember how they made all of us learn something physical in school?"

She laughed and I did too. We'd shared this bond since we were little girls. I preferred to be indoors with my studies and she with her sketchbook, and we'd both resented being forced into activities by adults who insisted we become more well-rounded. I'd opted to learn folk dancing, been bad at it, and complained a lot. She'd studied...

"Archery," she reminded me. "I kind of liked it, more than I expected to, maybe because this thing with my vision made me better at it. It's fun to be good at something. I kept it up while I was in school. A friend of mine," she paused, "he heard about it and my long-eye and convinced me to pick up my bow and start practicing. He says it's a good skill to have in uncertain times. I think he's spooked about these stupid Mongols, like everyone else. Anyway, I'm back at it." She smiled and pointed to her lightly tanned forearm. "See? I'm even getting a little sunshine."

How interesting to discover a whole side to my younger sister I'd never gotten to know.

"Does having a long-eye make you a better archer?"

"It helps, but I can see farther than I can shoot with any accuracy. Farther than anyone can, I think. If my arrows went farther, my long-eye would be more helpful."

I stared at her in disbelief. "I have twigs that go farther when I throw them."

"Huh?"

"Olivine. Could you stay for another day or two? Please? Look, I know Kolada is coming and you probably wanted to celebrate it elsewhere, but I'm doing more than improving my abilities. I'm trying to find a way to use them for defense. Against an attack."

"Don't tell me you're obsessed with the Mongols, too."

"The threat's real. And the idea I just had would be amazing if it worked. I need a little more of your time."

She shrugged. "Of course. I didn't bring my equipment with me, though."

"I'm sure we have something you can use."

Joli and the other oomrushers were as dubious as Olivine. Having time to relax had done them good, but the break had also given them time to think. They questioned whether we were wasting our time. I agreed; the question was worth asking.

They thought my idea of giving a moving arrow more accuracy on a longer flight was beyond what was possible with our gift. I thought smoke, dust, and flying twigs could be helpful, but such tricks alone would never give us all we needed.

Olivine fidgeted as she stood at one end of the clearing for our lodge, a borrowed bow in her hands. My grandmother, most of the Conclave, and several dozen others had come outside to watch. I knew this was the kind of spectacle Olivine hated, and I wished I didn't have to make such a show of this.

"So you want me to shoot while you, I don't know, push?"

"Exactly. Push is a good word. For now, you don't have to aim at anything. Just shoot while I stand behind you." I had paced the clearing off. At its longest, it was three hundred paces. "I'll push on five of them, and Joli knows which ones. When you're done, she'll see if mine went a little further or perhaps stayed on course better."

Olivine was more adept with a bow than I expected. Arrows one, two, four, seven, and nine flew across the clearing to land in the dirt. Arrows three, five, six, eight, and ten, however, flew over the scattered pile of arrows and into the trees.

"Is that how you and your sister intend to kill Mongols?" Hana asked. "If they hold still, it ought to take only a day or two to get the job done." Idris and Natia giggled.

"No, it isn't," I said. "But if the Conclave will meet me in a more private setting, I'll tell them what I *would* do with this technique."

The Year of Extreme Distress

~ 9 ~

A Plan to Make a Plan

To my grandmother's credit, she shooed away most of the spectators as we made our way inside. When we sat down behind closed doors, only the Conclave was there, plus a few other women I'd met but never understood their function. Hana, Natia, and Idris sat in a corner together, whispering to each other.

I waited until everyone sat, then I didn't waste words.

"I don't want to shoot Mongols. I plan to kill horses. Sleeping horses."

The room erupted.

"The poor horses are not to blame. Why kill them?"

"Do you have any idea how hard it is to pierce a horse's tough hide?"

"Surely the Mongols travel with extras?"

Why is it the first thing people do when they hear a proposal is to find arguments against it? I chose to answer the last objection first.

"The horde itself travels with extra horses and more than most. But I've spent the last anks learning about them. Ilari will be a small conquest, one likely to be handled in a day or two by a group dispatched only with what they need."

"We're no small conquest," said Hana.

I ignored her. Her comment showed she knew little about our foes.

"They'll likely enter Ilari through the grasslands of Bisu. My idea is they will find our entrance deserted and the grass unexpectedly lush. We want them to stop and spend the night. We'll look into ways to make sure they do. Because our long eyes can see well in faint light, we'll attack their horses at the first glow of dawn, when none but a few guards are awake."

"It sounds dangerous." This came from a serious older woman I'd never spoken with before.

"The Mongols won't suspect archers before sunrise, and our people will be at least twice as far away as any normal bowman. Plus, we'll work with the Bisuites to construct camouflaged shelters for our teams to hide in."

"You think you can kill all of their horses?" asked Aliz.

"No. Not even close. I'm hoping for four long-eyed archers and four oomrushers strong enough for this. At best each team can get off sixty shots in the time between first light and sunrise. If we kill, say, two hundred of their horses, we'll have done well."

"That's your plan?"

"It is. I've good reason to think they'll enter Ilari with a thousand warriors. We'll try to send no more than eight hundred of them on to Pilk, where the Svadlu will have a better chance of defeating them. Understand. My idea is for the Mongols to encounter no one to fight when they enter. We want to diminish their forces, then send them on to our army. We let the Svadlu do their job. It's how we win, too."

"It's not much of plan," said Idris. She was right, and several others agreed with her aloud.

"No, it isn't, but it also doesn't risk many Velka, and it in no way threatens our home in the forest." This part seemed to please everyone. "Yet it may be enough to make a difference."

"It would be easier to kill the horses if the arrows had poison tips," a voice said.

Finally, someone with something helpful to say.

"It would be kinder to the horse as well," agreed another. I thought she was one of the growers. "We have mixtures that kill fast and without pain. We need to start making large quantities."

"I imagine dead horses would leave their fighters spooked, too, giving our Svadlu an advantage."

It delighted me to hear this positive response. Then ...

"No. Wait. This idea is horrible."

Everyone turned towards a soft-spoken grower sitting in the corner. I didn't know what rank she held, but I'd noticed others always listened to her with respect. I had no desire to challenge her.

"We can do better than murdering two hundred horses." She spoke to me. "If we make the poison right, the horses you hit will appear to be dead, but some, maybe even many, will come out of it. Think. We can use more horses here in Ilari, and I bet they have good ones."

"Yeah and the herders in Bisu would be happy not to have so many horses' carcasses laying around," Natia said. I guess she wanted to take any side opposed to me, but I happened to agree.

"That's brilliant. If it's possible," I said. "We have to make it strong enough to knock out every horse we hit; they must all appear dead. But yes, but the more we keep alive the better."

"Do you think they'll put two people on a horse, or leave two hundred horseless fighters behind?" This woman gave me the perfect lead-in to the last part of my plan.

"The Mongols only ride singly into battle because they fight too fiercely from horseback to do otherwise."

"So what happens to the two hundred of them now stranded in Bisu?"

"A surprise." I smiled. "For them, not us. I'm assuming they stay on the deserted grasslands while the others charge on, thinking they can ride double afterward to rejoin the larger horde.

While they're waiting, I want the herders in Bisu to take them as prisoners."

"That's ridiculous. We've no place to hold two hundred Mongols." Hana stood up as she said it, the better to be heard.

"Of course we don't, and we won't waste resources building one. We're going to hold them one prisoner to a household, for the remainder of the cold weather. I want to give the Bisuite herders some training for this. I figure the captured Mongols can earn their keep doing chores and we'll release them in small bunches after it gets too warm for them to fight."

"Are you serious? These are savages. We'd be fools not to kill them when we have the chance!"

"You'd think so," I agreed. "But the one thing we've heard repeatedly is that their leader, this Khan of theirs, places an unusual value on the lives of his fighters. Returning them could be what saves us."

Not everyone looked convinced, but I didn't expect them to be.

"All I'm asking today is your permission, and the resources, to begin this plan. The more time we have, the better thought out it will be."

"We don't have much to lose," said the women who'd once called my one-for-all platitudes goat scump. "It could help. *If* the participants are willing to take the risks. *If* you can get cooperation in Bisu."

"Thank you. I'll hope for both. If the attack comes this winter, my group will do what it can. If it doesn't come, then in the spring we'll expand our options."

"Perhaps by spring, your plans will have evolved to the point where we can have more confidence in them."

"Yes, Grandmother. I hope they will have."

Later that day, Aliz informed me Coral would arrive soon to spend the final anks of her pregnancy in the forest. Sulphur would accompany her and, for a few days until another cabin was ready, all my sisters would have to be housed in my room.

They arrived two days after the experiment with Olivine, in the middle of an archery session. Sulphur seemed impressed while Coral was too pregnant to care.

Crowded together over the next few days, I realized what I'd missed most while living with the Velka. It wasn't the wide-open sky, though that would have been my first guess. And it wasn't the chance to sleep every night with a man in my arms, though that would have been the guess of so many others.

I missed my sisters most. Not them specifically, to be fair, and certainly not the many petty squabbles we had. What I missed was having people in my corner, friends I knew I could count on. Joli and some of the other oomrushers had started to fill those shoes, but as I talked through my plans with the three women I was closest to, I felt whole again.

As soon as Coral arrived, she and I compared the information we'd gotten from Davor and Nevik. Between our two pivotal sources, we had a fairly good idea of how the Svadlu's plans for our defense were progressing. We agreed Davor and his cohorts would likely let Nevik and the other Royals think the invasion would be handled as they wished, with all or most of the army charging out to Bisu. Then, once word came the invaders were near, the Svadlu would insist they revert to the more drastic military plan. At that point, all Eastern Ilari would be lost.

Coral and I both worried about Sulphur. She was so happy to have been admitted into the Svadlu only anks ago, and we feared she wouldn't take our analysis well.

We were right. It took both of us to even get her to listen.

"If our military experts think we can't defend the outer nichnas, why aren't the Royals listening to them? We shouldn't be giving up territory, we should be training more Svadlu so we don't have to give up anything." She turned to me. "You put everyone in danger by planning to involve civilians in this fight."

"Everyone is in danger already," I replied. "Surely you've heard stories about what the Mongols do."

I could tell from her expression she had.

"Instead of sitting by idle, I want to offer those in eastern Ilari a way to defend themselves. I think they'll be happy to take it."

Coral tried another tactic. "Sometimes a thousand mosquitoes, or ten thousand ants, can do what a lion cannot."

Sulphur didn't appear convinced, but her silence told me she gave Coral's argument some thought. By the end of our conversation, she conceded that if the Svadlu *did* give up the eastern realm, my ideas would have some validity. But we'd need real soldiers like her to teach the herders fighting skills or they'd have no hope of capturing the horseless Mongols.

Over the next few days, the four of us brainstormed about Ilari's defense more than we celebrated Kolada. Joli joined us sometimes, as did other oomrushers. The more we talked, the more it seemed we needed another surprise or two to diminish the Mongol's numbers as they made their way westward. We decided on three unexpected attacks, all staged along a carefully controlled path.

"You've got a lot to figure out yet," Sulphur said. She was right.

"Do you think the younger sisters could help?"

It was a funny question coming from Olivine, given she was barely older than her twin. But for some reason, she'd always considered herself one of the "older girls."

"Maybe," Coral said.

"Don't be ridiculous," Sulphur answered at the same time and we all laughed.

They were both right. Given the various delicate natures of our youngest three, it was unlikely they'd be helpful. Yet, as the previous days had proved, we were most formidable when we worked together. We agreed to start by including Olivine's twin, Celestine. I'd invite her into the forest for a visit.

****

The next time I saw Nevik, I kept my promise to not discuss politics or war. That meant we didn't talk much, which was fine, at least for the afternoon and early evening. Yet after those couple of bouts in bed, I could tell he was tired.

"Everything okay?" I wanted to walk the fine line between concerned and nosy. I looked closer and saw the pain in his eyes.

"I'm fine."

Yeah right. I moved behind his chair, then placed my hands on his shoulders and began to rub them, trying to ease the tension I felt.

"I like it when you do that. It feels good."

"It's supposed to."

"She'd never do such a simple thing for me, not in a million years."

Oh.

"I'm sorry. You don't want me to talk about her."

I shrugged. I hadn't wanted him to, but I was pretty sure there was something specific on Nevik's mind, and we weren't going to have more fun together until he got it off of his chest. I sat back down and faced him.

"Let's make a one-time exception."

He looked away from me and mumbled. "I don't know if you heard. We had the wedding. Now we're trying to make a baby."

I hadn't expected that or how sad it would make me feel. I wasn't sure why. I didn't want his child.

"She gave me the three nights around Kolada to get the job done. I'll know in an ank or two if I succeeded."

I had to laugh. "Sounds terribly romantic."

"It wasn't. Frankly, I had to think of you ..." He froze. Something on my face must have alerted him to the danger of continuing. "I'm sorry. It's not something you need to know. She and I are done for now. We've agreed to make a similar effort every holiday until she is with child."

This was more sex than had been in their original agreement, at least as it had been described to me. I didn't comment.

"I guess I have to hope you were successful, then."

He reached for my hand. "What a mess I've asked you to live with."

I didn't want the conversation to go in that direction. "So tell me about one thing that *is* going well. Besides your time with me." I gave him the most playful smile I could manage.

"Well, your brother-in-law Davor isn't so hostile to me anymore. He's not such a bad sort once he gets past the stick he has up his arse about anyone born into royalty. We've gone out twice now and had a few ales. You'll be glad to know we're even finding common ground on devising a strategy for Ilari's defense. The Svadlu now recommend a contingent be placed at the gate in Bisu. At the least, they'll slow the Mongols down and give the eastern citizens more time to take shelter."

Would Davor do this? The contingent at the gate would likely be slaughtered unless it had most of our soldiers. And, any battle at our entrance would make a mess of my plans.

I tried to steer the topic away from military planning. "I guess Davor thinks he's had to fight hard for what's his."

"I suppose. It doesn't excuse ..." Nevik hesitated and I could tell he thought the better of what he was about to say. "I've said enough stupid things for one night."

"So, you want me to spend all night worrying about what you're not telling me? That's not kind, Nevik. You brought it up, you finish it. He's cheating on my sister, isn't he?"

"Yeah, but I think everyone saw that coming. It's worse."

"Seriously? What's worse?"

"He's in love. With someone else. A widow up in Tolo. Couldn't stop talking about her charms once the liquor was flowing. Of course, he has no idea I've ever met Coral, so why wouldn't he talk? I did my best to share a manly appreciation for this other lady but Heli ... Do you think your sister knows?"

"She may. I think her expectations for Davor are pretty realistic."

After that, we cuddled together and fell asleep, well before we normally would have. I guess we both needed the rest.

~ 10 ~

Sleeping Donkeys

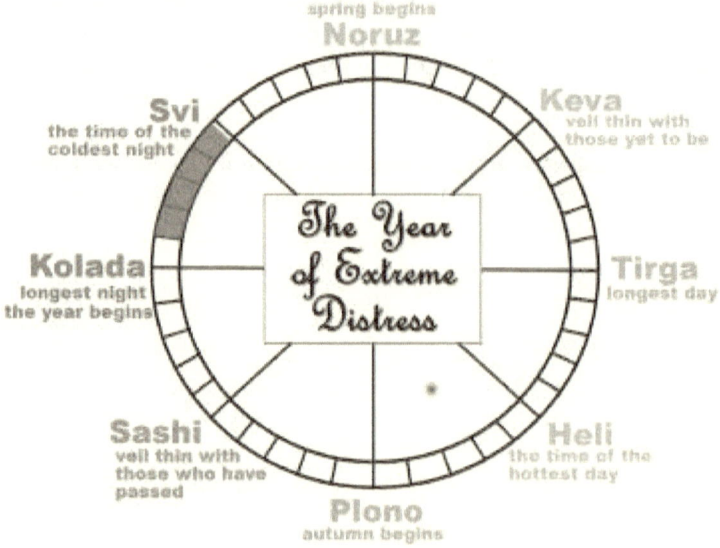

Most markets were open on all of the six working days of the ank, and then on one or two of the resting days as well. Of course, no one actually rested on those three days. People used the time to take care of personal matters, visit friends and family, and sometimes pursue hobbies, while farmers, herders, and fisherfolk scheduled their work and leisure around need and weather.

The Velka tried to have a presence at every open market. The little things we sold brought in most of our income, giving us all a more comfortable life and giving people like me the means to travel outside of the forest. But our presence served other vital purposes. It provided a way for Ilarians to approach us, to ask for charms and spells they professed to only half believe in but wanted anyway. It wasn't our way to mislead them, but the Velka had long since learned people sometimes chose to mislead themselves. In those cases, we obliged, feeling pleased when the charm worked as well as the purchaser had hoped.

Many of us came to conclude hope and belief were the most potent magic of all.

We seldom gave voice to our other purpose for being in the markets, but we all knew it. Because we went to every corner of the realm and returned to a common area, we had one of the two lines of communication in Ilari. The Svadlu had the other. Messages not important enough to warrant the time for a horseback ride, or the cost of a paid courier, were often sent via the Velka. We were happy to help. Not only did our service provide us with occasional sales, but it also allowed us to amass a wealth of information.

Two of the women who sat in on the explanation of my plans for the Mongol invasion were Recorders. We gave this title to those who kept track of the messages by writing them down, sorting, and filing them. As I began to firm up my plans, Aliz instructed me to keep the Recorders informed of all I did, and to allow them to provide me with any information they thought useful.

I was delighted. In exchange for a little of my time, I now had research assistants who were experts in current affairs. I soon got updates on the progress of the wall along Pilk's eastern border, reports on military recruiting and exercises, and even some occasional intelligence about traveler's sightings of Mongols. Helpful indeed.

I also began to use the Velka in the market to communicate with Olivine. She'd left here planning to talk to the three other long-eyes in her art group to see if any had proficiency with a bow and were inclined to help us. I'd learned one artistic long-eye qualified and he and Olivine were practicing archery as weather permitted.

I decided not to send any messages to Sulphur, however, guessing the Svadlu paid as much attention to her communications as the Velka did to mine. I didn't want to add to her problems.

Winter was no time for training anyway; I'd find a way to meet with her in person before spring.

While this was happening, Coral settled into a small cottage nearby, and Aliz took over the job of seeing to her granddaughter's health and comfort during these last few anks before the baby was born. Our trained midwives visited Coral often. I tried to get over there when I could, but I felt helpless. I knew so little about childbirth.

However, I did know about other things. Two eighths ago, I'd searched for a luski willing to give Coral more information about the ability to use one's voice to order others to obey. It hadn't been easy to find someone because most luskies hid their identity. Ewalina had reluctantly agreed to visit Coral at her home and, to my surprise, had decided my meek sister possessed this ability to command others.

Now, I made sure Ewalina knew Coral was in the forest with us. The forest was a safe place for luskies to visit, as the Velka knew better than to fear their skills. I sent word asking Ewalina to come work with my sister if she could find the time. I didn't want to push Coral too hard in her advanced state of pregnancy, but her skills could become a part of my plan.

Ewalina surprised me and made the trip and, after she spent a few days with Coral, Coral assured me she appreciated the distraction.

She was less than two anks away from her time to give birth when Celestine came. I'd planned to invite this other twin for a visit, but my grandmother and father had gone one step further and decided Celestine should attend the birth. My glamour-conscious musician of a sister wouldn't have been anyone's first choice for such an event, but my mother wouldn't consider a trip here, Sulphur and Olivine were both busy elsewhere, and the two youngest were in school for two more eighths. Everyone must have decided I was too busy as well, which I was. That left Celestine.

I stood in the clearing to greet her when she arrived. She looked flustered by the twigs and dead leaves deposited in her hair on the way in.

"You go through *this* every time you leave?" It was how she greeted me.

"You look beautiful, dear. Very nature-loving."

"Right." She brushed out her unusually full head of long coal-black hair as she dismounted and then she smoothed her fashionable dress over a slight and slender frame identical to Olivine's. After that, she hugged me.

"It's good to see you too," I said. "How are you and Olivine surviving as the kids in charge?"

"We'll be glad to see Iolite and Gypsum finish school. We need more people back in that house. There's too much attention on us."

I laughed because I understood.

"Well, this will be a nice break, I hope. I'd love for you to stay and have dinner in the lodge tonight, but I know Coral is anxious to see you. Come on. I'll walk you over to her place." I looked down at Celestine's shoes. I'd seen her wear worse. "Can you walk a thousand paces in those?"

She rolled her eyes. "I can run in them if I have to." I looked at the shoes again. I couldn't run in them, but maybe she could.

I saw little of either sister after that, so I assumed Celestine was helping Coral do get-ready-for-baby things, whatever those were. She did find time to come over to the lodge a few times and several Velka recognized her. I learned Celestine had acquired a certain amount of fame, both for her musical talents and her taste in fashion. To my amazement, I overheard more than one younger Velka bragging about how she'd had lunch or breakfast with *Celestine,* and *Celestine* was as nice and normal as a regular person.

I heard through the midwives that Coral remained healthy and progressed well, so I didn't worry about her as I dedicated my efforts to reading all the new reports on Mongol activity. Although the information was sketchy, nothing appeared to be moving in our direction. I became hopeful we'd be spared until next winter.

Days got colder, and we had two light sprinklings of snow. Travel would be unpredictable for many anks, making this time of year best for making plans by candlelight. Well, plenty of planning needed to be done to be ready when spring came. I woke at dawn most days, anxious to use every bit of the stingy daylight before I had to light the candles.

I began drawing a map of the realm on the wood of my bedroom wall, adding in what I knew of the surrounding areas.

Ilari's mountains, rivers, and marshlands protected us well, but they also served to isolate us from the rest of the world. Traders who knew of us made their way in, telling us they bothered because we were an oasis of relative peace and wealth, selling them fine goods and reliably buying their products.

Our legends said that long ago, magic had kept us completely hidden from outsiders. No one knew for sure if it was true but the idea had always intrigued me. Had the Velka done this? If so, why? And why and when had they stopped? I hoped someday to learn answers to these questions.

Today, our Royals had contact with the rulers of the nearby nations, but our natural barriers made interactions with our neighbors rare. Some of us did travel and bring back tales, and sometimes even mates. The occasional explorer or refugee from elsewhere stumbled upon us as well, sometimes stopping for a visit and sometimes staying for life.

This gave us sketchy information about the lands around us, but what we knew was incomplete. I pushed the Recorders for all the information they had and I added notes to my drawing to show potential problem areas along our borders.

Then I began sketching in the tilt of the land, to distinguish flat areas from steep ones. Terrain seemed important to me. I could see how those on horseback could be guided along the easiest path if we were clever, and then we could plant our various surprises along their route. I began to note where my efforts would be most effective.

My grandmother came in one afternoon as I worked on this. She said nothing as she studied my creation, and I feared she was angry I'd defaced my quarters. Finally, she murmured "excellent," and turned and left.

The next day, as I continued my work, I heard a commotion outside.

"Come on. You've got to see this. She's got six donkeys sound asleep in her yard."

Huh?

"Which one? The pregnant one? Or the famous one?"

Hmm. That had to be my two sisters.

"Both of them. The pregnant one is a luski and the singer keeps singing and it's the weirdest thing I've seen. They got cats doing dog tricks and a dog trying to meow."

I didn't know what was going on, but I was pretty sure I needed to find out. I grabbed a shawl and ran to Coral's cabin.

When I got there, the demonstration had ended but it looked like my sisters discovered something important. For reasons we could only guess, their combined voices nudged animals into actions much the same way Coral's voice alone could nudge another human's behavior.

"Would this work with horses?" I could hardly contain my enthusiasm. "If it does, we'll have the invaders right where we want them -- on horses that don't move. War over!"

Celestine shook her head. "Horses are too loyal to their humans to listen to us." She had a point. It would be a feat to get a horse to defy its human partner, but we wouldn't know if we could until we tried it.

"So, we need to get horses with riders they know and love. Also, we've got to try this with a lot of horses. Noise could be a problem."

"That means you need more luskies," Coral said.

"And singers," Celestine added.

Would sheer volume solve the noise problem? We had to find out. If we hurried, perhaps we could get some preliminary testing done before the weather turned its worst.

The weather held, but my sister Coral did not. The day before we were supposed to meet a group of horsemen at the forest's edge to run our first tests, she went into labor. My grandmother insisted we call the experiment off, claiming if we went on without Coral, we'd fail to understand what, if any, unique contribution she brought to this phenomenon.

Grandmother's analysis made sense, so as much as it pained me to delay, we sent messengers out to convey the postponement. I returned to my room to work.

To my surprise, a midwife came to fetch me. Coral wanted me with her as she gave birth. It seemed like such a personal time, but she wanted Aliz, Celestine, and me all there for support.

I understood better as time wore on. I didn't remember my mother's deliveries of my younger sisters, and I had no younger aunts or older cousins, so I didn't know the process could last days. Heli, I'd want all the people I could get to distract me, too. I did my best to cheer Coral on.

Finally, she gave birth to a healthy boy. He looked too much like Davor for my tastes, with a mop of the same dark hair, but my sister didn't seem to notice. As she held her newborn, gazing at him with adoring eyes, I wondered if it would be tactless to ask how soon she'd be able to travel.

~ 11 ~

A Frundle's Dreams

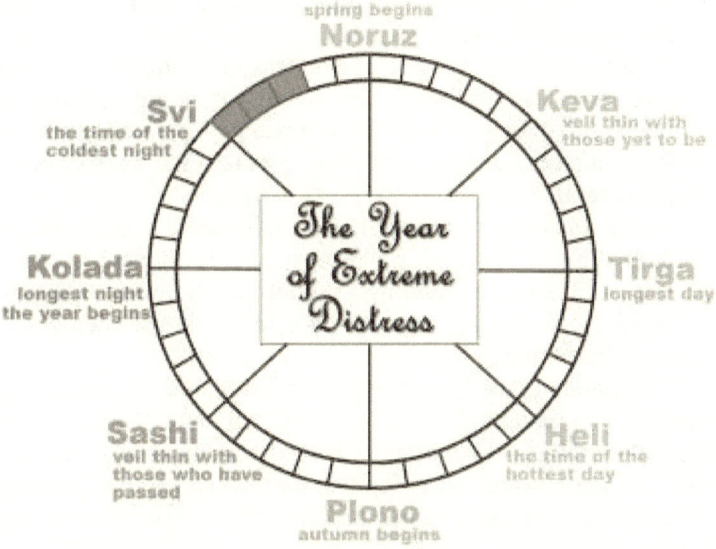

I admit I concentrated on little else while I waited for Coral to become strong enough to travel. I knew I needed two more plans to reduce the number of the invaders, and I was counting on Coral and Celestine's combined skills to somehow deliver one of them.

When the day of our rescheduled experiment finally came, I had little patience for excuses or delays. I'm sure I trampled on feelings, both within the Velka and elsewhere, as I herded everyone together, stood upon a large rock on the forest's edge, and barked orders to singers and horsemen alike. I had to face the unfortunate fact that those who would create order out of chaos seldom make friends while they are doing it.

As the morning wore on, our efforts to make horses fall asleep while being ridden failed miserably. Horses won't do that. We'd nearly given up on working with them altogether when someone suggested getting the animals to do something they wanted to do, instead.

Eating was a natural alternative, and I could see the usefulness of making a herd of war horses obsessed with feeding. Of course, a few of the farmhands began to make jokes about how the animals would rather mate than eat, and this lead to several horrible moments in which everyone was reduced to crude jokes and embarrassed laughter. It passed.

Then it dawned on me. There are instincts stronger than the sex drive. A startled horse has no interest in eating, mating, or anything else. Not once it's spooked. It rears up, possibly throwing its rider, as it struggles to appear larger and to place its front hoofs to best protect itself.

We could simply scare the horses, of course, which wasn't a bad idea, although I suspected these particular horses were too well trained to panic at anything we could do. So, why not startle them, then use our luski/singer combos to instill a deeper fear to overcome their training?

The group agreed, and even the farmhands in danger of getting thrown thought this was worth looking into and they could protect themselves. So we tried several variations and they all worked to some extent. The idea had merit. As everyone gathered up their things to head home before dark, my brain was still churning.

We could block the road coming into Vinx, forcing them to stop. The narrow passage between the forest's edge and the start of the cliffs of Vinx would be the perfect place.

Then, we'd stage something using fire or loud noises, or better yet both. In the luski-enhanced panic that followed, we'd get as many riders thrown as we could. One out of four was a reasonable target, based on what we'd seen. We'd get the riderless horses to bolt and encourage the horses with riders to gallop onward as well. That last bit was important: we weren't equipped to do battle with the angry warriors who hadn't been thrown. Once it was safe, the surrounding farm folk could move in and capture the thrown riders in the same way the Bisuites had captured Mongols earlier in the day. Hopefully.

The next step would be to test my ideas with far more horses and riders.

"We'll meet again in two anks," I announced from my perch. "Let's try to gather more people and horses so our testing can be more realistic. Great job everyone!"

They all smiled and waved, grateful to have found something that worked, and grateful to be headed home.

****

I had plans to meet Nevik the next day, but my grandmother came to my room first thing in the morning. I feared I'd crossed some invisible line yesterday by bossing everyone around. Was I going to be relieved of my duties? The idea distressed me more than I would have suspected.

She must have seen the worry in my eyes.

"You're doing fine, Ryalgar. Relax. You've annoyed a few people, but they're the ones who never liked you to begin with. I've no problem with that. It's not why I'm here."

"Coral? The baby? No ..."

"They're fine too."

I could tell from her expression not everyone was well, but it seemed silly to keep guessing.

"Who then?"

"Your sister Iolite. She's in a school in northwest Pilk, right? Inside the fork between the two rivers?"

"That's right. It's why I didn't visit her in my travels. The place is uncommonly hard to get to. Is she okay?"

"We're not sure. They brought her into the forest late yesterday. She's having some medical issues."

That didn't make sense.

"The trained specialists in Pilk are closer," I said. "Why bring her to us?" Academicians who studied the human body tended to approach medicine differently than the Velka, but we shared a common knowledge base. Why not take my sister to those nearby?

"Her issues aren't, un, entirely physical. They thought we were better suited to deal with her."

"Oh dear."

"Exactly. Ryalgar, I know your sister was born with certain challenges."

"You could call it that." There was no humor in my laugh. I looked into my grandmother's eyes. "She's a frundle."

Grandma raised an eyebrow. There is so much shame in Ilari associated with this condition that most family members never use the word. All Grandma said was "I've got a donkey ready for you, loaded with supplies, and a guide to take you and one of our best healers over to the corner of Pilk. You should leave now."

"She asked for me?"

"She ... asked for Coral, actually, but I didn't think it was wise for Coral and the baby to make another strenuous journey today. Now hurry. She'll be glad to see you."

I had plenty to worry about as I traveled. Frundles matured quickly and died young; few lived past forty. They tended to suffer from health problems, often many of them. For a frundle, Iolite had been uncommonly healthy. At least up to now.

A frundle can't produce a child so they usually live with their parents all their lives. It wasn't easy to grow up as a frundle, or to leave home as one to pursue higher learning. Frankly, I admired the Heli out of Iolite for doing what she had.

A lot of superstitions existed, so children were usually scared of frundles. So were a lot of adults, though many wouldn't admit it. It hadn't been easy having a frundle for a sister, either, but no one in my family complained, at least not aloud. My father was difficult to anger, but grumbling about Iolite was the one line he never allowed us to cross.

My concern as I traveled, though, was with the remaining trait of frundles. It made my heart pound in my chest as I rode.

They were, inevitably, different in the head. Some were unstable, prone to hallucinations or hearing voices. Others had disturbing dreams well beyond the norm. Often, these problems conveyed helpful information to the frundle about the future or about what was happening elsewhere, but in other cases, they only made the frundle's life difficult, containing a mix of true and false information no one could sort out.

My family was so thankful Iolite had never shown these tendencies.

"She's the most fortunate frundle who's ever lived," my father often bragged.

And perhaps she had been, until yesterday.

When we arrived, Iolite was resting, but she woke as I came in.

She stood to greet me, the top of her head well below my chin as she hugged me. Most frundles never achieve full adult height, though some come close, and Iolite has. The silver hair she's had since birth was shiny as ever as I held her close.

"Ryalgar. You're who I wanted to see!"

"You sure you weren't hoping for Coral?" Coral had been better at nurturing Iolite as we grew, and Iolite's devotion to Coral was well known. I regretted saying it, but Iolite took no offense.

"No. You. I've been riding with the Mongols, and I need to tell you about it."

"You've been doing what?"

"In the dreams I keep having. I'm riding with them. They're close to Ilari, and they're coming here soon. In a few anks."

Pruck. Could it be true? We were only two anks away from the start of spring and I'd let myself believe the invasion wouldn't come until next winter. If Iolite was right, I had almost no time to implement what little plans I had.

Maybe I could work with Olivine to kill a few of their horses from afar, maybe even get Joli and Olivine's friend to kill a few more? At best it would be way less than I hoped. And I didn't even know where to start with using the luskies and the singers.

"How sure are you?"

"That they're Mongols? Positive. That they'll be here soon? Almost positive."

"Okay." We sat on the bed next to each other, so close our legs were touching. I could look straight into her eyes. Iolite had the deep violet eyes typical of a frundle and although many found frundle eyes to be eerie, I thought Iolite's eyes were beautiful. They were a light violet, now. I'd heard it was the color the eyes turned when a frundle was deep in a trance.

"Tell me everything you can."

She started talking about their horses and their clothing and what they ate and I had to admit it matched well with what I'd learned. She described how she'd begun to understand them when they spoke, although when she talked, they didn't seem to hear her or know she was there.

"They've heard of Ilari. They're curious about us," she said. "We have a reputation of being something called a utopia. An isolated paradise." She laughed, and there was a hint of hysteria in the sound. "Obviously they don't know much about us."

Then Iolite started to talk faster, and I had trouble understanding her. After a few sentences, I realized she wasn't speaking in our language. I asked her to slow down and talk so I could understand her, but she looked at me like she'd never seen me before as she raised her voice and laughed louder.

Then tears began to pour from her eyes while she talked. She waved her arms and hands in gestures I didn't understand, alternating between yelling and crying. Then she bent forward and put her head in my lap, pulling my skirt around her face like she was a small child hiding from someone. She started to sob, and to rub her eyes with my dress, and her shoulders shook with the pain she felt. I didn't know what else to do, so I stroked her silver hair the way I would a little girl's. She cried a while longer and then she giggled a few times.

The next sound I heard was her snoring. She was sound asleep with her head in my lap.

When she woke, her body jerked in surprise. She raised her head, then sat up confused.

"Ryalgar? What are you doing here? What am *I* doing here? Why aren't I in school?" I could see panic growing in her eyes, eyes that had returned to the deep shade of purple I'd always known.

"It's okay. Everything's okay."

But it wasn't. Iolite remembered nothing of the Mongols, or her trip here, or of our conversation. She even argued with me that it hadn't happened.

"Now what am I supposed to do?" she asked

I answered her in a whisper.

"Say no more about this. Let them take you back to school." I gestured to the two women in the other room who had brought her.

"Act normal, like you're fine. I'll tell them this is an isolated incident. Let's assume, let's hope, it was."

She left soon after with her two companions, promising me she'd do as I said, and would send word to me if she remembered anything more. I left wondering how much I should believe her rantings, and whether I should try to put together a meager defense over the next few anks. Or not.

****

When I updated my grandmother and the others, Iolite's prediction of an invasion didn't concern them much. A frundle's first visions were often inaccurate, they said; it took most frundles several episodes to develop a feel for what was a near certainty and what was only a distant possibility. Even experienced frundles reported information they believed but had misinterpreted. I should ignore what Iolite said.

Despite that advice, I turned to the Recorders more often, checking for reports of Mongol activity. I knew our potential attackers moved in a group of thousands, peeling off smaller parties for lesser jobs like taking over little realms such as Ilari. Every day the Recorders told me there was no sign of a Mongol hoard anywhere. Every day I became more skeptical of what Iolite had told me, even though my sister believed what she'd said.

Perhaps she was mistaken, like my grandmother suggested, and it was another, similar realm they'd been about to attack. Or maybe they'd been headed our way when things changed. Either way, by the day of our second experiment with horses, I'd abandoned the idea of setting up some minimal defense.

On that day, my dad brought at least fifty horses and riders from surrounding farms, and several wagons full of straw to protect our riders. There were fourteen Luskies this time, all wearing masks of some kind over their eyes to keep their identities hidden. How had Coral had convinced so many to attend? Someone had also persuaded experts on working with fire to come help us, and Celestine got over forty singers to show up as well.

I sought out my dad to thank him for the extra horsemen he'd brought.

"People talk, dear," he said. "Everyone's scared about the Mongols and nearly everyone knows you're doing something, they're not sure what, to keep us safer. It wasn't hard to talk others into being here."

This time we proved that even amidst crowds, noise, and confusion, many trained horses could be persuaded to throw their riders. By our third and most successful run, nearly one out of three landed in the piles of straw. We'd found our next plan.

I had one more experiment I wanted to conduct when I saw a cloud of dust in the distance. No matter who it was, being discovered wasn't good. I ordered most of the people into the forest, leaving only the farmers and horses to pretend they were engaged in some innocent activity once the distant horsemen arrived.

~ 12 ~

An Awkward Meeting

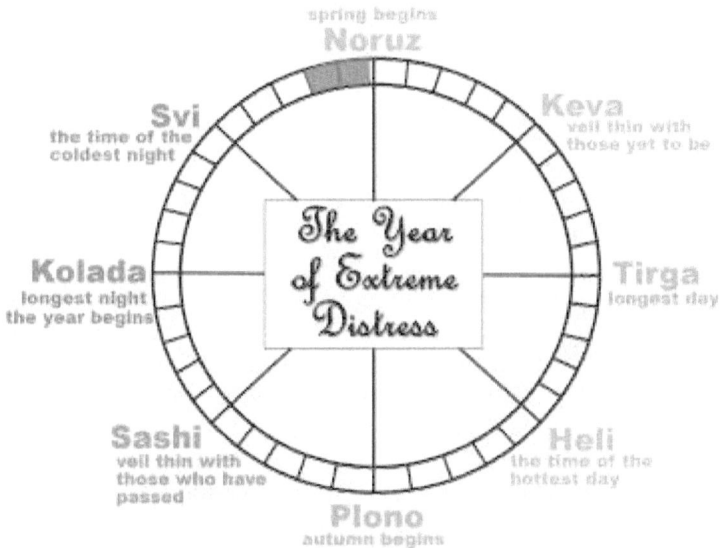

Nevik sent a terse response when I canceled our rendezvous because of Iolite, and I still hadn't received an invitation from him for another time. Well, winter *was* a tougher time to travel, and I supposed he was as busy as me.

On the other hand, Coral received a request from her husband, one long overdue. An ank later, she left with a guide to ride to the border of Pilk to introduce her son to his father.

I helped her pack her things, as we both thought Davor might want the two of them to stay for a while so he could get to know his child. But she was back before dark.

"It didn't go well?"

"No, it was fine, I suppose. He, he doesn't have room for me at his place."

Probably because he has another woman living there. I thought it, but of course I said nothing.

"Um, we, we have another sort of problem," she said. "We, uh, well …."

"What is it?" I don't remember when I'd seen Coral so hesitant to tell me something.

"Remember the day you tried all that stuff with the horses, and we had to leave fast when we saw a group riding towards us in the distance? Remember how you left Dad and his neighbors to talk to whoever it was?"

"Of course. It was a sensible thing to do. Dad didn't mind." Something in her tone made me defensive.

"Well, the group that rode up was the Svadlu. A group reporting to Davor."

"Pruck."

"Exactly. Whatever Dad said, Davor concluded our dad wants to create his own make-shift army to fight the Mongols and Davor is *not* happy about it. I found out the real reason he called for me was to order me to go spy on my dad and report back to him."

"That's ridiculous."

"It is, and Dad was facing serious trouble for it. I didn't know what else to do, so I told Davor the truth."

"What truth?"

"That *you're* developing the make-shift army he's worried about and Dad has nothing to do with it."

She raised a hand to stop me from saying anything.

"Think about it. They could lock Dad away, but they'd never touch a Velka. What's more, so many people know you're doing this that sooner or later you're going to end up explaining it to the Svadlu anyway. You may even want to tell them because this whole plan could go way better if you don't have to bother hiding it from them."

I squelched the burst of fear inside. She had an excellent point.

It had bothered me for a while that my plan assumed the Svadlu would ultimately use the defense strategy they thought best and be nowhere near the entrance to Ilari when the attack came. But they'd already promised Nevik they'd station soldiers along the fence in Bisu. If the Royals forced them to follow through, those fighters would be in my way. And I'd be in theirs.

The most helpful thing the Svadlu could do would be to loudly announce their intent to defend only part of the realm. Then I'd have a lot more support from the farming and herding communities, too.

I flopped into a chair, wondering how I could have missed the obvious. Anks ago I'd been desperately hoping for Nevik to prevail. Now, what I needed most was for him to completely fail and get out of my way.

"You okay?" Coral looked at me with concern.

"You're right. I thought of the Svadlu as our enemy, but we need to work with them. They could render what I'm planning useless."

I would have preferred to consult with them this summer, when my ideas were further along, but I didn't want Dad in trouble. Besides, it would be better to have time to change my strategy if the Svadlu and Royals weren't willing to cooperate with me.

"Okay. So Davor knows what I'm up to, thanks to you. He's fine with what I'm doing?"

Coral laughed. "No. Of course he isn't. But he did agree to hear from you in person. He wants you to come to Pilk for Noruz, and tell him your plans. He'll let you know which of them, if any, the Svadlu approve of."

I tried to control my irritation. As far as I was concerned, when the Svadlu decided to sacrifice the land I was born on, they lost the right to tell me what I could or couldn't do to defend myself.

"I'll explain my ideas, but I can't promise I'll hold back on anything to keep Davor happy."

"I don't want you to. I only want you to keep Dad out of trouble and get as much Svadlu backing as you can. We're on the same side, remember?"

I thought we were done, but as I turned to go, Coral reached for my arm to stop me.

"There's one more thing. Ryalgar, I'm so sorry about this, but Davor wanted me to warn you he'd be bringing a member of the Pilk royal family with him."

"Whatever for?"

"He thought his boss, the prince in charge of training the army for the invasion, should hear your arguments as well."

"He's bringing *Nevik* to this discussion?"

"I .... What could I say? It makes sense. The man *is* in charge of training troops for Ilari's defense. He should hear your plans, too."

So now I would not only have to ask Davor to override Nevik's impulse to do what was right, I'd have to ask him to do that with Nevik watching? I wanted to pound my head against my fist, but all that would do was give me a headache.

"Fine."

"You'll do this?" she asked.

"You have a better idea?"

Of course she didn't, and I didn't either. We were going to Pilk.

****

I ran the situation by my grandmother only. I didn't care to have the entire Conclave analyzing the pros and cons of my affair with Nevik. She understood my desire for discretion and gave me a quiet okay to speak on behalf of the Velka and to report the results of the meeting in Pilk directly to her.

"We'll find a way to involve the others, once you're back here and we know more."

"Grandma?" I was fairly sure I'd never called her that before. "We may need to wait to involve others. I'm designing three small attacks against our invaders as they make their way to Pilk, and what I once considered treachery or cowardliness on the part of the Svadlu is now central to my plan. I'll be asking them to warn the realm they are giving up the eastern nichnas, with plans to move those citizens to safety. The Velka's role in requesting this action would best be kept quiet for now."

"I see." She took both of my hands in hers. "Well then, let's not make any decisions, yet, about who we'll tell what. Not until we understand more about the situation. Travel safely, Granddaughter."

I squeezed both of her hands before I let go.

She and I were placing a lot of trust in each other.

****

A few days before Noruz, Coral and I set off at dawn, with the baby she'd named Votto bundled against her chest. I had to give Coral credit, she'd become adept at traveling with that little kid attached to her.

This was my first trip out of the forest without a guide, and I wanted to find every marker as I rode so we'd make it out without problems. I knew Coral thought this was a poor time for me to test my navigation abilities, but I'd grown tired of needing an escort when I wanted to leave. I'd also hoped the lack of another person would allow Coral and me to talk more freely, but we rode in near silence as she concentrated on suckling Votto while maintaining her balance and as I checked off markers in my head and sought the next one.

Davor sent a soldier to meet us with proper horses to ride into town, allowing us to use the donkeys to follow behind with our belongings. I appreciated the courtesy.

Coral learned days ago that Mom and Dad planned to come to Pilk to see Iolite and Gypsum over the holiday. She and I hoped to surprise them, and we debated finding them before our meeting. I argued against it, wanting to use the short time to refresh ourselves instead.

"We'll see them tomorrow," I said. "Let's get this over with first."

But Votto became uncharacteristically fussy as we tried to rest, and the more Coral tried to soothe him the more agitated he became.

"I can catch up with you once I get him to sleep," she said. "You want to go on ahead without me?"

"You bet your sweet arse I don't. I want you there for every awkward moment of this." I was trying to be funny but I gather from the look she gave me I didn't sound as light as I'd hoped.

By the time we made it to the agreed-upon tavern, Votto had fallen asleep. One soldier showed us to a back room where Davor and Nevik waited, and another let us through the door.

I hadn't seen Nevik for over an eighth, the longest we'd gone without being together since we met. The last time, he'd been exhausted from trying to make a baby with his wife. I suppose the idea had put a damper on things, at least for me. Then, he'd failed to contact me after I canceled on him, and now I didn't know what to expect.

His eyes lit up when I walked in, and I glanced away. His reaction pleased me and part of me wanted to rush into his arms, but the rest of me understood that was an unbelievably bad idea. As I looked away from Nevik, I forced as much coldness into my face as I could. Davor, the fourth person in the room, didn't strike me as particularly astute, but we couldn't take a chance of him suspecting a thing.

Formalities for meeting royalty were minimal under such circumstances, so a slight curtsey got the proprieties out of the way so I could focus on my brother-in-law. I intended to speak to him as an equal, no matter how difficult he made it. I started by talking before he could take control of the conversation.

"Thank you for inviting me here and for hearing me out." Davor started to say something but I kept going. "Let me give you my reasoning, please, so we can have a more informed discussion. You know the Velka are well connected around the realm. Multiple sources have confirmed the Svadlu would rather not defend the eastern and lesser populated nichnas of Gruen, Vinx, Bisu, Scrud, K'ba, and Eds."

There, at least I made it clear to Nevik I had no intention of revealing him as a source of my information.

I kept talking, without pausing to breathe, lest Davor interrupt.

"Although my sister and I are from Vinx, I speak today as a representative of the Velka. Should the Svadlu abandon these areas, the Velka would be surrounded on three sides by Mongols and on one side by Zurians. We don't believe we'd survive long under those circumstances."

Davor stopped trying to interrupt me and gave an impressed nod. I supposed he was appreciative my approach hadn't involved accusations or, worse yet, a woman's emotions. At least so far.

Nevik, on the other hand, seemed uncomfortable with the didactic woman in front of him discussing military tactics in a staccato manner. He kept trying to catch my eye. I ignored him.

"Therefore, we've deemed it in our best interest to support your approach and to do what we can to ensure the invading Mongol army is, in fact, something the Svadlu can defeat. Easily."

I exhaled and Davor raised one eyebrow.

"How in the name of my grandmother's arse could the Velka possibly accomplish such a thing?"

I almost laughed aloud at his vulgarity, but neither Coral nor Nevik seemed amused.

"I'm here to ask you to not only give up the eastern nichnas, but to be quite vocal about it before the conflict. The Velka will protest along with everyone else, of course, but in reality, we'll be making plans to pick away at the invading army as it makes its way to the wall you're building. By the time the Mongols reach you, we hope to have reduced them by more than half and scared them considerably. Then, once you defeat what's left of them, all of us are safe."

"You don't even want us to *try* to stop the Mongols as they enter Ilari?" Davor seemed relieved at this request.

Nevik was not. "That's unacceptable." He glared at Davor. "How many times do we have to go over this? We will meet any invasion at our eastern border and do our best to stop it there. *Only* if we're overpowered will we fall back and sacrifice what we must. The Ruling Prince of Pilk has decreed this."

"The Ruling Prince of Pilk may not know as much about the Mongols as the Velka do," Davor muttered. He looked at me. "What makes you think your ragtag militia on the eastern border won't be slaughtered?"

"We don't plan to fight. We'll keep most of the population out of sight. We believe the Mongols will ride until they encounter resistance." His puzzled expression told me he had no idea what I intended. "We'll be relying on other skills to reduce their numbers. Those talents the Velka are known for, and a few others less well-publicized." I tried my best to sound ominous, as though we perhaps kept dragon eggs ready to be hatched in our potting sheds. "We'll need to get nearby farmers and herders to clean up behind us, though, once the danger has passed. So, they'll need training in the basics of fighting and taking prisoners. That's what my father was helping with when your soldiers came upon us."

"I see."

"I don't," Nevik said. "Ilari is not the sort of place where our citizens need to take up arms. We're a civilized realm."

"With all due respect, sir." For the first time I looked him straight in the eye, and I made sure there was no trace of a lover's longing in my gaze. "My extensive research gives me every reason to believe when these invaders come, we are in for far worse than you expect. We shouldn't wait to find this out. We'll need every capable adult and some of our older children trained and ready to fight for their lives."

"You think it's that dire?" Davor appeared to wonder if I'd moved into hysteria after all.

"I'm sure it is. Please, sirs. Allow the outer nichnas to know you *will* abandon them. Allow the Velka to rile them up enough so they wish to learn to defend themselves. Allow some of your soldiers to train these farmers and herders. Finally, allow us to use our little magic tricks to deliver you a lesser foe. All of Ilari will benefit, and we can work together to ensure this looks good for everyone once it is over."

I saw Davor putting together the pieces in his brain. "You're not interested in badmouthing the Svadlu or, worse yet, stirring up some trouble with the farmers as you do this, are you?"

"Are you kidding? We're not even interested in taking credit for our part of the victory once it's over. It's not our way."

Davor wasn't my favorite human, but he understood a good arrangement when it was handed to him.

"So after we defeat the Mongols, the Svadlu reveal how the abandonment of the outer nichnas was our clever military plan all along." He nudged Nevik. "Extreme danger involves extreme cunning. Everyone will be grateful when it ends well. You Royals will be praised for crafting a victory. What do you say, prince? These ladies are offering us a gift."

Nevik gave me a dubious look. I read it as *where in Heli did this scheme come from?*

I smiled the vaguest, least informative smile I could manage, thinking this had all gone as well as it possibly could.

That's when the guard came through the door.

"Your Majesty. Sir, we need to leave now. The Mongols are here. The invasion has started!"

What?

Outside the door, I could hear people beginning to yell.

"Get out!" "Hide." "Take Cover." "Run!"

"You two go do your jobs," I said to the two men and their anxious guard. "We'll be fine."

"Mom, Dad, and Iolite are here in town," Coral added. "We'll get to them now."

After the men left, I was more confused than scared.

"How did this happen? How could we not have known?" I was sure we'd have gotten warnings from travelers coming into the realm.

Coral and I made our way out into a street filled with frightened people. Some yelled for help, others pleaded for safety. A few looted newly-abandoned merchants' stands. The only thing missing from the chaotic scene was an actual Mongol.

"Where are they?"

"In Pilk Center," a man told me. "They're outside the offices of the Ruling Prince of Pilk."

Most people headed away from Pilk Center, fleeing towards their homes. Coral and I looked at each other. Neither of us said a word as we walked towards whatever the crowd fled from, hoping to find out what the pruck was going on.

~ 13 ~

Or What?

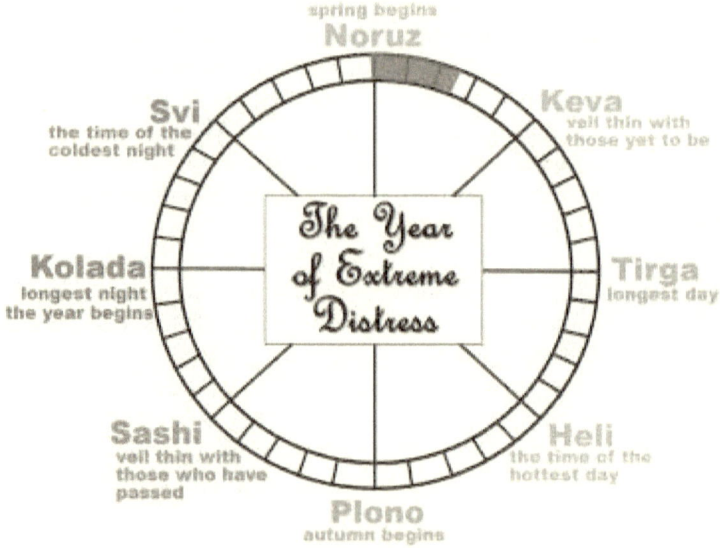

By the time we got to the square, the crowd had thinned and the Mongols were gone. As people talked about what they'd seen, we learned a small group had come to Ilari to demand tribute to the Khan. They'd left after voicing their demands.

No one around us knew what those demands were, exactly, only that they'd ridden into the central square to declare their ultimatum and our leaders had done an admirable job of refusing to give anyone any fraction of Ilari's wealth. The crowd around us cheered every time that part of the story was told.

I had to stop the revelry to ask. "Or what?"

"What do you mean 'or what'? Get out or we'll kick your arses, that's what. Their arses, of course, not yours," he added.

"I understand that part. What did the Mongols threaten *us* with if we didn't do what they asked?"

"Oh, I don't know. I guess that they'd come back and try to kick our arses instead."

"Yeah. Like anyone could defeat our Svadlu," another man said.

"How soon?"

"How soon what?"

I was losing patience. "How soon until they want their tribute. How long do we have?"

"Oh, a long time. Like till next winter."

Thanks be to every incarnation of the Goddess who was ever praised.

I turned to Coral. "We need to find Davor and Nevik and finish our conversation."

Finding our two men wasn't easy and in all the confusion we couldn't get a Svadlu to listen to us. Coral finally found one who knew Davor had married a redhead from Vinx. After squinting at her hair he offered to give him a message. We thought it best to go back and wait at our place of lodging so Davor would know where to find us.

We heard nothing the whole evening. After a while, we persuaded the innkeeper to bring us supper. Coral bathed Votto and I penned a better outline of my plans, on paper I'd brought for the purpose.

The Noruz merriment got louder outside our window, and as darkness came it turned towards the adult celebration it always became. Judging from the enthusiasm we heard, the strong spike of fear caused by the Mongols had prompted more drunken revelry and casual sex than usual.

"Do you miss being out there having fun?" Coral asked me. When I didn't answer, she said "I mean, under the circumstances, I wouldn't fault you if you wanted to wander off for a while and enjoy yourself. I'd keep it between us."

I had to laugh. "It's a nice offer but I never took to that sort of thing …"

"I understand. Look at me. I'm happy here, taking care of Votto." On cue, he gave her a tiny smile filled with baby gurgles.

"And I'm happy making plans to defend my homeland." I was, of course, but what I wanted to do was celebrate Noruz with Nevik; the one thing I'd never get to do.

Was his new wife pregnant? I didn't even know. If she wasn't, they'd be at it again tonight. Had she agreed to more frequent sex because of pressure to produce an heir? Or because she found Nevik less disagreeable than she expected? Probably both.

I dipped my pen into the small dish of ink and pushed thoughts of his wife out of my mind.

I was devising a plot to save everyone I loved.

I bet that was something she couldn't do.

The first thing the next morning, someone knocked on our door.

"If you ladies would allow me to meet with you in your quarters, I'd appreciate the convenience."

"Of course, Your Highness." I put enough sweetness in my voice to choke a bear. Coral hurried to pull her blouse together, as she eased her teat out a sleeping baby's mouth.

"Shh." As I opened the door to Nevik, I motioned to the baby lying on the bed.

His eyes flicked over me with the longing I'd seen when we met yesterday, then he took control of his face.

"I'm sure you two heard about the envoys who arrived yesterday. We allowed them to leave Ilari unharmed and under the impression we were considering their offer."

He said it as he entered, working to keep his voice low. Davor wasn't with him. "My father spoke with the envoys. I heard your sister Iolite was involved in the conversation, too."

"Oh no ..."

"She was helpful, Ryalgar. I know this isn't good for her, but it is for Ilari. She appears to have a connection with these people, and it could be useful. My father says your parents left early this morning to take her back to her school."

I didn't say anything. The Velka often worked with frundles and I, more than the rest of my family, understood what this "connection" would cost my sister.

"After the Noruz revelers head home, we'll circulate rumors about the Svadlu's plans to move many of the citizens of Ilari to safer areas before next winter so we can maximize our defense by minimizing the area we have to defend."

"That's a clever turn of words."

"It's what you requested. We'll allow the citizens of Ilari to know we expect the worst to happen after we fail to provide the first yearly tribute. Their ensuing fear should buy you all the cooperation you need."

"That's, uh, wonderful. I didn't expect such a lack of argument, nor for you to act so fast."

"Well, several of the royal families met after the envoys left, and we discussed your ideas until late into the night."

Oh, so he hadn't been with her. I tried not to smile.

"I came here this morning to give you official word that the Royals of Ilari have agreed to let the Velka proceed with their plan. I also came out of concern for you, Ryalgar. I hope you understand the full implications of what you're doing."

I thought I did. Was I missing something?

"If you succeed, you deliver us a foe who is easier to defeat, and we all benefit. But if you fail, you become the one who's given the Svadlu the political cover to do the cowardly thing they wished to do all along. The thing I tried to prevent them from doing."

"What?"

"Think this through, Ryalgar. Even if the Mongol army blows by whatever you set up, we have a country easier to defend. If we lose that, too, then the situation was hopeless from the beginning. On the other hand, if we defeat them, then *you've* allowed the Svadlu to use the strategy I and my father abhorred. *You've* allowed Ilari to give up your homeland. If the outer nichnas are devastated, it's your fault. Be sure you understand this."

He was angry with me. Angry I had thwarted his, what? His noble stance to defend every square inch of the realm? I appreciated his vehemence for doing the right thing, and I had all along. But because of what I knew about the Mongols, I saw the defense of Ilari in a wholly different light. I needed to get Nevik to see my point of view.

"Please understand. What you describe isn't possible. The Svadlu like the idea of a smaller area to defend because they're thinking about this like other military skirmishes they've had. It isn't. These invaders are fierce and they don't take a portion of a realm, then let the rest of it be. They just don't. Either my plan saves us all, or it doesn't work and they destroy everything. The scenario you describe could never happen."

"Then I have your answer."

"You do."

Our eyes locked. I was not going to back down. But perhaps he was.

"How sure are you that you're right?" he asked.

I blew the air out of my mouth slowly, preparing to give the answer of a lifetime.

"Enough to bet everything and everyone I love on it."

He looked away first, glancing over at Coral, then back at me. When he looked back, I saw something other than anger burning in his eyes. He wanted me, perhaps all the more so because I'd forced the entire realm to take such a gamble.

Coral turned to busy herself with something on the dresser. He stepped towards me, and I felt those silly flutters I used to feel as a young girl when a boy I liked came towards me. Then his arms went around me and he kissed me and of course, I kissed him too.

"Can I see you soon? Please?" he said.

"You mean any time after Noruz is over?"

"It's not an issue. She's with child."

"Ah, well then."

"You need to know this, Ryalgar. If you are *so* certain of this, then I believe you."

If I thought my heart was fluttering before, at those words it broke into a wild dance.

He turned towards Coral again.

"I was just about to take the baby out for a walk," she said.

By late morning, Coral hadn't returned. She'd given us far longer than our quick burst of passion required, so we used the extra time to get caught up on each other's lives, make plans, and exchange a lot of stupid sweet words that made us both feel better.

Then we shared our thoughts on how the realm would respond to the news we were about to unleash.

"Do you think we're manipulating Ilari's citizens?" I asked.

"Not really. Davor and his crowd were pushing hard to do exactly what you've asked them to do; they'd likely have prevailed in the end. I know that. You've pleaded for people to know the truth in time to craft a scheme to defend everyone. I can't work up a lot of moral outrage about that."

I started to agree when Coral knocked on the door, then entered.

"Ready to go when you are."

Nevik lingered as we packed our last few belonging into our saddlebags.

"Davor did ask me last night if I would see the two of you, and the baby, safely out of Pilk. Coral, he says he assumes you'll go back to Vinx now that the immediate danger is past and resume teaching?"

"Yes. I guess that's what I should do." She looked a little confused she wouldn't be seeing Davor before she left.

Nevik fumbled with something in his pocket and brought out a trinket he gave to Coral. It was a necklace, nothing lavish or expensive, but pretty. "He, uh, he sends his love to you, along with this little gift."

I wondered it if was from Davor or whether Nevik was improvising, trying in his way to make my sister feel better.

****

My grandmother and I may have been an unlikely pair of co-conspirators, but we adapted well. As we wandered off to hold more frequent and longer private discussions, we each let it slip how much we enjoyed becoming re-acquainted and sharing tales about our family.

In reality, we'd chosen to hold a secret between us. The rest of the Velka were not to know of the request I'd made to Davor and Nevik. At least not yet.

Publicly, we decried the cowardliness of the Svadlu for not defending all. We vowed to use the power of the Velka to aid the poor discarded citizens of the Eastern nichnas.

Privately, she encouraged me to strengthen my planning and to begin training sessions on all fronts as the weather improved. She would use the time to put a more formal organizational structure in place.

When she told me her first proposal, the idea appalled me. She intended to take Hana, Natia, and Idris and turn them into my deputies, telling the others their relative youth and vitality were the reason.

"I can't work with those women," I said. "They hate me and everyone knows it."

"They do. That's why this option is the best one. If they have a stake in your success, they may realize you're not so bad, and help make this plan work."

"And if they don't?"

"Then their duties and travels will keep them too busy to cause you as much trouble as they'd like, and you and I will both have a good reason to watch them closely."

I conceded her point.

I liked her second idea far more. She wanted Joli to join the Conclave. No other woman from Zur had been given this honor, but Grandma thought Joli was a worthy choice. Then Grandma intended to elevate Joli to be my second in command.

"Smart leaders utilize existing relationships," she said.

Grandma scheduled a gathering of the Conclave in two anks, and I knew a great deal of private conversations followed. Before she asked her questions in public, she wanted to be sure the group would give the answers she wanted.

She intended for me to be assigned a Recorder full time, along with a guide to train my entire leadership in getting around the forest on our own. If others agreed, the Conclave would grant us unlimited use of donkeys, coins up to a generous amount, and the services of other Velka as needed. Oomrushers, potion makers, and growers would be at my disposal.

As the evening of the gathering neared, I decided Joli was right. My grandmother had to be whatever supreme leader the Velka had. When she stood in front of the blazing fire in the main room of the lodge the night we gathered, outlining her proposal in detail, everyone nodded as if her ideas were their own.

I'd wanted to ask her how she'd ascended to such a powerful position, but after watching her that evening, I didn't have to ask.

~ 14 ~

Hermits and Naked People

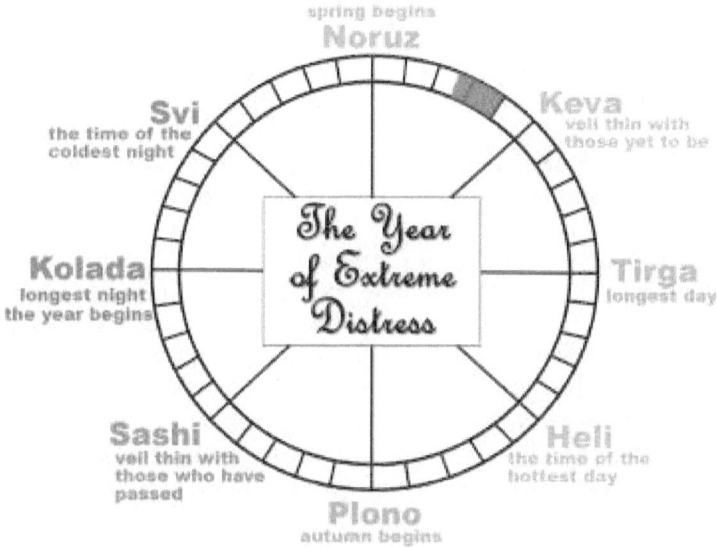

A few days later a Velka who tended a market stall in Vinx brought me a lengthy note, handwritten by my father. He seldom wrote to me. He said he'd hoped to have a conversation with me in Pilk but this would have to do instead.

He feared for Iolite and her frundle episodes if they continued. Meanwhile, he'd tried to meet up with Gypsum while in Pilk but when he sought her out, he learned she hadn't been at her school for anks. He hadn't been able to talk to anyone in charge, but other students reported she'd either been expelled or had chosen to leave. He got both stories in equal measure.

He'd had less success when asking where she'd gone. Most looked too embarrassed to answer. Finally, one young woman suggested he look for her where the nichna of K'ba met the forest.

I read those words and couldn't decide whether to laugh or cry. In the open-minded realm of Ilari, few things were too embarrassing to mention, but the little piece of land the student referred to held one of them. There, where the scrubbiest northern edge of the forest met the bleakest part of the desert of K'ba, lived a group of adults who managed to make grown Ilarians blush.

Of course Gypsum would go there.

My father felt it unwise to try to find his daughter in such a place and decided to hold off telling my mother until he knew more. Mom and Gypsum had a contentious relationship and my dad didn't want to make matters worse with incomplete information.

So. In between devising schemes to save the realm, would I please ride through the forest towards K'ba to see what I could learn?

Of course I would. No matter how much responsibility a woman has, she doesn't say no to such a request from her father. I found the woman who brought me the letter and asked her to send word back. I would do his bidding soon, over the next few days.

A journey through the northern forest provided a perfect opportunity to practice finding my way around, so I persuaded Joli and our new guide to join me on an expedition exploring areas where the Velka were less congregated. I thought we could seek out the women choosing to live in solitude. Perhaps some had skills to contribute or strategies to suggest. We could also scope out places to hide our most vulnerable farmers and herders and places to stash supplies like poison arrows where they'd be out of harm's way.

I confided in both women about the personal part of this outing and got chuckles from each one.

"You girls are a troublesome lot," Joli said.

"What do you mean?"

"Come on. You're difficult enough for seven women all by yourself. But no, you've got a luski sister. And you've got one that's joined the Svadlu. There's one who's a long-eye and a Heli of a shooter. Another who, I'm not sure what it is she does but when she sings, she makes horses buck. Hey. Then you tell me you've got a frundle in your family. At this point, I'm impressed."

I hadn't quite looked at it so objectively. "We're not that bad."

"Yeah, right. Now I find out another little sister has run off to join the reczavy." Joli barely blushed when she said the name. Maybe she didn't blush at all. That impressed me.

"We don't know if she's joined. She's probably just curious and went to find out more. Gypsum's always been one to push boundaries. My father wants reassurance she spent a couple of days with them, then moved on."

Our guide chirped in. "Tell you what. I'll take you to a half dozen or so Velka places hidden deep in the forest. Some of these women haven't seen outsiders in years. It'll give your sister a few extra days. Maybe by the time we make it to, to that place, she'll have left and you can share the good news with your parents."

Yeah. I wished the idea of Gypsum joining the reczavy didn't sound so much like it had been in the cards all along.

****

The women we visited lived alone or in twos and threes. They differed from the Velka I knew and resembled what outsiders feared. They were older, with hoarse voices and vague looks in their eyes. Their pale skin hadn't seen sunshine for decades, and their hygiene was poor at best. While the Velka I knew spent time socializing, these women devoted entire days to contemplation and their arts.

Some refused to come out and talk to us; I suspected others hid and we never knew they were there. But of the couple dozen we spoke with, I could feel the strength in each of them as an energy pulsating from within.

Mindful of my mission, I took the time to explain Ilari's predicament to each woman, asking for her advice or better yet her help. Not one had useful ideas, and not one was willing to join us.

"If we do nothing," I said, "the Mongols will make their way into the forest and destroy every one of you. You'd be fighting for yourselves and your lifestyle, too."

"One doesn't *fight* for this lifestyle," a woman who looked at least ninety years old told me. "One lives it until it is gone. Then it is."

We got similar responses from the others we spoke with. The best I got was a reluctant promise from a few to help me hide the sick or injured or to allow me to stash supplies nearby. Some of the women let me know they wouldn't even tolerate that.

As we stopped to eat our lunch, one woman must have watched Joli and I through the trees, recognizing us as sister oomrushers. She flung a rock at Joli's face in fun, thinking Joli would stop it in midair I guess, but Joli couldn't get the job done. The stone grazed her face just below her eye, drawing blood. The old woman emerged, embarrassed, identifying herself as Yarnya.

We introduced ourselves. "It's okay," Joli said. "I should have used my hands. I thought I could stop it. I had no idea you were so strong."

Yarnya responded with a hoarse, crackly laugh. "Well, that kind of strength is what forty years of doing absolutely nothing else will give you, sweetie,"

I'm sure Joli thought the same thing I did. *No thanks.*

As we approached the northern edge of the forest, I said what I'd been thinking. "Pretty much a disaster, huh?"

"Really?" our guide said. "No one attacked you, well except for the one rock and that was meant in fun. No one told you not to set foot anywhere near them again. A few were even a little helpful. I thought it went pretty well."

Keva was only an ank away, and the buds on the trees had begun to unfurl, each into a tiny yellow-green leaf. I realized my time of relatively open space in the forest would end soon.

We saw several colorful tents peeking through these bright leaflets as we got closer to the northern edge. We stopped and exchanged a look. The reczavy's fondness for full or partial nudity was one of their most well-known traits. I knew it was why my father hadn't considered seeking out Gypsum but had sent me.

However, half or more of the reczavy were male.

Well, we'd all seen a naked man before. We'd all seen several. We'd just never seen more than one of them at a time. Something about a whole group of penises bouncing around was different.

"We're doing this?" the guide said.

"You can wait here in the forest if you like."

She laughed. "Are you kidding?"

We knew the reczavy to be friendly despite their boisterous playfulness, so I saw no reason not to secure our donkeys, walk into the circle of tents, and say hello.

A surprising number of them wore clothes. It was a cool day, and there was a breeze, so I guess they were being sensible. A few wore jackets with nothing on their bottom halves, but they kept close to the fire. Some were entwined with each other. I kept my eyes away.

"People," one of them remarked.

"Hi, people," another said.

"Hi, Recs," Joli answered, using the slang term I'd been told was mildly insulting but none of them seemed to mind.

"Whacha want?"

"My sister." These were people of few words; it seemed wise to get to the point.

"The new girl? Gypsum?"

"Yeah, she said she'd family she thought'd come looking," another said. "Sisters. Dad too embarrassed. Mom too outraged. You the sister?"

"Yup. Just want to say hi. No trouble."

They all laughed when I said "no trouble."

"No one makes trouble with us," a pantless young man said. He had a juggling stick in his hand, and he began pounding it hard into the palm of his other hand. "We know too many tricks."

"I bet you do." I gave him a wide smile. I'd always considered these people to be the scariest in the realm because they were so different. Suddenly, they were a potential ally with as much to lose as I. And perhaps with tricks I'd never considered.

"That's the other reason I came," I said.

"Ooh," another young man turned to his companion. "Big sister wants a little of the trouble you're famous for, bro." They bumped fists.

"Not that." Heli. I knew I was blushing. "Let me talk to my sister. She can explain it to you better."

"Gypsum!" one of the women shouted. "You wanna talk to your family?"

"On my way." Gypsum's voice came out of one of the tents, then she appeared wearing a multi-colored robe that appeared to have been pulled on in haste. She gave me a careful look.

"So, you drew the short straw and had to come talk to me, huh? I don't care what you say. I'm not going back to school."

"Okay. But do you want to stay here?"

She looked at me. "Didn't our parents send you to tell me to get my arse back to my studies?"

"No. Mom doesn't know you're here. Yet. Dad was too shy to come. I'm here to make sure you're okay. Where you want to be."

"Hey, we don't hold anyone prisoner," one of the men said. It was the first time any of them had sounded offended.

I held up my hands, palms out.

"I don't know much about you so I'm just making sure. Gypsum?"

"I heard you like it with the Velka," she said.

"Yeah. I think I found a home there."

"Good. Then you understand. I think I've found one here."

I looked around at the tattered tents and half-dressed people and knew that many, including my parents, would never understand how a well-raised child such as Gypsum could feel at home in such a place.

Gypsum's grey eyes were filled with defiance. It wasn't exactly an unusual look for her. I sought soothing words.

"Wonderful. I'll send word back to Dad that you're well. He'll be glad to hear it."

We looked at each other for several more long seconds.

"You three want some dinner?" one of the guys asked. My first thought was I wasn't sure I wanted to eat anything they'd be serving. My second thought was saying no was not the way to make new friends.

"That'd be great. While we eat, can I tell you about this other thing I'm working on?"

They all shrugged. "Maybe. Is it anything interesting to us?"

"It ought to be. I hope it is."

~ 15 ~

Uneasy Allies

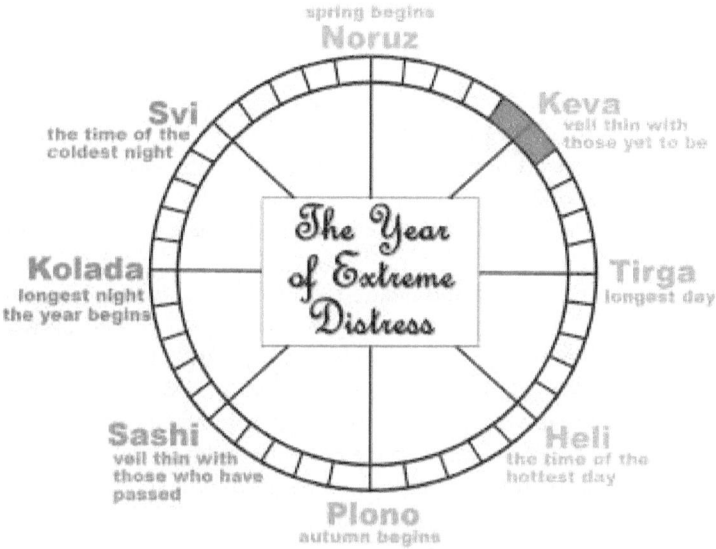

The reczavy showed more interest in my project than the Velka of the deep forest did, although that wasn't saying much. They let me talk for a while before one of the women said, "We've already heard a lot of this."

"From whom?"

She pointed her thumb at my sister. Gypsum shrugged. "After you visited me at school, I asked the professors what you were up to. I got some pretty interesting reports. Some of them kept me up to date afterward. So when I came here, I started thinking about ways we could help you."

Heli, she'd been on my side all along and I hadn't even known it.

"I'm sorry I didn't include you more. I had no idea you'd be interested."

"It's okay." Another shrug.

The pantless man with the juggling stick spoke up. "We know we don't get to live this life under Mongol rule. Or under most people's rule. So, you don't have to convince us to help you. What do you need?"

"What can you do?"

The whole tent full of partially clothed people laughed.

"Pretty much anything," he said.

"No, I'm serious."

"So am I. We do tricks. Illusions. Carnival acts. Pranks."

"You work with fire, right?"

"Yeah, but a few of us are already working with your horse people on that one."

"Oh." I hadn't realized. "Okay. I'm looking for a third way to reduce the number of invaders. I've got, I hope, six out of ten of them still on horseback and headed to Pilk, thinking they're going to win this thing easily despite my two setbacks. I need another way to slow them down, spook them, and capture more of them."

"Why don't you start by sending them somewhere other than Pilk? I mean, make it look to them like they're heading there, but I don't know, route 'em south to the river instead."

"Yeah. Then we can throw rotten eggs at them."

"Eggs filled with itching powder."

"Thrown with catapults."

The tent erupted in laughter again.

"Is that possible?"

"Which part?" It was juggling-stick-man again, and I noticed he was grinning at Gypsum and she was grinning back.

"Any part of it."

"It's all possible, big sister. How about we make Gypsum here your official lee ayes on." He said liaison like it was three separate words. "You two sisters work out the specs. We'll deliver."

I gave Gypsum a questioning look, trying to discern if this was something she wanted.

"Does this mean I get to come visit you at your Velka place?" she asked.

Oh, that's right. I hadn't invited her yet and I promised my sisters they'd all get to visit me once I settled in. Every other one had, besides Iolite.

"It probably means you'll have to come there a lot. And I'll come here too, of course."

"You'll come here?" The defiance in her grey eyes had melted and in its place was something I hadn't seen there often. My troubled sister looked happy. "And you'll handle things with Mom and Dad?"

That part wasn't going to be easy, but if it bought me the aid of this resourceful group, I'd find a way.

"Sure."

****

By the time I returned to the lodge, I was overwhelmed by the enormity of what I was undertaking. I couldn't afford to be paralyzed by fear, but Nevik's words, and my emphatic answer to him, echoed in my head. *I'd bet everything and everyone I loved* ... The proof of the direness of my situation lay in the fact that I'd just accepted the help of the reczavy. With eagerness.

I felt the little tendrils of fright growing in the corners of my mind as I stared at the map on my wall. I focused on making the tentacles shrink.

I had advantages. I knew important things. I needed to remember that.

One. I was sure of the size of the attacking army. I had reason to believe they wanted to be outnumbered. I'd learned a realm our size should have raised an army of two or three thousand by now and such an army probably would have lost, much to the Mongol's delight. It was our hubris and our lack of wartime experience that made us think five hundred Svadlu was plenty. The thousand attackers we faced would be disappointed by how fast they defeated us.

Would have defeated us. Had I not convinced Nevik to agree to the Svadlu plan, many of our fighters would have died on the grasslands of Bisu, defending the entrance to our realm. One of them could have been Sulphur. That image did nothing to quell my fears.

But knowledge was power. I knew their numbers.

I also knew when they were coming. We'd been given until Kolada to amass their tribute, and been told to signal our agreement by placing wagons filled with grain and preserved foods along the fence separating Bisu from the open grasslands to the east. No waiting wagons, no mercy. A brutal attack would follow, immediately or at least within days. Preparations could be paced to take advantage of this knowledge. How many leaders had the luxury of such information?

Finally, I knew the direction from which to expect the attack. Or did I?

It was hard to imagine the bulk of the riders entering Ilari any way but through the flat, easy path in Bisu, and hard to imagine them doing anything other than taking the well-maintained road leading to Pilk. Brute force, not subtlety, was their style.

Yet, their success ratio suggested they weren't always predictable.

I studied the map again. An army on horseback had to avoid a wide river and a canyon river as well. Ilari was blessed with one of each and, between them, they protected nearly two-thirds of our perimeter. The marsh around the lake to our southeast was equally unfriendly to an army on horseback.

I tried to think of Ilari as a bladder holding liquid. Where did it leak, so to speak, besides at the grasslands of Bisu?

Well, coming into Tolo over the high mountains to our north was possible, but the trip would be slow and dangerous, and much of the mountainous area was heavily forested. I couldn't see how entering through there would gain the Mongols anything but trouble.

There was another way in, though, in northernmost Eds along the ridge between the Cliffs of Tolo and The Canyon River. The advantage here was an almost complete lack of trees to block the way. Any path would still be narrow and rocky, and require navigating around steep hills, but it was possible. Did I need to be preparing for some of the Mongols to enter this way? It depended on what the terrain looked like on the other side of Ilari's borders.

Unfortunately, our neighbors to the north were our least friendly, and information from that direction was the scarcest. But before I bet my life on all of the attackers entering Ilari through the most obvious route, I needed to send an expedition to Eds. That wouldn't be easy, but nothing I was doing was.

After we'd celebrated Keva, I had five tasks I dreaded but could put off no longer. Three of them involved meeting one on one with each of the hostile assistants Grandma had saddled me with. Over the last few eights, the petulant threesome seemed to object less to the role I played. Perhaps with the end of winter, my work felt more like an academic study to them. I liked appearing as less of a threat but I suspected once I started giving them instructions their relative goodwill would evaporate.

The woman I picked to speak with first wasn't any older than me but she'd been with the Velka for ten years, having joined soon after her menses started. Idris was skinny and irritable. Her people from Eds tended to be both of those, but I knew it wasn't wise to judge someone by their kin. I knew many in Eds had little use for the Velka, but when I asked Idris why she joined us, she said it was none of my business. In fact, she refused to share any information about her past. That told me enough.

I felt certain she was running from someone who'd treated her poorly. There were lots of ways that could have gone, and it didn't matter much which one was true. She was distrustful and angry and probably had good reason to be. She'd gotten chosen for the Conclave at the request of her two friends, whom she spent all her time with and idolized. It surprised me that Grandma had agreed to include her as she seemed more of a follower than a leader.

"What part of this effort would you like to be in charge of?" I thought my best shot was to get her doing something she enjoyed.

"I thought you were in charge of all of it."

"I am, ultimately. But if we're going to get this done, I need people to handle different parts. Travel. Maybe even live outside the forest for the summer, if that's something you think you can do. I know some don't. What makes you happy?"

"Happy? Not having some varming rantallion tell me what to do makes me happy."

"Me too."

I made a conscious effort not to blush as I asked her the next question.

"How do you feel about the reczavy?" I knew there was a great deal of animosity between them and the Eds, but I was determined to judge Idris by her own response.

"That's where I wanted to run, but it was easier to get here."

Really?

"Well, Idris, I've just learned my youngest sister is one of them."

That earned me the first friendly look I'd ever received from Idris.

"She's coming to visit me in a few anks, and she's going to be working closely with me to devise ways the reczavy can help us. I want to work with her, of course, but I can't be running back and forth all the time. If you'd be willing to join us, meet her, and talk to her, we'll find out if you could be the person who makes half those trips for me and some of the decisions, too."

"I could do that."

It wasn't hard to guess we might lose Idris to the reczavy if all this ended well.

****

Joli was a logical choice to lead the oomrushers and long-eyed archers, and she agreed without hesitating. By this time I'd filled her in completely on my Noruz meeting with Davor and Nevik, and she knew how the Royals and Svadlu had secretly agreed to give the Velka the time and space to mount their own first line of defense for the realm.

My second request was more difficult.

"I'd also like you to be the one to work with Sulphur and the Svadlu on training the farmers, if you don't think it's too much on your plate."

"Glad to do it, but wouldn't you like to coordinate with Sulphur?"

"I would, but, um, actually, we kind of have a problem. One that makes you a better person than me to deal with her."

"You two have a problem?"

"No, and I'd like to keep it that way. Sulphur doesn't know we and the Svadlu are coordinating and as much as I want to tell her, it's a bad idea."

"Why? Truth is always better. You know that."

"Yeah, but right now I'm sure she's outraged her beloved army is not going to do the right thing and fight the Mongols at our border. Her anger is real. If she knows the truth, then she has to pretend, and I don't know a worse liar than Sulphur. Not only is she bad at it, lying eats at her soul. I don't want to put her in that position."

"So you want me to keep her in the dark."

"Yeah, I know. It's scumpy to lie to her, but we can't untell her. Let's at least start by keeping our cooperation with the Svadlu from her."

"That means I have to keep it from every single soldier helping us."

Sheep scump. I hadn't really thought this through.

"For now, I guess we have to do that. Let them think they're doing this on their own time, with no support from their superiors. Otherwise, they'll talk and then some farmer will overhear them and tell everyone we're conspiring with the army and not trying to help the people at all."

"Pruck, I hate this kind of nonsense."

"I know." I had to smile. "So does Sulphur. Do what you can for her, and her Svadlu buddies, for as long as you can."

"Then what's your plan?"

"We'll tell everyone everything eventually, and beg them all to understand."

****

Two tough tasks down and three to go.

I met with Hana next. She was the clear leader of the trio and the oldest of them. A tall, thin woman, she wore her brown hair pulled into a tight bun on top of her head. It gave her a harsh appearance, but it matched her outspoken confidence. She came from one of the finer families in Pilk and I guessed she'd entered the Velka with the powerful ambitions she'd been advancing for years.

She'd already challenged me several times, and I was sure we'd never be friends. I'd only lose face by trying to get along. So, what *could* we be when I was a roadblock to be removed?

"Let's not pretend we like each other," I began. I wanted my rude opening to get her attention. "I don't want to die for many decades. Do you?"

I could see I had her off balance. "What kind of game are you playing?"

"I'm not. Playing. I will someday, but before we resume our contest to rule the Velka, I suggest we both show the good sense a leader needs."

"What makes you think I want to run the Velka?"

"*Don't* play games with me," I said. "We need to live through this invasion first. If we waste our energy sparring, we could both lose everything. I propose a truce, one in which I put you in charge of a major part of this operation. You'll get all the credit you deserve when it's done, and we'll both get something better."

She didn't hesitate. "We get to stay alive."

"Yeah. So, let's agree this is an emergency and act like it. You do something to make me distrust you? I'll listen to your explanation, not jump to conclusions. I step on your toes? You don't go behind my back; you tell me and I back off. Agreed?"

"What were you thinking of asking me to do?"

"I saw you there when my two sisters made the donkeys fall asleep. And you beat on one of the drums the day we got all the horses to throw their riders. You have a fondness for working with animals? Or for music?"

"Music, I suppose. I didn't get much opportunity for it though. My parents wanted me to teach fine needlework, the way my mother did."

"Well, I'm putting you in charge of our entire luski and singer project. Horses, gongs, fire … you got it all. Somewhere at the entrance to Vinx, you need to get about a quarter of the Mongols thrown off their horses. You can handle that?"

"I can."

I wanted to add *and can you do it without prucking me over?* But I didn't.

~ 16 ~

Half a Year Left

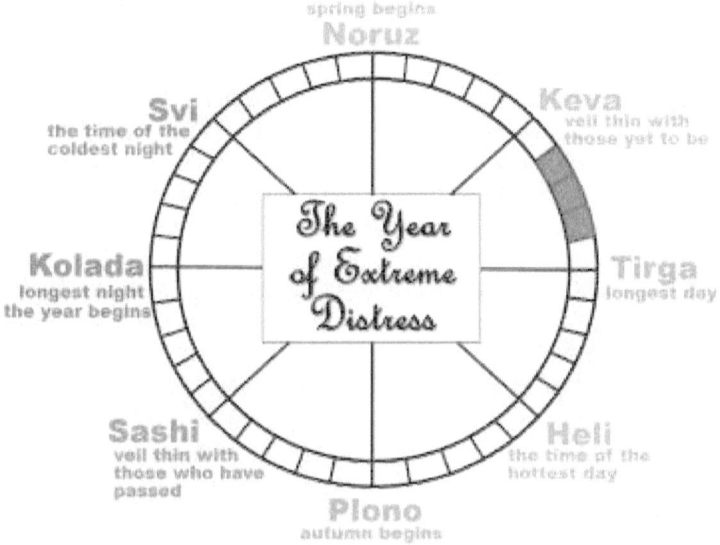

Hana's agreement brought me to my next onerous task and probably the most difficult of the five. I wanted to put it off till last but knew I couldn't. I packed a saddlebag and secured a donkey large and strong enough to be ridden all the way to my parents' farm in Vinx.

This would be my first solo trip out of the forest, with no guide, sister, or friend going with me. Despite the large leaves blocking the sky, knowing I could go knocked my claustrophobia back a notch. I hummed as I rode away from the lodge.

My need for my family's help made this trip urgent. I'd assigned Hana, my most ambitious assistant, to work in Vinx in part to keep her visible to my parents and sisters. I needed them to keep an eye on her from the beginning.

I wanted to trust Hana and hoped I could, at least as far as our shared effort went. But we couldn't afford to fail because she saw a chance to sabotage me and couldn't resist. My family could be formidable watchdogs.

Before I asked, though, I owed my parents an update on Gypsum.

My mother hung laundry out to dry and saw my horse in the distance. By the time I arrived in the yard, there was fizzy green afternoon wine and a plate of little cakes. With her daughters now scattered around the realm, I suspected my mother experienced something new. Loneliness. I knew she'd longed for quiet years ago, but perhaps the silence no longer suited her.

We chatted about everyone else in the family first. She told me of Iolite's letters from school saying she'd had no further episodes and would finish her studies by Tirga. Mom even asked about my grandmother. After that, we had no more excuses.

"Did you find your sister Gypsum? Your father shared his suspicions with me and told me he asked you to look for her."

"I found her. She was where Father suspected. She's been there for a while."

"I see." My mother didn't say anything for a few seconds. I'm sure her questions were many. *Was she naked? Having sex with multiple men?* Instead, my mother asked, "Is she well?"

"Quite well. The place was, um, less shocking than I expected."

My mother smiled. "The worst of rumors do have a way of becoming well known, don't they?"

"I suppose. The people around her were nice, Mom, and they seemed, well, pretty normal. A little protective of her, too. As if they cared for her. She assured me she was there of her own will and wanted to stay, at least for now."

"I see."

"They also offered to help me with the plans to repel the Mongols. They have as much to lose as any of us, maybe more. Gypsum will coordinate with me, so I'll have the chance to see her often. I'll be able to check on her, make sure she remains well."

"That much is good. Now, tell me all about this plan of yours to protect Ilari? How does a woman, much less a perpetual student like you, end up in charge of such a thing? It does seem a bit far-fetched."

The conversation about Gypsum had ended. Mom would pass along the devastating news to Dad in her own fashion, at a time of her choosing.

I answered Mom's questions, sharing the story of my plans for stopping an invasion. I left Nevik and Davor out of the story and tried to minimize the ways my sisters were involved, but those were the two things that interested my mother the most.

"When did you last see Nevik?" she asked.

"I'll meet him on my way back home tomorrow. We'll spend tomorrow night together."

She sucked in her breath. "As a woman, I understand your love for him. I do. He really is both attractive and kind, isn't he?"

She didn't wait for my answer but kept talking. I took a long sip of wine and listened.

"While I don't condemn you, I *do* worry for you. The whole realm is talking about how his wife is pregnant, and how his older brother has failed to accomplish the same feat even though he's been married for two years. The rules in Pilk are such that if Nevik has a healthy son who turns three before his older brother produces a pregnancy, then Nevik becomes the ruling prince. Surely you understand you can't be having an affair with the ruling prince of Pilk?"

I didn't know what to say. "I honestly haven't thought that far ahead. Right now, my goal is to live through Kolada."

"Of course."

I'd brought the conversation back to where I wanted it and I intended to keep it there.

"To that end. I'm going to need some help. Here's what you and Dad can do, if you're willing."

****

The next morning I left the farm with a few supplies and headed out to the far eastern edge of Vinx. I needed more information about the height of the cliffs and how far one could see standing at their edge. I followed them along the north edge of

Vinx until they were small enough for an agile person to climb up and down and then I traced them until they were gone altogether, taking measurements as I went. A horde of invaders would enter Vinx here to make their way onward.

Then I rode to Vinx's south side, making more measurements of where the rock face thinned and died out, providing a wide area for people and animals to move into Gruen without effort. A horde of invaders would turn right here and head to Pilk. I needed to stage my third and final act somewhere after that turn.

When I was done with my day of scouting, I met Nevik at the familiar little cabin in the corner where Pilk and the open forest touched. We kept our promise to let no one, not a pregnant wife, a scheming assistant, a sister of mine, or a brother of his, intrude into our night together.

Perhaps because we'd been apart for so long, not counting the brief tryst we had in Pilk while Coral took the baby for a walk, this night reminded me of the time in the cabin in the mountains where we'd made love over and over while the snow fell. We believed back then we'd have all the time in the world to do this as often as we liked.

This time, though, there was no snow. The long days of Tirga approached and spring thunderstorms moved in late in the day. At night, the crickets chirped to greet the warmth.

Tirga. It was exactly half a year from Tirga to Kolada. Half a year to turn my wild ideas into well-thought-out plans. Half a year to enjoy Nevik as often as I was able. Half a year to drink sweet dessert wine and smell spices from far away and feel silk against my skin. To laugh with my sisters and joke with Joli and finish getting to know my grandmother. Half a year for all that and so much more.

I sat up in the small bed gasping for air.

"Ryalgar? You okay?" Nevik woke, putting an arm around me.

"I can't breathe."

"It's okay. Relax. You're okay."

I wanted to ask him how he knew, but those tendrils of fear had grown all over my brain while I slept and now, they shut off my breath. I sat there trying to calm down.

"There isn't. Much time. Between Tirga. And Kolada," was all I could manage.

"I know." He put both arms around me and held on tight.

****

When I rode back to lodge the next morning, I was calm. No one would follow someone who woke up in the middle of the night in a panic. I had to believe I could do this, so others would believe it, too.

"Did you have a nice trip?" my grandmother asked as I entered the lodge.

"Yes, of course. I enjoyed being able to ride out on my own."

"I thought you would. Your family is well?"

"I only saw my mother. She inquired about you."

I saw the faint bit of a smile in response. "Please give her my best the next time you see her. And the man you sometimes spend the night with?"

It was my turn to smile. She never referred to Nevik by name. "He is well also."

"He isn't going to be a problem, is he?"

"Oh no. At the moment he appears to be my biggest supporter."

She nodded but the worry on her face didn't disappear. If I didn't know better, I'd have thought she'd been conferring with my mother.

****

I had one more conversation to get out of the way before I could return to my drawing, analyzing, and researching. I needed to speak with Natia, the last of the three assistants my grandmother had stuck me with.

Idris, the first woman I'd talked to, had already brought me an impressive list of ways the reczavy could help us, based on what she knew about them. I'd sent an invitation to Gypsum to visit me right after Tirga, and she'd accepted. I thought she and Idris would get along and make a formidable team.

Hana, on the other hand, seemed to have become obsessed with the idea of luskies. I kept trying to steer her towards their effect on animals, my primary concern, but she hoped to use them in other ways. She wanted luskies to coerce the invaders to rest in Bisu and to follow the roads we picked. She wanted to use luskies to calm the Mongol prisoners to make them easier to handle. Her ideas made sense to consider, even though Coral had gone to great lengths to explain how a luski's power was limited and how few if any luskies would agree to manipulate humans in any public setting. To be honest, Hana's fascination with luskies concerned me.

As soon as I sat down with Natia, I realized I hadn't given her situation enough thought. Idris' outward belligerence and Hana's position as top dog in the group had led me to craft a particular approach with each one. I hadn't thought about Natia because she was friendlier. She had soft blonde hair and a pleasant face and, while I knew she was Hana's closest friend, she'd always been gracious to me, at least compared to the other two. Frankly, I was less afraid of her.

Sitting across a small table speaking with her, I realized she could be the most dangerous of the three. Idris wanted respect. I could provide that. Hana would consider an arrangement benefitting us both. I could provide that. Natia, however, only wanted to advance the interests of her best friend Hana. To that end, she'd act nice and say what I wanted to hear, and then do as she pleased. The more we talked, the more I understood I had no currency with which to buy her cooperation. She only cared about my demise.

The best I could come up with was to assign her some piece of this plan where she could do as little damage as possible. Yet, no piece seemed unimportant enough.

Wait. I could send her off on an expedition to scope out the possible second entry into Ilari. Someone had to go marching through Eds to see what the terrain was like on the other side of the border.

"I have an extremely sensitive and important assignment I am hoping you'll tackle," I said.

She smiled at me. Her smile said *like scump I will*. Her mouth said, "Of course."

As I gave her the details, I did my best to reassure her. "I'm confident I can get a Svadlu or two on leave to accompany you and see to your safety. We'll add a couple of Velka to your team, too. Women who have considerable experience camping and hiking in the hills. You'll be well supplied and have the experts you need to be comfortable and cared for."

"Why not just send this group without me, then? I'm not sure I have much to contribute." She had a point.

"Oh, no, you have a lot to contribute. Decisions will need to be made on the fly, decisions we can't predict but will require the broad knowledge about our plans that only you will have. And, the information you bring back will be vital to our planning. I can't tell you how important this is."

Of course, she realized she'd be out of my way for anks, in a place where she couldn't possibly do me harm. I wasn't lying to her, though. This information was important.

What's more, if she went, I had to share a lot more with her. I needed to teach her basic map-making skills and she needed to learn about elevation, terrain, and how to commit this information to paper.

Hoping for something encouraging, I asked "If you hadn't become a Velka, what would you have chosen to do?"

"Oh. Design clothing. For women. You know, really fashionable clothing."

Well, that wasn't so helpful.

"Or maybe houses. I always thought it'd be fun to design beautiful homes for people, with lots of staircases and spectacular views."

That's right. She was from the lovely hills of Lev.

"I think you're going to like making maps, then. It involves drawing, so it's a bit of the same thing."

She gave me an *I doubt it* smile but I thought Natia would do great with this assignment.

~ 17 ~

Fifty Vital Words

spring begins
Noruz

Svi
the time of the
coldest night

Keva
veil thin with
those yet to be

Kolada
longest night
the year begins

*The Year
of Extreme
Distress*

Tirga
longest day

Sashi
veil thin with
those who have
passed

Heli
the time of the
hottest day

Plono
autumn begins

Before Tirga arrived, it became too warm even in the shade of the forest. With all the hard labor facing us, we didn't need an unusually hot summer. I took comfort in hoping the heat made the Mongols more uncomfortable and I fantasized about it driving them back to their cold mountains.

I couldn't imagine an army as successful as theirs rode into any land uninformed. I guessed their envoys had done more than trot into Pilk and demand tribute. They'd probably ridden the width and breadth of our realm first, noting our population centers, roads, crops, and natural protection.

This was good news. A well-armed party of ten people in unusual clothing wouldn't have escaped notice. I could find out what nichnas the group had scouted. Better yet, if the summer heat had sent them running, I could begin to alter Ilari. What would confuse them the most?

Removing the Bisu fence and gate would mean they wouldn't know when they'd entered our realm. The farmers could do some dredging, extending the swamp outward to narrow the entry. We'd need to be careful, keeping the changes subtle enough to avoid suspicion, but things did change over six eighths of a year and their memories would be uncertain.

The reczavy and their fondness for illusions made me think of more drastic ideas. I remembered standing on the road leading south out of Vinx. We *could* cover most of the wide road headed to Pilk and then widen the road going south through Gruen instead. The one leading to the river. If we made it gradual enough and had enough vegetation to make it look natural, we could divert them without their knowing it and launch one last attack on them at the river's edge. Eggs filled with itching powder wasn't a bad idea. If we could get the horses uncomfortable enough, perhaps they'd swim out into the water. Could I find enough strong swimmers in Ilari to grab them? Faroojers were known for their prowess in the water.

By the time those remaining on land realized they weren't where they thought they were, their army would be further reduced. Four hundred riders instead of six. Would they ride on towards Pilk once they got re-oriented? I hoped so. We needed a defeat so thorough they never wanted to come back.

Changing the landscape required many strong people with lots of shovels. I'd need trees and shrubs to hide the old road and similar growth to make my new road look real. That took people who could make almost anything grow anywhere fast. Lucky me. The Velka had women who devoted their lives to the plant kingdom.

Oh, and my father the soil expert could help, too. How much of Ilari could we remake in half a year, if we worked as if our lives depended on it?

I went back to the map on my wall and started drawing.

****

As soon as Tirga passed, I sent an invitation to Sulphur so she, I, and Joli could move along the plans for training our farmers and herders. I couched it as a social visit, but I knew Sulphur would understand my meaning. She agreed to come, but when she arrived she wasn't the sunny sister I remembered. Her stance was defiant and her eyes bored into mine as I came outside to greet her.

"It's been too long since we've visited," I said. "You've had a tough half year?"

She rolled her eyes before she turned the force of them back on me.

"Yes. Tell me, are you happy your dire predictions were right? Are you pleased the Svadlu plan to use the cowardly approach you suspected all along?"

"Please, Sulphur. I understand they have different priorities for defending the realm. The Velka want to work within those realities to keep everyone safe."

She glared harder at me. "You want my help, don't you? What can I do but give it? If I don't, I betray my own family. If I do, I go against those I've sworn loyalty to."

Her misery showed in the way she slid her eyes away from me after she said it, and held her arms crossed tight against her chest. She felt she couldn't win. If anyone in the world hated not being able to win, it was Sulphur.

"This is never going to work." I said it to her and myself.

"Of course it will. I'll help you, and I'll lie to those I fight with about what I'm doing with my free time. I'll do it because your strategies have left me no choice."

Prucking horse scump. My sister hated me now.

"Listen to me. The Svadlu *know* what we're doing. We've told them, so they won't interfere. They're not only okay with it, but they've also turned our ideas into part of their strategy." There, I said it. I couldn't keep my sister in this kind of misery any longer.

"Don't add more lies to the mix," she said. "I won't believe them."

"I'm not lying. I asked, no I begged, Nevik and Davor to use the best military strategy for defending Ilari. We all realize a small force at the entrance to the realm would almost certainly be wiped out by fighters whose expertise is charging in on horseback, with arrows flying and swords drawn. And yet, if we place the entire army there and we lose that battle, then we've lost the realm."

"So, what is it you claim they've decided to do?"

"We've *all* decided to hide the entrance to Ilari, hide the people who live near it, and offer no force to stop them when they ride in."

"Well now, that sounds like a great strategy."

"Hold on. We're in the same fight here. The Velka, and the people who live in the outer nichnas, will be taking other, more stealthy measures to hamper the invasion. By the time the Mongols get to part of Ilari the Svadlu can best defend, there won't be near as many invaders. Or there won't be if you'll help us."

"Yeah. So why haven't you told everyone the Svadlu and Velka are working together?"

"Think about it. Our farmers' anger at the army helps us gain their cooperation. I don't like the deception, either, but it's our best shot at surviving. I believe it and so do the Svadlu."

She looked at me for at least as long as it takes to put on one's shoes. Finally, she spoke.

"Are you scumping me?"

I wasn't sure which fact she referred to, but no matter which, I had my answer.

"I scump you not. I'd have told you all this sooner, Davor would have told you sooner, but I know how much you hate lying."

"How much I hate lies," she corrected me.

"Yes. Well, how could we ask you to train the people of Bisu and Vinx while pretending you didn't know things you did. I was trying to protect you. To make it easier for you."

"You failed at that."

Joli walked in near the end of the conversation, but I knew she'd overheard all of it.

"Lucky for you," Joli said to Sulphur, "you don't have to deal with your well-meaning sister's handling of this." Sulphur gave her a questioning look. "I'm the one who's working directly with you and the Svadlu."

Joli turned to me. "Let me take over. We'll be fine."

I gave Sulphur a pleading look, but she wouldn't even glance in my direction. I knew she hated being lied to as much as she hated having to lie.

"She'll calm down, once she sorts through it in her mind," Joli said to me. Then she turned away. "Okay Sulphur. Here's what we've got to deal with so far. It's a lot to get done, and it's all important."

I left, closing the door behind me, trusting my closest friend to move forward and my sister to forgive me in time.

A few days after Sulphur left, the guide who'd taken me to the reczavy offered to go fetch Gypsum for her visit.

"The others are nervous about going, but I know it's no big deal. Plus the reczavy know me now. I'm the best one to go."

"Would you mind taking Idris with you? She's going to be handling a lot of this for me, and the sooner she jumps in the better."

"Sure. Why not. She has some idea of what to expect?"

"Idris is more informed about the reczavy than anyone I've ever met."

The guide raised her eyebrow but said no more.

When I saw Gypsum's pale blonde hair through the trees, at first I thought it was Sulphur returning. All seven of us wore our hair long or braided, as women did, except for Sulphur who'd gone after her thick blonde locks with a kitchen knife when she was eight and had refused to let her golden mane grow below her chin ever since.

This blonde head had fairer and better-behaved hair than Sulphur's, but it too had been cut short.

"Gypsum?"

I recognized her, of course, once she entered the clearing. She was built differently, with a tall, slender body and long limbs that moved gracefully without her giving it any thought. She hopped off her donkey and gave me a happy hug. Happy to be invited, happy to be included. It was the Gypsum I'd grown to love and appreciate years ago.

"Your sister and I had the best talk on the way here," Idris said, dismounting as well. It looked like my instincts had been good concerning this partnership.

Word had already spread around the lodge about my sister's current living situation and Idris's fascination with it. For once, the social status of my trio of rivals held an advantage. Thanks to Idris, Hana let it be known the reczavy were now valued partners, deserving of all the open-mindedness we could muster. It became suddenly fashionable to be tolerant of them rather than dismissive. Gypsum got a warm welcome.

To her delight, she got to stay in my room with me. Joli, Idris, Hana, and Natia spent considerable time in there with us as we concentrated on the giant drawing of Ilari on my wall and on ways to use our landscape and all of our talents to befuddle and reduce a foe we couldn't possibly defeat. I won't go so far as to say we all liked each other by the time Gypsum left, but we got along well enough to amass a long list of ideas to build on.

I wondered if I'd made a poor choice planning to send Natia off to Eds but I decided to trust my instincts. She had an artistic eye with a flair for capturing the terrain on paper. Even if her absence wasn't an advantage, perhaps turning her into a mapping expert would be.

****

Soon after Gypsum left, I returned to Pilk. I wanted to scout the landscape in Gruen more and I needed to talk to people in academia with helpful knowledge who I'd overlooked during my trip last year.

I met with three language experts. One knew a man who'd once been held captive by the Mongols. This former prisoner was Persian and his skill with languages was so great that during his four years as a captive he'd learned Mongolian despite the effort the Mongols made to keep outsiders from learning their tongue. Five years ago he'd escaped, braving the elements for anks until he collapsed on the road into Bisu, too ill to travel further. A family of herders nursed him back to health, and he'd stayed on.

This former captive didn't know it yet, but he'd become one of the most important people in Ilari. He, and probably he alone, could teach my would-be jailers the words to calm their prisoners, to order them around as needed, and to free them eventually.

"Why not kill these vermin right away?" the language teacher asked me. I knew I'd have to answer this question many times, so I crafted the shortest and most convincing reply I could.

"Because they are more valuable to us alive." I explained to him what I'd heard about the importance this Khan placed on his warriors. "We can defeat the Mongols once, maybe, but we can't possibly stage performances like this every winter. We have to ensure they don't send an army to conquer us again."

"You're going to try to defeat them once, then persuade them to leave us alone? I don't think these barbarians bargain with anyone."

"We won't be just anyone. We'll be the people, probably the *only* people, who chose not to kill hundreds of their fighters. Heli, if things go well we might even be able to give them back some of their horses."

The teacher shrugged. "You may be on to something. The little I know of their language indicates a code of honor. Given the lack of alternatives, your gamble could be worth taking."

"How much of the language do you know?"

"Enough to realize it's hard to learn. I could teach you what I know in an afternoon."

"This afternoon?"

"Why not."

I left before the sun went down, knowing all the Mongolian he knew. It was pitifully little, but it included the most basic words of survival. Hello. Please. Listen. Stop. I want … Will you… Pardon me. Take this. Thank you. Go away. Good-bye.

I'd practice my fifty words and phrases every day, and once I found the former captive in Bisu, I'd learn more. Maybe someday these words would save my life. Maybe they'd save my realm.

Next, I sought out other experts I'd neglected the first time. I spoke with historians about the techniques of war; I learned of famous treaties. I sought out stories of those who'd tried to persuade outsiders to leave them alone. I listened to those who claimed to understand the workings of the human mind. I talked to medical professionals about poisons and yes, even about itching powder.

I knew a morsel or two of information would turn out to be vital to me, but I had no way of knowing which morsel it was. So I gathered them all, writing them in my best tiny lettering and hoping, when the time came, I'd find or remember the one or two that mattered.

~ 18 ~

What to Call This Thing

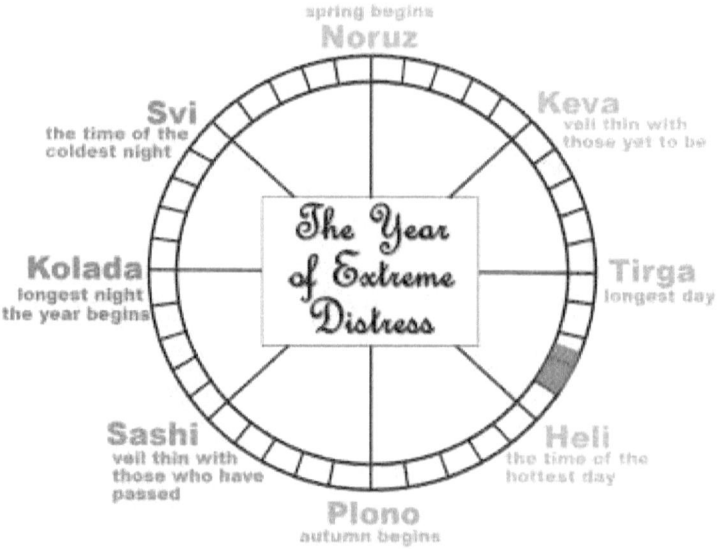

I left Pilk Central to meet Nevik at a famous old inn on the other side of the river, just inside of Faroo. We knew he'd be recognized anywhere so close to Pilk, but Nevik said the owners understood his need for discretion and would have a picnic supper for us waiting in his room. They'd offered to bring me to his quarters through a back hallway so I wouldn't be seen.

I found sneaking in distasteful and it brought back all my mother's worries. However, once I entered the lavish room and saw a table covered in tiny egg and cheese pies surrounded by ripe peaches and plums, the inn didn't seem so bad.

We greeted each other in the way we'd both hoped, with barely a word said between us. My head ached from all the facts I'd crammed into it, and once we laid exhausted in each other's arms, I explained my new fascination with a clever Greek fighting technique in which each warrior protected his neighbor with a large circular shield on his left arm.

"It's called a phalanx," Nevik said. "Worth knowing about, I suppose, but I can hardly imagine the Velka crammed together in a V-shape, marching in lockstep to defeat the Mongols." He laughed at the image. "You're better off developing the things you do well already."

"I know. I just, I don't want my ignorance of anything to be our downfall. Surely you understand."

"I understand that no one, not even a lady as smart as you, can know everything. You think too much. Give your mind a rest."

I laughed. "That's what all the neighbors used to say about me. 'She's the one who thinks too much.'"

"Your neighbors had a point." He said it playfully, making it hard to take offense.

When I asked him what was on *his* mind, he waited until we each held a goblet of red dinner wine in our hands. He inhaled deeply to take in its rich aroma, then he answered.

"Her pregnancy is half over. The midwives say she's likely to go full term and give birth in three eighths of a year."

That changed the tone of the evening.

"At Sashi?" I asked.

"Yes. A mere eighth before the Mongols discover we've chosen not to be their vassals."

"That's an unfortunate time to have a newborn child."

"It is."

We ate and drank in silence.

"She's told me she wishes to reconsider our arrangement once the child is born. She intends to give up her lover and become a loyal spouse. She wants me to do the same. She thinks we owe the child that much."

I stared at him, stunned. How could he bring up this horrible idea over dinner, as calmly as if he were discussing a change in our breakfast menu? Of all the scenarios I'd played in my head, this one had never occurred to me. I set my goblet on the dresser lest I drop it or, worse yet, fling it to the floor.

"Are you considering it?"

"Of course not. I love you."

Okay. Perhaps that's why he found his wife's request of such little importance.

"What did you tell her?"

"She's with child, Ryalgar. With my child. I told her we should make no decisions now, but wait until the baby is born."

"What?? A coward's answer if ever there was one!" The angry words were powered by my surprise, and they flew out of my mouth with no thought. He looked as if I'd slapped him across the face.

"It was the answer of a sensible man."

"And how did she respond to this *sensible* man?" If my tone improved, it wasn't by much.

"She reminded me if the child is a son, and if my older brother and his wife are as infertile as they appear, this child will make me the ruling prince of Pilk in three years

"That nonsense again," I said. I was speaking of every nichna's convoluted rules for accession to the throne of the ruling prince, but he misunderstood me.

"Yes, the requirement of being male is silly. A woman is every bit as capable of ruling a nichna, and everyone in Ilari knows it. But I can't change the way things are."

"I don't care about rules of ascension," I said. "Not now, anyway. I care about the idea of never being with you again!"

"And I care as much as you do. Maybe more. But Ryalgar, why should I upset her now when there is so much yet to happen. Will it be a healthy birth? Will it be a boy? Will any of us be alive after Kolada to care? I'm not afraid to tell her no, I just see no point in turning her into a hostile enemy for both of us until we get past all those other hurdles."

For both of us? My mother's words came back to me.

"Does she know who I am?"

"I've never told her, but she's a clever woman and she's made allies at the palace. I assume she knows. She's never referred to you by name, if that's what you mean."

It wasn't what I meant. I worried that even if I survived the Mongol invasion, I wouldn't be safe from her. Not as long as I had relations with the man I loved.

"It's a long way down the road, Ryalgar. Please. Let's make this a problem for another day."

"Then why did you have to tell me?"

He looked genuinely puzzled.

"I tell you everything. Everything that matters to me, at least. I don't want to stop doing that."

Heli. There was no response to those words. I shoved my plate away.

"I've lost my appetite. I'm going to sleep."

"Now?"

"Now. I'll see you in the morning."

I got into bed and pulled the soft goose down duvet over my head, to block out the candlelight and any further words coming out of his mouth. I fell asleep and dreamt of an evil sorceress sending phalanxes of elderly Velka after me. Their pale skin hadn't seen sunlight in decades, and they cackled as they rattled their shields together and chased me into a reczavy tent where I was afraid to open my eyes.

When I woke up in the morning, for the first time in our relationship, he was gone.

****

I'd planned to return to the forest that day, but the way we'd parted left me dazed. I couldn't afford to be so distracted by personal problems and hoped a good hard ride into Bisu would clear my head. There I could scout out the swamp in more detail, which I'd been wanting to do, and could talk to the valuable man who spoke Mongolian.

It wasn't a well thought out plan, but fate was with me that day. After riding along the swamp's edge, taking what measurements I could, I found this former captive where my teacher said I would.

His name was Zirab, and he'd taken a wife in recent years. The two of them had a small place on an undesirable parcel right along the marsh and barely inside the realm. I guessed it wasn't far from where he'd been found five years ago, nearly dead. I wondered if that was on purpose.

"I've forgotten all of the language," he said before I'd gotten more than a few words into my request. "I've spent five years doing my best not to think of those times and the last thing I want is to bring those memories back."

His wife stood behind him, and she began rubbing his neck as he spoke.

"They treated you horribly?" I asked

He gave me a funny look. "Not particularly. They weren't cruel, but they did own me, own every second of my life. I'd be happiest to never hear their tongue again."

"I'm sure you would, and no one could blame you for that. However, we have a little problem."

I explained about the Mongol envoys and their demand that tribute be put pretty much where his home sat. He'd heard of nothing of this. I described my ideas for thwarting an invasion, and the role he could play as a valued teacher. While I talked, his wife left the room and returned with a child of maybe a year on her hip. The little girl looked as if she'd woken from a nap. The woman held her on her lap as I finished talking, stroking her hair and swaying gently to soothe her awake.

"This job you have for me. Where would you want me to do it?"

"Anywhere you like. Of course."

He looked again at the woman and child. "I'll need a house and a decent plot of land to go with it. In Vinx I think. Upon these high cliffs I look at every day. Can you arrange that?"

I hadn't considered this sort of answer. Yet, Zirab was not of Ilari, and he barely lived inside the realm. He probably didn't feel his fate was interwoven with our survival. He did care about the survival of two particular Ilarians, however.

I looked at the woman and the child. Being timid would not serve me well. I knew many of the families who lived along the cliffs and none would give up their land easily, but it didn't have to be easy to get it done.

"I can make such a thing happen."

"I can start teaching as soon as you do."

I held my tongue about his sudden ability to remember Mongolian and left promising to send news soon.

****

I knew I needed to return to the lodge, but Joli surprised me when she met me as I dismounted.

"You forgot? Today's the day all the oomrushers are practicing together to figure out who is the best and what archers we need to be paired with."

So that's what nagged at the corners of my memory. I'd originally planned to be back days earlier, but Nevik ... then Zirab ....

"Where?"

"At the forest's edge in Vinx. Come on. We're leaving now."

More were there than I expected. All the oomrushers in our original group stood ready to take part, along with other women I'd never seen. Perhaps they lived further away? My grandmother sat with them.

What was she doing here? Didn't she trust Joli to handle this? Then I remembered my father telling me Grandma was drawn to the Velka because she was an oomrusher, too. She was auditioning, just like the rest of us.

Olivine outdid herself, bringing five more long-eyed archers with her. Three of them were men. So that's why we hadn't met on the clearing in front of the lodge. Perhaps the Velka needed more flexibility regarding male visitors? A discussion for another time

Today, Joli had the organization well in hand. Every combination of oomrushers and archers would be tried, and then she'd select teams to begin training.

"And what about those remaining?" one woman asked.

"Remaining oomrushers will audition to join a team, to see if they can extend the path or improve the accuracy of the arrow. We'll pick a few as understudies well-enough qualified to fill in for anyone, and the rest will be assigned to assist in another part of, of the ...." She turned to me in exasperation.

"What are we calling this thing, anyway?"

Ah, I hadn't spent all that time studying Greek history for nothing. I'd given this some thought and I liked my answer. A lot.

"The Chimera. We're calling the big plan, the entire illusion, the Chimera."

"What in name of my great uncle's arse is a come-here-uh?" one of the unknown Velka said.

"Kuh-mere-uh," I corrected her. "It's a make-believe animal with three parts. The Greeks thought it was a lion, a goat, and a snake, but it's anything made up of three disparate pieces. Like our plan."

"I've heard of it," Arek, Olivine's artist friend, said. "I heard it describes something impossible."

"It can. Others say it describes something wildly imaginative, implausible, or dazzling. I think that covers what we're doing."

Several laughed and agreed.

"Can we be the lion part? I want to be the lion."

"Nah. That's got to be the folks making all those horses throw their riders."

"How about we be the goats?"

"I think the reczavy are the goats."

"That settles it," my grandma said. "We're the snakes."

"Not exactly a complimentary mascot."

"If you're trying to be sneaky and deadly, it is."

"A Chimera isn't all that lovable." Arek spoke up again.

"We don't want to be lovable. We need to be frightening."

Joli took control then, sending us off for our tryouts.

As we tried different combinations, we learned our best shots came from two oomrusher friends working with one archer. If one of the two oomrushers was exceptionally strong, then another with whom she had rapport made her stronger. More oomrushers than that mucked things up.

We had two women who worked well with everyone, and Joli chose them to be understudies. The remaining six women would work with the Lions or Goats, as we were already calling them.

My best companion? My grandmother. She wasn't a strong oomrusher, but I seemed to bring out the best in her and she in me. I figured we'd be working with Olivine, making it an all-around family affair, but Joli and Olivine made our single strongest combo by far, with no other help needed.

Joli assigned Grandma and I to work with Nikolo, Arek's boyfriend. He coached archery in Gruen and was the strongest shooter in the group. Odd trio that we were, only Joli and Olivine surpassed our distance and accuracy.

We left before sunset, exhausted but satisfied, and with a clear plan for regular practice. It appeared I would be both a general and foot-soldier in this odd Chimera I'd created.   ·

~ 19 ~

The First Man in
Three-hundred Years

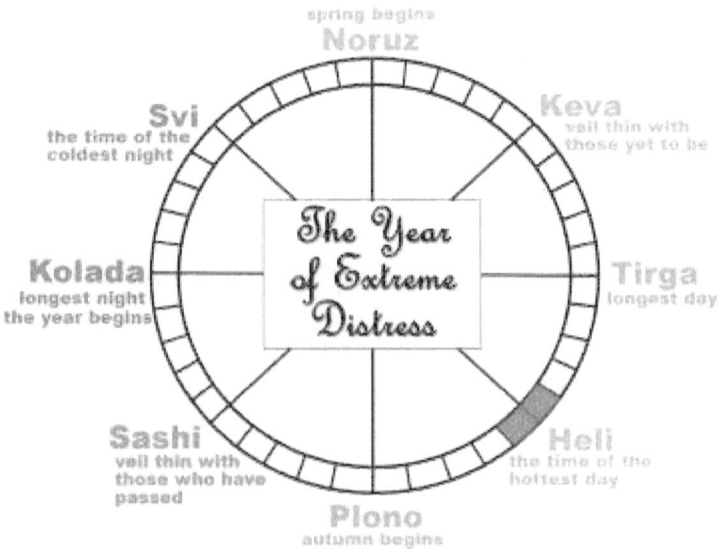

spring begins
Noruz

Svi
the time of the
coldest night

Keva
veil thin with
those yet to be

Kolada
longest night
the year begins

The Year
of Extreme
Distress

Tirga
longest day

Sashi
veil thin with
those who have
passed

Heli
the time of the
hottest day

Plono
autumn begins

I turned to the Velka Recorders to verify the Mongol envoys had gone scouting around Ilaria before delivering their ultimatum.

"Why do you care?" one asked me. I'd learned to accept their direct style and knew they meant no offense by it. They talked to everyone this way.

"Well, if they didn't scout us out back then, it means they'll be back to look us over before they come riding in. We don't want that. As it is, I'm hoping they're so sure of themselves they don't bother to send spies ahead to check on us. I don't think they will. We're such a small conquest, so innocent and poorly prepared. And it's so hot." I made a helpless face, and the Recorder laughed.

"There is much about Ilari they would have trouble learning," she said.

"True, and I'm hoping nothing they saw gave them reason to think that."

Stories began trickling in after a few days. Yes, the group tried to enter the forest of Zur from the south. They waded out into The Wide River in Kir. They walked around the marshes of Gruen and stared across The Canyon River in Scrud. One witness claimed he saw them try to throw a rope over the canyon to the other side.

They also rode up into the hills of Lev and sampled the wine. Several vintners said the unusual group found their beverages quite acceptable. Reports found them in Tolo next, a few days before Noruz, where they found the springs creating The Little River. Word was they followed it into Pilk Center and checked out the stores and restaurants. Someone decided they were Mongolian and sent up the alarm causing the yelling and commotion that interrupted my conversation with Davor and Nevik. After the mayhem ensured, they delivered their message to our leaders and left.

I was satisfied. They had reason to think they knew us and knew our land. Now we had to prove them wrong.

As the reports kept coming in, I worked to get my newly deputized mapmaker Natia on the road to Eds. I secured two Svadlu escorts. A Velka guide with expertise on our northern border agreed to go with the group. Then I added a fifth member because Natia asked me to.

She had an old boyfriend back in Lev whom she'd never married and the affair had rekindled recently. She wanted to bring him along, using this time away from the forest to enjoy the pleasures of an ongoing relationship. Perhaps I did have a currency with which to buy her cooperation.

"Pitch your tent a respectful distance away from the others," I said as I agreed to her request.

The issue of no male visitors inside the forest became a problem sooner than I expected. My next chore involved seeking the advice of my father about my efforts to redo some of Ilari's terrain. I couldn't possibly copy all the details in the map on my wall and no amount of paper scraps could convey the sense of scope given by my mural.

I needed my grandmother to make a short, one-time exception for my father to visit. But he was her son. Better for someone else, anyone else, to give him permission, so I asked her to convene the Conclave.

"Don't you think it would be best if you told me what this was about?"

"Yes, almost always, but I've found one of those exceptions. Trust me, Grandma. It's better if you're surprised by my request."

I may have given her enough information to figure it out, but she said no more, and she looked as flustered as I could have hoped when I explained my needs to the group.

"No exception has been made in over three hundred years," I was told. Then everyone began talking.

"It's a slippery slope once we go down that path."

"We've nothing against men, mind you. Some of us are quite fond of them."

"But we have power over our own lives here and we cherish this."

"In such an unequal world, only our isolation makes our freedom possible."

"Surely you understand. Once males come and go, our lives change."

"Yes. In subtle ways at first, but it will happen."

"If things were equal outside, they could be so in here."

One woman conceded a point. "Of course, we do recognize Yasen is Aliz's son and your father."

"That's not why I want him here," I said. "Let me show you. Please. Come to my room."

I got puzzled looks but they followed. Most of them, of course, hadn't been inside my quarters. There were plenty of murmurs as they entered.

"Well, she *did* end up with a nice one, didn't she?"

"Look at all those windows."

And then, finally …

"Look at that mess on her wall."

Everyone stopped to stare.

"Well slap the Goddess on the arse. I do believe that is Ilari."

"My goodness, girl, how did you ever manage such a thing?"

Finally, I heard what I'd hoped for.

"You need your father to see this?"

"For important reasons," I said.

They nodded, almost as one.

"Very well, Yasen may spend a day here but he must leave by nightfall."

Another woman turned to my grandmother. "You did well, Aliz, to recuse yourself from this decision. Very smart."

"Thank you," she said. Once the woman turned away, she winked at me.

My dad arrived two days later. He exchanged a long hug with his mother, and I could only guess at the undercurrent of emotions that must have run through each of them

"I'll join you and Ryalgar later for lunch," she told him, then gave me a nod as she added, "I know you two have a lot to cover before the day ends."

Dad looked around the lodge with a bemused smile on his face then followed me to my room. He'd already heard about my mural and had brought sketches of his own, but I don't think he was prepared for the scope of my work.

"I've never seen anything like this. Those lines have to do with steepness, don't they? How did you get a sense of how fast the ground rose?"

"I started by balancing a full cup of water on a flat board held even with my eyes. Then I'd climb to the rock or twig it pointed to, knowing the point was two paces high, like my eyes. I'd pace it off from where I'd stood so I'd have two sides of a triangle. You know."

My dad laughed. "Yes, I do know. You made calculations from there."

"Of course. I kept up the pacing, and I'd redo the height thing every so often because the steepness kept changing and then I'd average things in between. If I didn't do it too often, it didn't take so long. My results aren't exact, but …"

"They're great, Ryalgar. Amazing. Now, I see you've got four, no five, places where you want to change the shape of the ground. Let's talk about the soil in each of those areas."

My dad and I fell into a familiar cadence, one where we worked together to get a thing done. This time we didn't fix a plow or repair a wheel; we sought to extend a swamp or build a ridge. By the time Grandma arrived with two women carrying lunch supplies, we had a plan for every problem.

After lunch, my grandma brought in our best growers. The Velka's roots, literally, were in cultivating herbs for medicines and growers remained central to our culture. We possessed agricultural knowledge surpassing anything in Pilk and often relied on techniques not given much credence in academia. Our women could convince plants to do the improbable. How they did it was anyone's guess.

Besides our medicine-making endeavors, this group dedicated their energy to keeping the boundaries of the forest thick and fire-resistant. That was a full-time job, and they'd already agreed to produce enough poisons for my arrows, too. But I needed more from them.

My ideas required trees and bushes where none grew now, so raw earth would look like it hadn't been altered. Rich grasses in Bisu had to last through the cold of autumn. In select areas, I needed dead brush dry enough to ignite. My dad and his workers could move soil and transplant trees, but only the Velka could make the flora of Ilaria grow abnormally fast and behave as we needed it to.

My dad didn't spook as easily as most farmers; his close kinship with two Velka helped. Soon he and the most cantankerous of the green witches laughed together at how blinded the Mongols would be by their joint efforts.

As the sun neared setting, the others retreated to their quarters and he and I reviewed the plans for who would do what and when. We agreed he'd work with Joli and the Svadlu to recruit workers to help him with the hard labor. I'd come to the farm right before Plono to ensure all was on schedule. As the coming dark hastened our goodbyes, he walked out of the lodge

First man in three hundred years. I wondered how long it would be until the next.

****

The Heli celebration tended to be the most subdued of the eight, due to the intense heat at that time of the year. Festivities often involved swimming and some skipped nighttime merriments altogether, although skinny-dipping remained a popular alternative for couples in love.

I hardly noticed the holiday as my sheaf of notes grew and I made more plans.

Hana communicated less with me than Joli or Idris, but as the leader of her trio, I thought her omissions reflected her habits more than an attempt to keep me in the dark. At least I hoped so.

Once she heard about my Greek-legend-inspired name for our efforts, she sought me out at dinner. Others had told me how much she liked her group being dubbed "the Lion."

"I studied Greek history, too," she told me as she passed by the table where I sat alone with a stack of reports from the Recorders to read as I ate. "The Chimera is a great choice. Just want to assure you the Lion is getting ready to roar."

I gave her the friendliest laugh I could manage. "Good to know. I'm hard at work learning to hiss like a snake. How are my sisters doing?"

"The singer, Celestine? I swear people think she's the most fashionable thing ever."

"She's always been the best dressed one in the family. But is she getting you the singers you need?"

"Are you kidding? She's got choirs rehearsing all over Ilari. The latest one is composed entirely of Zurians. Can you imagine a group as disagreeable as them forming a choir? It's insane."

"That is interesting. Do you have enough luskies to work with all of those singers?"

An expression of panic flashed across Hana's face, disappearing as fast as a strike of lightning. I knew I hadn't imagined it though.

"The luskies are a disappointment. All that mask-wearing is tiresome. Why won't they proclaim their powers and be done with it? And they're *so* reticent to push the limits of their abilities. More scaredy-cats than lionesses. It's a shame."

She made an exaggerated frightened face, I think to make me laugh. I didn't.

"But do we have enough of them?"

"Yes and no. Plenty of people, mostly women like you said, though we got one guy. Most are weaker than your sister, so we'll use 'em in groups and do what we can. I think with all the gongs and fire and everything else, those horses will buck and run. Once they do, though, we won't have much control over the Mongols on the ground."

"Controlling Mongols with luskies never was part of the plan. The farmers of Vinx will handle the thrown riders. Joli and Sulphur have that covered."

She looked at me. "I thought there could be a better way to do it."

"Keep on roaring," I said. It was the most neutral thing I could think of.

"Keep on hissing." She laughed as she walked away.

~ 20 ~

Often Gone

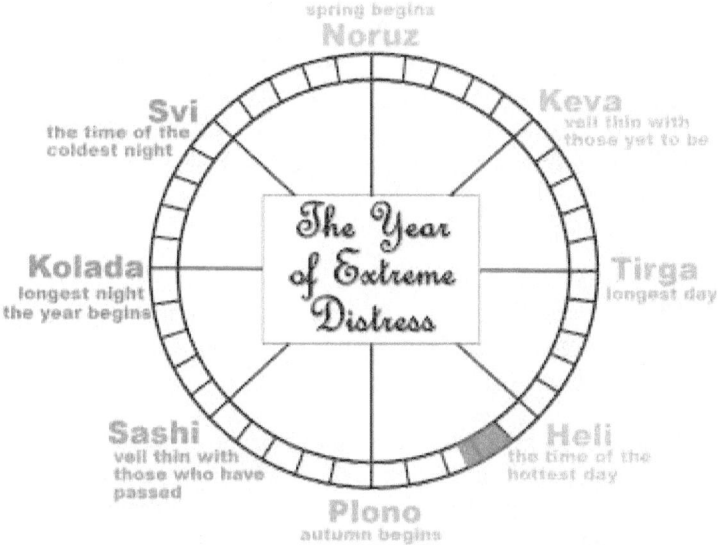

After the way Nevik and I parted, I worried he found ignoring me easier than dealing with me. I finally heard from him an ank after Heli when he invited me to meet him high in the mountains of Tolo. The location pleased me. It was cooler and further from the curious eyes in Pilk and the trip would allow me to scout out one more part of the realm with which I was less familiar.

"Can't wait to see you," his note said.

"I'll be there," I wrote in reply.

I decided to bring a Velka guide along to help take land measurements before I met with Nevik. A second person would make my process simpler and, although I felt safe traveling alone in most of Ilaria, Tolo was one of the few places where I preferred a companion.

The guide and I rode along the northern border of the Zurian forest to The Little River as it poured down out the mountains. The people of Zur may have seen us from a distance, but none gave us trouble. Then we followed the bank of the river along the Eds border, where many of the Edsers lived. They left us alone as well. During this strange time of waiting, everyone avoided conflict.

After we entered Tolo, our most remote nichna, the guide and I spent two days making notes and taking measurements. My map of this area would be much improved when I got back. She assured me she'd be fine riding home alone and left me to my lovers' rendezvous. I wondered if she knew how much I appreciated her doing it without a single smutty joke.

****

"Talk or don't talk?" Nevik greeted me with those words as I entered our cabin.

"Decide later?"

"Good call."

We reached for each other with an eager anticipation fueled by a long separation. Darkness came before we returned to conversation. He started a fire while I busied myself laying out the provisions he'd brought. There was fresh bread, soft cheese, grapes, cherries, and a smoked duck. A jug of one of Lev's best dinner wines sat on the table. One doesn't eat poorly when one dines with a prince.

"Talk," I decided.

"I'm so glad."

That night, I heard more about palace intrigue than I ever had. I think I helped Nevik by letting him speak freely. His brother had sunk into depression at his inability to produce an heir. His brother's barren wife now hated Nevik's pregnant wife, who had cleverly allied with Nevik's mother.

His father chafed under laws demanding he transfer the crown to any son with a three-year-old male heir. Like many a ruling prince before him, he'd been happy to force *his* father into retirement, but he wasn't ready to end his own rule.

Everyone was concerned about the Mongols, and there was talk of sending Nevik's wife west across The Wide River to visit her homeland once the baby was born. Nevik didn't like the idea. I held my tongue until I heard his reasons.

He believed the Mongols would attack the lands west of us next and would do so sooner if thwarted here. He thought they'd be thwarted alright, and he wished for his child's safety. I translated his thoughts. He wasn't saying he wanted his wife around. He was saying he thought I would succeed and was willing to bet his child's life on it.

Before the night was done, I availed myself of his neutral ear, too, as I complained about Velka power struggles. He nodded in sympathy through most of it, but when I got to the part about Hana and her fascination with getting luskies to control people, he gave me a funny look.

"Is this Hana from Pilk?"

"She is. I know her mother teaches needlepoint there. Do you know her?"

He laughed. "Oh yes. I spent some time with her. Once." There was an emphasis on the *once*.

"*That* kind of time?"

"Yeah. She's several years older and I was rather young, but she was single and eager. She scared me off, though, when she confessed to me she wanted to rule Pilk."

"It's probably a common dream, you know."

"I suppose, but she told me the best she could do as a woman was to find a way to control the man who ruled Pilk. That scared me."

"Hmm." I had to laugh. "I can see how it would be a little creepy in your case."

"She's quite ambitious," he said. "I'd tell you to watch your back, but I bet you already are."

"Every day."

On cue, he started to massage my back, and we both understood the talking part of the visit was over, at least until morning.

****

Once I returned to the forest, I spent only a night at the lodge before Grandma and I headed into Gruen to practice with Nikolo. I guessed he and Arek were lovers, living together in K'ba where people were more open-minded. Unmarried couples rarely lived together anywhere else and certainly not couples of the same gender. I realized Nikolo and Arek were fighting for more than I was; they were fighting for their right to be together.

Yet, they were adamant about not holding practice sessions where they lived. It puzzled me, but I knew little about K'ba so I didn't argue.

Nikolo was a natural coach, and he started our training by teaching Grandma and me about archery. He was right; the more we understood how the bow worked and why the arrow flew, the better we'd be at controlling it.

"Would you be willing to share this with our entire group?" I asked

"Of course."

After some questions and answers, with practices in between, Grandma and I got noticeably better. We hoped our poison tips would make it so our arrows didn't require much velocity when they hit their target. If so, we easily sent arrows twice as far as any archer I'd seen. The further away we could be, the safer we were. Beyond some radius, our enemy wouldn't come searching for us.

We agreed to practice on our own and meet for a group practice on the fourth day of every ank. As we walked back to our donkeys, I noticed my grandmother's face in the harsh summer sun. She looked younger in the forest, where her features were softened by its shadows. I saw her struggle, a little, to mount her donkey and wondered how old she was. I had no idea.

"I'm not as young as I used to be." She startled me with her answer. "I saw you watching me. You're right, I can't hop up on an animal the way I once could, but I still do get around. I want you to know, I'm also not nearly as old as I intend to get."

"I'm glad to hear it." I meant it too. I hoped she'd be around a long while.

****

Gypsum invited me back to her camp, sending word through Idris. I didn't have time for socializing, and I didn't want to step on Idris' toes, but something in Gypsum's tone sounded important. I sent a message back. I'd be there tomorrow.

I'm not sure what I expected to find, but it wasn't a woman with a sheaf of notes and concern on her face.

"Idris is great." It was how she greeted me. "But she's not much for putting together something like this. Neither, really, are many here. Look. I need you. I need someone to listen to this plan and tell me whether I'm brilliant or crazy. Or both. If this was just for fun it'd be one thing, but it's not. People will die on this day, and I won't pretend otherwise. So listen to this like you know there will be deaths, and then tell me what you think."

No, this was not what I expected.

I settled into a soft thing on her floor, one I supposed was meant to be used as a chair. At least I hoped it was. I checked for stains and saw none, so I stayed put.

"We use towels," she said, noticing my scrutiny of the furniture. "You needn't worry." I know I winced. "It's okay, Ryalgar. I understand. Now listen."

So I did. I heard about diversions, illusions, and the by now infamous eggs filled with itching powder that had begun as a joke, at least I thought it was a joke, and then had stuck as a plan. However, instead of attacking the Mongols by unseen forces when they were surrounded by nothing, like the first two groups, my Goats planned to slow the invaders to a halt and then surround them with the surreal. The actual inhabitants of Gruen Town, the settlement along the river, would be replaced by the reczavy, who would dig deep into their bag of tricks.

I thought it could work, at least as part three of the plan, when the seeds of fear would already be growing. I hoped some of the frightened horde would regroup and move on to Pilk, where they'd encounter our Svadlu, fresh and ready to fight.

"This is excellent." I meant it.

****

It bothered me I'd hadn't heard anything about Iolite in a while. She'd told my parents she'd be done with school during Tirga, yet we were well into Heli and I'd received no news of her being back at the farm. I asked one of the Recorders if she could find out if my sister was still in school.

"She isn't."

"Oh."

Why did she have that answer at her fingertips?

"Is she home with my parents?"

"No, she's not there either."

Well, this wasn't good.

"And you know all this because?"

"Because a few days ago your grandmother asked the same questions. She was surprised we hadn't heard anything about Iolite, and wanted to make sure she was well."

"Have you found her?"

"No. We've been unable to determine her whereabouts and your grandmother wants you to contact your parents. But you've been often gone and she's been waiting for a good time to talk to you."

"I see. Where's my grandmother now?

"She's hoping you'll join her for afternoon wine in her room."

Well, that was convenient. I guess I would.

~ 21 ~

Ten Thousand People With Shovels

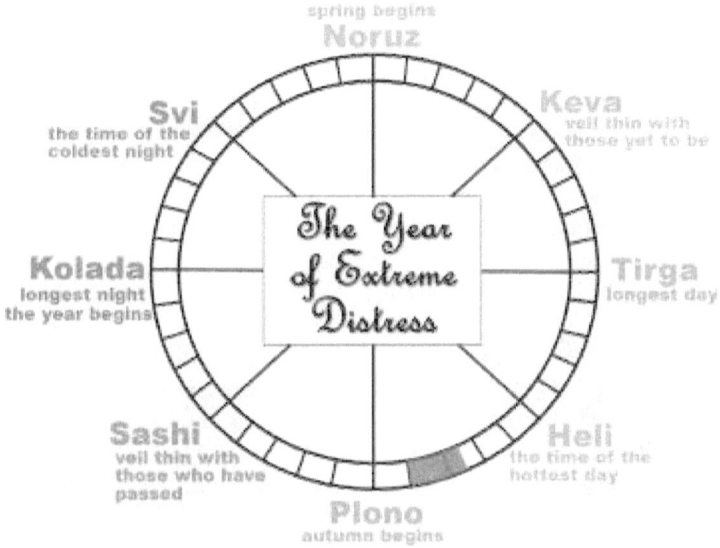

My grandmother sipped her pale fizzy green afternoon wine. "Please. Join me," she said as I entered and closed the door behind me.

"I hear you're searching for Iolite," I said. "How long has she been missing?"

My grandmother set her cup down, gestured me to a chair, and sighed. "After we got back from practicing with Nikolo, I discovered she left her school three eighths ago. That's a long time. It worried me, so while you were with Gypsum, I did something I swore I'd never do. I went to the market in Vinx and sought out anyone from your family. The only one there was your mother, of course, and I begged her to speak with me."

I couldn't imagine this scene in my head.

"Did she?"

"She hesitated, but I think she saw my concern. She looked at me and asked 'Which daughter?' When I told her it was Iolite, she nodded and followed me into our tent. She's worried too. She and Yasen have received several short letters from Iolite assuring them she's fine. Students usually finish around Tirga, so once it passed and your parents didn't hear anything, they traveled to Iolite's school to check on her and discovered she'd left before Keva. Her teachers said she finished early, and everyone thought she'd gone home."

"Why would she lie to them like that?"

"No one knows, but days after your parents returned home, they got another short letter from her saying she was safe, handling important matters, and not to worry. *That* was over an eighth ago, and they haven't heard a thing since."

"My parents must be so scared."

"They are. I asked our Recorders to look into it. They can be thorough when they wish and they found nothing. Your sister has disappeared."

I remembered Iolite's deep purple eyes and imagined them peering at me, asking me for help. Where was she? Was she safe, or had she lied about that too?

"What are we going to do?"

"I've asked the Recorders to dig deeper and I haven't heard anything back, but I'll let you know when I do."

I left Grandma's room upset I had one more reason to be anxious. I think it's a good thing we don't know our future. I'm not sure I'd have made it through the day knowing by nightfall I'd face more disturbing information.

****

The days were still longer than not as we approached Plono, and I was headed into the lodge at dusk after practicing my oomrushing in the woods. I worked with leaves, getting them to sway without a breeze, mindful of how often I'd ended up breaking my promise to practice every day.

I needed to do more. Working with green plants calmed me, but also made me feel stronger. I wondered if the myth of the Velka drawing power from plants came from some deeper truth I didn't understand.

As I washed my hands in our outdoor basin, two women rode in on donkeys. I recognized Natia and her guide escort from across the clearing. What was she doing here? We'd estimated her mission would take two eighths, maybe more, and she'd been gone little more than one.

She seemed relieved to see me once she recognized me in the fading light, and she hurried over, leaving her companion to deal with the animals.

"Ryalgar. We must talk. It's worse than you thought."

Great.

We sat together on the front porch. I confess my first reaction was relief she took her responsibilities seriously, and my second was relief she'd returned unharmed. Yes, I knew I had it backward.

"Tell me." It was both a plea and an order.

"Okay. We walked that area in Eds where you told us to, between the mountains and the river. I tried to take measurements like you said but it wasn't easy. It's pretty steep in some parts, so steep you couldn't trot on a horse, much less gallop. But you were right, a horse could walk without climbing up or down much and there are hardly any trees. In some places, it opens up and you could make better time."

"That's what I guessed but it's good to know for sure. So what happens after you leave Eds?"

"Well, I thought the border would be marked somehow, you know, but it isn't. There's a town near the border higher up in the mountains, and you can see it from below. After you get past it, you figure you've got to be out of Ilari but you're not sure."

"I'm surprised the Edsers haven't put up a fence to keep their goats in, but this is good to know, too. What happens after you get out of the realm?"

"Not much. At first, the land gets steeper and narrower, kind of a natural break near the border. Then it gets flatter and it's more fertile the further away you go. Maybe it's open pasture there, not part of any other realm? There's no homes or farms, just like the open pasture when you leave through Bisu."

"Yeah, but that one is open specifically because of a treaty with the east. We made that agreement to stop all the arguing over lost livestock."

"Maybe this is by agreement, too. It's not like the Edsers wouldn't go and make a treaty on their own and not tell anyone, right?"

"Good point. How long does this open pasture go on for?"

"At least half a day's ride. It's just open land and you see fewer goats as you keep going."

"So the Edsers don't have up a fence because it gives them more grazing land."

"I think so."

"And except for the narrow place past the border, would it be pretty easy to come in that way?"

She nodded. Her eyes had widened, and even in the waning light I could see how pale she was.

"So when you kept going, what happened? Did you find yourself in another realm? Did you meet the people there?"

"Maybe and no." She looked at me like she didn't know how to answer me.

"What then? Speak up."

"We got to this point and then everything was charred. All of it. Burnt to the ground. You could see parts of a few buildings here and there, made from stone. There were dead animals. Dead people. Dead children. Dead, half-burnt bodies everywhere. Half rotted. Half charred. It was … It is the most horrible thing I've seen in my life." She looked away from me. "I don't think I'll ever stop seeing it. What did these people do to deserve such a horrible fate?"

I thought I knew. "They failed to pay the tribute the Mongols demanded."

"Are you serious? Can't we just pay it, then? Giving them everything we have would be better than what happened to those people."

She was right. But I already knew nothing she or I could say would convince the proud yet naive people of Ilari to become the servants of the Mongols. She knew it, too.

"What are we gonna do?"

"We're going to make more swamp at our entrance. Moisten the earth. Drench everything so Eastern Ilari won't catch fire."

"And the people? We can't drench them. Isn't this even more reason to hide those who can't fight? They need to go into the forest."

"I agree. And now that we know this, we'll get them there. We'll also have to think of better ways to hide those who do fight. We've got to be prepared for our attackers riding in and trying to set fire as they go. You've brought us something terrible but valuable. Natia, listen to me. What you saw was horrible, but your knowledge could be the thing that saves us."

I relieved Natia of her duties, ostensibly so she could rest up from her arduous journey. I would ask my grandmother if the same could be done for the guide who'd gone with her. I could do nothing for the two off-duty Svadlu who'd been with them, or the former boyfriend who Natia had failed to mention.

I hoped whoever commanded the soldiers had the wisdom to recognize their situation and give the two of them some time off as well. As for the boyfriend, I'd try to get more information from Natia in a few days.

****

The next day was the fourth day of the ank and as I rode with my grandmother to meet Nikolo for our practice, I told her of what Natia had seen.

She shook her head. "No one should come upon something so awful." I saw doubt in her I hadn't seen before. "Are we in over our heads, Ryalgar? Way over our heads?"

I'd been wondering the same thing but been afraid to say it.

"Do you have a better idea? At this point?"

She kept silent for a few moments, considering. I suspected she thought of trying to convince the Svadlu to guard the Bisu border after all, and the odds of them being effective. I'm certain she tried on the idea of attempting to convince those in charge of the realm to capitulate to the Mongols' demands. I'd considered both options after talking to Natia. I hadn't been able to think of another, except maybe to run away and hide alone deep in the forest in hopes of living a while longer. I suppose she considered that option, too.

"No," she said. "I don't have a better idea."

If we surprised Nikolo with the intensity of our practice that day, he kept quiet about his observation.

As we rode home, I asked her "Do you know of anyone in the Velka who can influence the weather?"

"What? Why?"

"We could use some rain. A lot of rain. Right before Kolada."

"We're a realm of farmers, Ryalgar. We can always use more rain. If the Velka could manage that trick, we'd have been running Ilari a long time ago."

"How about fog?"

"I do think some of the oomrushers can move fog. Perhaps part of the mist over the lake and the swamps could be coerced into covering Bisu? Would that help?"

"Yeah. It's one more little thing that could matter. Would you be able to find time to coordinate that?"

She looked pleased at being given a part.

"I'd love to." She smiled. "You can call us the Water Snakes. At your disposal."

****

Nevik and I met almost every ank as summer neared its end but after the one night of sharing all our political troubles, we didn't talk about other people again. He didn't mention his wife's pregnancy or her ultimatum. I didn't ask about them, and I didn't offer updates on the Velka or the Chimera. Instead, we had glorious nights making love like there was no tomorrow. Because maybe there wasn't.

As Plono neared, the number "two eighths" loomed in my head. Two eighths to go. Two eighths of a year to make every part perfect. Two eighths to enjoy my life, in case a vital detail or two brought us all down.

I'd stayed the furthest from the plans involving Joli and Sulphur. I wanted to give Joli all the room she needed to run her show, and Sulphur all the room she needed to forgive me. But, as

Plono neared, I needed to make sure all was well. I knew big picture items Joli did not; I needed to be coordinating at a larger, more strategic scale.

I approached Joli and asked for a formal update.

"About time." She launched into the details of Bisu herders and problems with hiding them. "We're working on tunnels where we can and deep trenches where we can't."

"Isn't that rather drastic? And labor-intensive?"

"Extrapolating from what Natia learned, if my herders are found, they'll be killed. I figure nothing is too much work to prevent that."

I agreed. "So you've got people digging all over Bisu?"

"No," she laughed. "I've got people digging all over Bisu, Vinx, and Gruen. I've also got a road crew working with your dad to build a fake road in Gruen, and he and I have people with shovels narrowing the entrance to Ilari and reforming the cliffs of Vinx on two sides. Everybody has people digging everywhere! We've got wide trenches to divert the horses along the chosen path, and we've got mounds of dirt in places just to slow them down. It's amazing what ten thousand determined people with shovels can accomplish in a summer."

"You've got *ten* thousand people out there digging?"

"No one's counted but it's probably more. Overall, I'd say the old women and children aren't as effective as the bigger people, but even they're surprisingly strong. People are digging for their lives."

"Shouldn't some of those people be practicing how to capture and subdue prisoners?"

"Oh, no. Those are separate groups. The reczavy have about six hundred Faroojers building rafts and practicing swimming in The Wide River. That's for the goat part. Sulphur now has over a thousand herders from Bisu and Scrud figuring out how to separate and capture two-hundred horseless riders. And last I heard, she's got over eighth hundred wheat farmers out there learning to chase away runaway horses, deal with mounted fighters who don't move on, and round up the ones who've been thrown. That's for the Lion part. I think people from Eds are helping with that one."

"And these people? They're doing well? They believe this can work?"

"These people have been told you've woven a magical scheme to protect them from an invader who wipes out realms like ours before lunch. They believe in what we're doing. Now, why don't you stop asking questions and come with me tomorrow and see all this for yourself? It's about time you got your head out of your reports and showed up."

"Will Sulphur be there?"

"Of course she will. The Svadlu have given up on her as a soldier, for now, and told her to work with us."

~ 22 ~

How a Leader Behaves

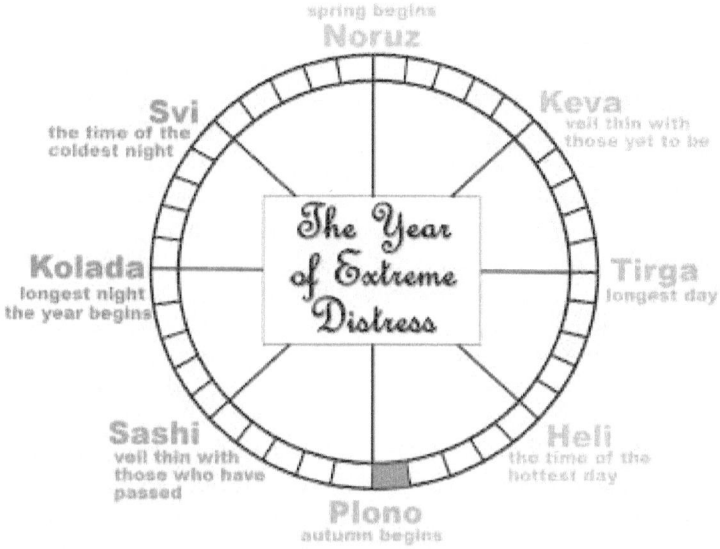

I rode up as six Bisuites surrounded a man trying to imitate a Mongol. He waved a sword, yelling and cursing as he jumped around. I thought our fake Mongol overacted a bit, but he succeeded in intimidating the six people trying to capture him. Two large men, two teenagers, and a grown woman and an older man with sacks over their shoulders all surrounded him. They kept their distance, wary of his sword.

"Rocks. Now." Sulphur yelled it. The older man picked three big stones out of his bag and hurled them at the face of the sword wielder, who then charged at him.

"Down. Now." Sulphur yelled again. The two teenagers lunged towards the man's knees from either side. As the fake Mongol turned to run his sword into one of them, the woman hurled a handful of pebbles into his eyes. Before he could react, one of the larger men in the group grabbed his sword arm from behind, pushing him forward as two teenagers held fast to his shins. The fake Mongol hit the ground and the largest of the men sat on his back while the other five worked fast to hogtie his ankles and wrists together.

"This is where you come in." I didn't think Sulphur had noticed me riding up, but she had, and she spoke to me.

"These people need words. 'Surrender. We won't hurt you. You're our prisoner. You'll be returned to your Khan. Don't be stupid.' Whatever you can manage to teach them. When are my words coming?"

I guessed having her address me at all was a positive thing.

"No one along the cliffs would relinquish any land to our language teacher, as I expected, so I had to get the ruling Prince of Vinx involved. He's been on the throne less than a year, you know, and he hates offending anyone."

"Yes, Prince Giorgi. I've had a few dealings with him in my new role." Her tone suggested she was more impressed by Vinx's new ruler than I was.

"When he hesitated, his father and mother both told him to get off his arse and take care of this. He did come up with a rather good plan then, forcing four farms to each sell a small corner of their parcel to the crown. The language teacher has got a cottage going up now and says he'll start teaching your people Mongolian next ank."

"Good. Thanks for handling your part."

I gestured out at the many identical teams of six talking and practicing among themselves. The two smaller and sometimes older members of each team carried bags of rocks. Each group had two people young and limber enough to dive for a man's knees, and each had a strong fighter capable of hanging on to that crucial sword arm. Finally, each team had one exceptionally large person capable of holding down anyone on which they sat.

"Looks like you've got a solid plan. Thanks for handling your part."

We looked at each other and said no more, but our exchange acknowledged mutual respect if nothing else.

Joli walked us around to the various groups, introducing me. Many, maybe most, looked at me in ways I'd never been looked at before. Their smiles shone with thankfulness for giving them hope; their eyes begged me to win the gamble I was taking with their lives.

It shook me. What I'd set in motion over a year ago, motivated by a desire to save my own family, and maybe a desire to please my grandmother and fit into my new surroundings, had morphed into a plan involving tens of thousands of people depending on me. This was not what I'd signed up for.

I thought of Nevik and all the Royals, and I realized they lived with these sorts of responsibilities every day. Why did common people aspire to have these problems? Such obligations were frightening.

I also understood that with my role came responsibilities I'd shirked. Like it or not, a leader needed to be seen. More to the point, a leader needed to be seen caring about her followers.

I turned to a teenager and asked "What do you think of diving for the knees of a sword or knife-wielding Mongol? Are you comfortable doing this?"

"No, I'm scared," she said. "And I'm angry at the Svadlu for not defending us like they should. But if they won't, this is better than just getting murdered. Right?"

"It is," I said. "And I saw the way you did your part in practice. When the time comes, you'll be great."

The smile she gave me back had more confidence in it.

A leader needs to do this. I made a promise to do it more in the anks ahead.

****

I gave Natia a couple of days to rest, then checked in on her in the small house she shared with Hana and Idris. They were both away, and she welcomed me in.

"I'm here to make sure you're okay."

She responded with a bitter, unamused laugh. "No, I'm not okay. But I am better than when I got here, and I suppose I appreciate your asking."

"I had no idea what I was sending you into. I hope you know that."

"Yeah. I wouldn't accuse you of sending anyone into such horrors."

Then, before I could open my mouth to respond.

"Don't say it. I know. *I brought back valuable information.*"

"You did, and I'm sorry it came at such a cost. To you. How did your boyfriend handle it?"

Finding out more about the unmentioned boyfriend was part of the reason for my visit.

"Oh, him."

"It didn't bother him?"

"We'll never know. He lasted through about three days of my taking tedious measurements before he declared the whole thing was a stupid waste of time and left. He wasn't with us by the time we rode out of Ilari."

"I'm sorry."

"Don't be. It reminded me why I chose not to marry him to begin with. I'd sort of forgotten about that side of him."

"Well then. Is there anything I can get for you? Do for you?"

She gave me a quizzical look.

"You've got it backward. You need to tell me what I can do next. Turns out I'm prucking good at taking tedious measurements and sketching them out. Have you looked at the maps I made of Eds?"

I had. They looked more meticulous than mine, but I'd wanted to study them closer before saying anything. Then so much had clamored for my attention. I'd met with the women making the poisoned arrows and spent a whole day with those trying to alter vegetation, in anticipation of my trip to Vinx to meet with my dad. I hadn't gotten back to Natia's maps, but she didn't need to hear that right now.

"They're fabulous. Better than the ones I make. You know, we do have another mapping problem facing us. I've learned how much we're redoing the landscape. We need to capture that information and alter our map accordingly.

The tiniest bit of light shone in her face. "I'll get you the revisions. It goes fastest with two assistants. Can you get me two? And horses? The donkeys are so much slower on the open prairie."

"Done. I've got a list of Velka who want to help. I'll find two suitable ones and they'll be ready to leave when you are."

****

My dad met me at the edge of the forest with my mare. There was always a surge of freedom when I mounted her and took off onto the wide-open prairie. I let exhilaration overtake me as I galloped with the sun on my face and the wind in my hair. Dad said nothing as he trotted to catch up with me, but I think he understood.

Once I slowed my horse and caught my breath, we talked. The Velka growers' accomplishments amazed him and he bragged about how his fake road to Pilk would fool even a native Ilarian.

"I understand Gypsum is part of the plan to capitalize on my road work. Her and her, uh, friends."

"It's true. The Velka and the reczavy have formed an alliance of need. They, too, have a useful bag of tricks, and Gypsum is leading their efforts."

"You think she'll stay on with them when this is over?"

That was what he cared about. I wanted to tell him no, because I wanted to comfort him. But I didn't think it was the truth.

"She seemed happy there, Dad. You probably need to consider this may be what she wants. For good."

He inhaled loud enough for me to hear him, but said no more.

On the way to the farm, he took me to see the long mounds of earth being created along the flat plains of Vinx to keep our attackers inclined to stay on the path we'd chosen for them. The first ones we passed were made a while back, and the Velka had done their best to cover them with enough growth to look natural and discourage horse traffic.

We came upon another set in progress and, remembering my earlier promise to act more like a leader, I asked my father if he minded stopping. He seemed surprised, but pleased, by my request.

"Of course. Let me introduce you around."

I could hear the pride in his voice, as the workers responded much like the fighters Joli and Sulphur had been training.

"You think this is going to work?" one man asked me.

"I do. How about you?"

He shrugged. "It all sounds pretty farfetched. I wish the Velka had stayed out of this. Then maybe the Svadlu would have changed their mind and done their job here."

"I understand, but we didn't think that was going to happen."

"Yeah, well, I'd have preferred it. But I'm glad you have some solid ideas. Don't get too fancy, okay?"

"We won't," I promised him. "Trying to keep it simple and effective."

He nodded. "Good. That's the way to go." Others nodded too, and they all waved as I rode off.

Mom met me at the door to the farm with the traditional apple nut bread, baked to celebrate Plono, only a day away.

"We've had so many holidays now without a child here with us," she said. 'It's not worth making these things for me and your dad. Here. Have a piece. It may be my best ever."

I wasn't hungry after my ride but I took a little off the plate she held out towards me, to be polite. As it melted into my mouth I reached for another, larger piece. Her apple nut bread *had* improved. I suppose these days she had more time to spend on her baking.

Once she seated me in the kitchen, with hot cider and more treats in front of me, I turned to my concerns.

"Have you thought about where you and Dad will be when Kolada comes?"

"Your father won't take shelter. He insists on staying with his workers in case more alterations are needed. Perhaps you can change his mind." She looked at me. "Probably not, though."

"And you? What will you do?"

"Well, I wanted to stay here at the farm, but I've been told that's a foolish choice. When Aliz and I spoke about Iolite…" She paused to give me time to comment on this unusual conversation but I passed. "Aliz told me you and she are part of a team of, of somethings, I hear, and you two will be out on the battlefield along with Olivine."

"Well hidden," I assured her.

"Whatever. You won't be sheltered. Neither will any of my other children, it appears. Sulphur will be fighting with the Svadlu, while Coral and Celestine are doing something confounding somewhere else, and Gypsum..." She faltered here and paused. "And then Iolite..." At this point, I heard a sniff and realized she'd begun to cry.

"How could I possibly have had *so* many children, and they're all going to die young!"

The sniff made its way to an outright sob and she covered her face with her hands.

"All of them," she said. "Every one."

She cried hard and I knew I should put my arm around her and say something comforting, but when she said "every one" my mind just flashed back to the drunk man at the celebration years ago who'd called us all pruskas.

"All of them. Pruskas, every one." The words slipped out of my mouth. She moved her hands away from her face and stared at me in absolute horror. I thought she was going to scream at me, or perhaps even demand I leave the house.

Then her face melted and she started to laugh. It was hoarse, like she hadn't laughed in a long time. It began small but it grew louder and more full of life until she laughed as if I'd said the funniest thing in the world.

"You're right, Ryalgar." She managed the words as she tried to catch her breath and discretely wipe away the snot running out of her nose. "You're exactly right. Seven pruskas is what I raised."

She stood up and she hugged me like I can't remember her having ever done before.

"Aliz invited me to take shelter in the forest," she said. "Near her quarters, right before Kolada. I accepted because Coral will bring her baby there and when Kolada comes I'll watch Votto. I'll be there for him if all the rest of you die."

With that, she patted her hair back in place, wiped the last of the tears from her eyes, and got up to clear the table. I could tell she'd finished talking by the way she kept her back to me as she rinsed the cups in the basin. I watched her for a bit, then I went to bed and fell asleep to the pleasant sound of her laughter ringing in my head.

~ 23 ~

Problems a Stargazer Can Solve

Up until I left my parents' house the day after Plono, I felt as if time sped along on a galloping horse, moving so fast my surroundings blurred together. There had been so much to do, to learn, and to coordinate. Yet on that day, as I rode through the plains of Vinx feeling the first traces of fall in the air, the world seemed to pause. Like most Ilarians, I wasn't particularly religious, but perhaps for the first time in my life I felt the balance of the equinox, the brief time twice a year when day and night sit in harmony. For as I rode, I heard nature holding her breath.

Then, time crept.

Nikolo, Grandma, and I practiced together. I supposed we got better, but it was hard to tell.

The reczavy met with us again. Idris lived with them now and most people thought she wasn't coming back to the forest. Hana stiffened any time anyone mentioned Idris and I suspected she blamed me for the loss of her friend.

Natia returned from Vinx with a remarkable amount of information detailing the impressive landscaping done by my father, Joli, Sulphur, and thousands of Ilarians willing to do anything to increase their chance of survival. As she and I annotated the messy map on my wall, I knew my responsibilities had shrunk down to a few key problems.

How many people would be stationed where? And when? How many days could we keep them in place? Did the Mongols often show up late, to prevent a staged resistance such as ours? How would we warn each other as they made their way into the realm? How could we respond to the unpredictable?

Of those not fighting, who was being sheltered where, and how, and when would they get there?

Because I'd set this in motion, everyone looked to me for answers. The Svadlu had barely been seen in Eastern Ilari in any official capacity. A good call on their part. Royals had retreated into their castles, content to leave the specifics to us underlings as they issued vague proclamations about maintaining hope and working together. The leadership of the Velka had followed Grandma's lead and stepped out of my way.

So? Who else was going to orchestrate the specifics?

I picked up my quill and paper and began to write out the ninety days from Plono to Kolada, marking the tasks needing completion and how many days each would take.

You can do this. I muttered it several times as I wrote.

****

Celestine sent me a note. "I need to speak with you, as soon as possible," it said. I turned to the woman who'd brought it. "It's still morning."

"I know. I left the other woman alone at the market because it sounded urgent."

"You did well. Ride back, find my sister, and bring her here. Oh, and please take someone with you to help the woman in the marketplace."

She nodded. Over the past few eighths, our business had more than doubled in the eastern nichnas, as the population turned to us in so many ways. One lone woman couldn't handle all the customers anymore.

"I'll be back soon."

Celestine's note concerned me, and I took my work out to the porch to watch for her as I read through reports from Recorders in Pilk. The Mongols remained absent during the long hot summer, as expected, but now that the days cooled, I expected some activity. I wasn't disappointed. A traveling caravan from the north reported coming across two separate groups of ten Mongol envoys, each apparently on their way to deliver ultimatums to other realms. Luckily for the caravans, the Mongols had never shown an interest in attacking small groups of travelers. Perhaps, being nomadic, they had a certain respect for other wanderers.

What was the timing like for an ultimatum delivered in the fall? Was tribute expected after the hardships of winter? It seemed cruel to force people into near-starvation during the harshest season so they could make their expected payment in the spring.

Or maybe these realms were given only two eighths to make their decision? Maybe they needed to amass their tribute before winter began? I found that more likely. Ilari might have benefitted from a lucky fluke, by being visited in the spring and given a whole six eighths to prepare.

Or maybe it wasn't luck.

If mere efficiency dictated some lands received more warning than others, our reputation as an idyllic place could have put us on the shortlist of those unlikely to cause trouble. Perhaps the Mongols felt certain we wouldn't put more time to good use. I hoped that was the case. I liked the idea of being underestimated.

I looked up to see two women accompanying the Velka messenger. One was my sister, her long curly black hair as unmistakable as her fashionable clothes and shoes. The woman with her was new to me. She was dressed in the soft grey wools and leathers often worn by teachers in advanced subjects, and she seemed at least ten years older than my sister. One of her instructors perhaps? Why?

I looked closer.

Although Ilari is isolated on many sides, those from elsewhere do settle here, as wanderers, as refugees, and sometimes as the lovers of returned wanderers of our own. Thus, it's not uncommon to meet an Ilarian with different features or darker skin than usual, and often this person's family has been here for as long as anyone can remember.

I assumed the woman with Celestine fell into that latter category.

"This is Firuza," my sister said as she walked towards me. "She's come to offer her help."

As the woman began to speak, though, her heavy accent told me she came from elsewhere.

"I'm an astronomer. I teach and work with your father."

"Pleased to meet you. Yours is an interesting profession, but not one of much use at the moment." I gave her what I hoped was a polite smile. My sister stepped forward.

"You have needs you probably haven't thought about, and they do involve the heavens."

I'm sure I raised an eyebrow for several reasons. Celestine had never spoken to me this way, with a certainty she was right and I was wrong. And, I was quite sure I'd well considered all my needs, and a stargazer could solve none of them.

Firuza pulled something out of her pocket. It was a tube, about twice as long as my foot and thinner than my fist, hammered out of metal.

"What is that?"

"Look through it." She handed it to me. I put the thinner end of it in front of my right eye, which I generally favored, and looked at the sky. I was in the clouds. A bird flew past and, for an instant, it covered my vision before it flew on.

"You've turned me into a long-eye! Or rather your device has. What manner of machine is this? Do you use magic in your science?"

"I do not." Her laugh was warm. "I made this. It's based on something my people do. If you grind a curve into the glass, the picture coming through it is different than the reality. Smaller, or bigger, or warped if you do the glass wrong. It's tedious, but it can enhance the vision of those with poor sight. I put several such glasses together because I've always wanted to fly to the moon, and thought if I could get enough of the curved glasses, it would almost be as if I had done so."

"Is it?" This was incredible.

Her warm laugh came again. "Somewhat. I'll let you use it one night when the moon is nearly full. You can see for yourself."

I liked this woman. Yet. "I still can't see how flying to the moon helps us." Then, of course, I stopped. "Wait. If you stand on a cliff and look out over the land ..."

"You can see an invasion coming from a long way off ..." Her smile was as warm as her laugh. "Your long-eyes can do the same, of course, and perhaps you were planning to use them for such, but I know you only have a few and they're needed elsewhere. Also, I've spoken to two of them. My moon glass sees further, and it never gets tired."

She didn't have to convince me.

"There are tricks to using it well. Let me train another and we'll be your lookouts. We'll camp on the cliffs of Vinx from Sashi on, and take shifts, from dusk to dawn, to be sure there are no surprises."

"Thank you," I said. "Having this certainty of a warning will make such a difference."

Celestine flipped her hair out of her face in that way she had. "Hold on, big sis. We're just getting started."

"Perhaps you'd like to have a seat?" I gestured to the chairs on the porch. "Let me get someone to bring us some light breakfast wine and pastries.

"Why just have two of you as lookouts?" I asked Firuza as we settled into our chairs. "If you went with four people, or eight, you could divide the day into smaller portions, so you'd stay more alert. And you could keep watch at night, too. If the moon is out, our enemy could advance in the dark, and you could detect them. Or maybe you could see their campfires far away."

Firuza shook her head. "I want to keep this simple. Eight people? No ...."

I understood. "I know a cottage on the cliffs that will become empty after Sashi. I could put you there, in charge, and my sister in the Svadlu could find someone agreeable to you to be your second. She, or he, could manage the people and let you focus on the job."

I could see she was considering my idea. I pushed harder. "I'd really like to have more people on this. It's too much work for two, and this early warning could make all the difference."

Inside, I cringed. How many times had I told people they were making *all the difference*? Well, maybe they all were...

Firuza agreed, but Celestine interrupted with something else for me to consider.

"Won't you be needing to get word to people about what's happening? Lots of words, to lots of people?"

"That's one of our biggest problems. There's no such thing as an instantaneous message, but it's what we need. At the least, we must communicate faster than the Mongols ride. I've no idea how to do that."

Celestine's smile was almost mischievous. "Between Firuza and me, we have three ideas."

"Three?"

Firuza spoke. "Mine's the worst because it only works if we have the good fortune to be attacked on a sunny day. But I think you should have people standing by to use it, because if we're lucky, it's faster than anything else and conveys more information than the other methods."

"You use sunshine?" This astronomer was more useful than I'd have guessed.

"I do. When it reflects off a small looking glass, sunshine can be seen half a realm away. One can cover it to make it blink off and on, using codes to transmit words. Whole sentences. I'd be glad to work with anyone you want to set this up. Between now and Sashi, that is, when I leave for the cliffs of Vinx."

"Absolutely. Consider it done and we'll hope for a sunny day." I turned to Celestine. "Does your idea somehow involve music?"

"No, but it does involve musicians."

"Okay...."

"When a show's been canceled, or the time or place has been changed, there can be a lot of people to notify. So, the director hangs a flag outside the venue to let the performers know. A red square means no show tonight. A green triangle means it's on as planned. And so on. You could use this idea but, you know, make the flags a lot bigger and put them high up on poles. Then you could have a series of these running from Bisu to Pilk, with somebody stationed at each pole. As soon as the next flag over changes, they change theirs. It must be a simple message because there are only so many colors and shapes everyone can tell apart. But, it's pretty close to immediate."

It would be faster than the fastest horse could ride, even allowing for the time to change the flags. And, it wouldn't require dozens of fast horses. "You thought of this yourself?"

She gave me a bit of an indignant look.

"Yes, I did."

I guess I deserved the look. "It's brilliant. Give me as much of a code as you performers have, and we'll add what we need. This, this could be what makes all the difference…"

I stopped before I finished, and I saw Firuza smiling. "I thought my moon glass out on the cliffs was going to make all the difference?"

"It, too." I shrugged. "A lot of things are."

We talked for the rest of the morning, about the people best suited to be lookouts and the logistics of making and placing tall poles at intervals. How tall? How far apart? Could we find long-eyes not involved in archery who would contribute their exceptional sight to relaying messages? The further apart we could place the poles the better. Who could start making flags? What messages were most vital?

Firuza was full of sensible ideas, and she seemed to bring out a side of my sister I'd seldom seen but appreciated.

"You can't have whole settlements sitting around watching a flagpole," she said. "So my third idea is if you get a message when the flag changes, and it needs to go out to the whole group, you do it like gossip."

"I beg your pardon?"

"You know. Every person who sees the new flag quickly tells three other people who don't already know. Pretty soon everyone knows."

I had to laugh. It would work.

We parted with my promise to get back to them with details soon. As they left, I marveled at how much my situation had changed. I'd woken up struggling with how to communicate vital facts across the realm. Now, I had more ideas than I could handle, and I needed pole climbers, flag designers, and mirror flashers. I needed people who could sew, make up codes, and see far away.

I didn't have a communication problem anymore, I had a recruiting problem. I needed a lot more people.

~ 24 ~

Lunch at the Palace

After talking with Joli and Grandma, I decided to use a variation of Celestine's gossip approach to recruit my specialized workers. I gathered the women who worked in the marketplaces and explained the message I needed them to spread.

The war effort now needed many more specialized skills. Anyone who had them, or knew anyone who did, should send word back. We had less than two eighths to gather the Ilarians we needed for this final piece of the plan for our survival.

I wasn't surprised when I had many takers after only a few days, but I was surprised by how many of them were from the Western nichnas. I'd assumed they considered this defense scheme of the Velka to be an Eastern Ilari problem. Not so.

Both Zurians and Tolovians offered the trunks of their tallest thin trees for our flagpoles. Each wanted to send their best climbers. Pilk's intellectual community jumped at the chance to design efficient codes and make mirrors. The seamstresses of Lev volunteered to produce flags made using the best dyes.

To my surprise, eight more long-eyes materialized, none with artistic talents or archery abilities, but all with a willingness to sit in a high perch and observe. Several others claiming merely excellent normal eyesight volunteered to spend an eighth on the cliffs of Vinx working as lookouts.

I didn't abandon my initial plan, which had been to set up a relay of messengers on fast horses, and a second relay of Velka guides who could cut through the forest at great speed. Neither would be our best choice, but both made reliable back-ups to these better ideas. I wanted all the back-ups I could get.

I was at the market in Vinx talking to some of my recruits when I saw my mother in the distance. She ran towards me.

"I can't believe you're here." She greeted me with a long hug, unusual for her in such a public place.

"Are you okay, Mom?"

"Yes. I was trying to find the Velka to get word to you. We got another letter from Iolite."

"That's wonderful."

"Well, maybe. Iolite wrote to ask us not to look for her. She said she's sorry for causing concern but needs more time. I guess we give it to her?"

Iolite had sense. I had to believe she had a good reason for her odd behavior.

"I guess we do."

****

After Plono, Nevik and I found it more difficult to get together. He spent a lot of time motivating the troops. I bet all the Royals counted on him to remind the people how much their monarchy cared about their welfare. Nevik probably did his job well. He was born into his life, and the obsession of much of the realm with the birth of his child only made him more effective.

I knew his wife neared the end of her pregnancy and I saw less of him because of that, too. Nevik would be a dad, soon. I tried to imagine the man I loved having this other life with a child he adored, and me being no part of it. Yet, he needed this child to become the ruling prince and I suspected his ambitions in this arena had grown. Once people tried on the idea of having power, they often liked it.

Her situation wasn't so different. She'd started this arranged marriage resigned to a façade and to seeking her happiness elsewhere as best she could. But once the possibility of being the consort of the ruling prince was on the table, I bet her take on the marriage changed.

If I looked at the situation with all the cold logic I could muster, I understood why she wanted me out of the picture. I knew why she'd at least pretend to care for Nevik. Or maybe she'd really care for him. Sure, she'd receive some extra privileges as the wife of the ruling prince, but her real power would lie in her ability to influence Nevik. That power would be stronger if I wasn't around and I had no reason to think she wasn't smart enough to know it.

Should I let Nevik go? Resign myself to having enjoyed a harmless fling and let him and his princess develop the relationship the whole realm wanted them to have? Cold logic favored this. He could probably find some happiness with her, eventually, and I could find other men to mingle with at the forest's edge. No, they'd never matter to me like he did, and none would be as much fun. But after a while, I'd get used to it.

Should I let Nevik go?

No matter how many times I asked the question, I got the same unwanted answer. I didn't care what made sense. I didn't even care what was best for the realm I was working so prucking hard to save. I would give my all to this battle, but I was *not* willing to give him up. That was that.

Surely the woman who saved Ilari was entitled to a life-long love affair with the ruling prince of the richest nichna?

Well, even if she wasn't, I didn't care.

****

I decided to travel to Pilk. Yes, I hoped my proximity would make it possible for Nevik and me to have a night together, but I also had plenty of business to tend to. I wanted to see the operation of the sun mirrors and check over the codes being developed. We could design a shorthand for some words, rather than spelling out the letters of the alphabet like Firuza proposed. I knew those keywords better than anyone, and this was best done in person.

Zirab, my former Mongol captive turned language teacher, had been in Pilk now for anks, teaching Mongolian to the officers of the Svadlu and those assigned to train the farmers and herders. I wanted to go over keywords and phrases with him, making sure my amateur country recruits were armed with the most useful terms they could have. Again, best done in person.

As I traveled around Pilk I made my presence known every way I could, hoping a message from Nevik would come. It didn't. After three days I'd exhausted all reasonable activities except for a visit to the Svadlu. I sent word to Davor that I needed to have a short conference with him before I left.

Word came back via courier almost at once. Today he conferred at the palace with Nevik. Would I please come by and join the two of them for lunch?

Seriously? Again?

I had plenty to discuss with Davor so I decided to go. I cleaned up as best I could, smoothed my hair, and headed over, preparing to once again pretend like Nevik and I had barely met.

A servant showed me into a small parlor where Nevik and Davor chatted as though they hadn't a care. Either their relationship had improved over the last few eighths or they both faked friendliness well. I guessed it was a mix of both.

Nevik's eyes lit up in their usual way when he saw me and I looked at the floor and gave a small curtsey, hoping my expression didn't give me away.

Davor let out a belly laugh.

"You're not much of an actress, dear sister, so please don't bother on my account. Your man here has been dying to get his hands on you since you set foot in Pilk. Haven't you, Nevik?"

I gave Nevik a horrified look.

"Oh don't blame him, blame the pint of hard liquor I forced down his throat. I thought there was something funny about you two last time we met. Nothing like a little drink to get to the truth, eh?" He stood up to go. "There has got to be some emergency somewhere requiring my attention. You kids have fun now." He pointed to a small couch on the other side of the room and laughed.

Under other circumstances, the smirk on his face as he left would have infuriated me, but Nevik had his hand on my thigh and all I could think about was wanting Davor out the door.

I did have the presence of mind to mutter "How could you have told him?"

"Trying to get along," he said as he began to kiss me. "Shouldn't have drunk so much." Another longer kiss. "But Heli, he pretty much figured it out." The third kiss went on for quite a while and it signaled my acceptance of his explanation.

We were on the couch together before I managed to say "Here? In the Palace?"

He answered while untying the leather cords of my bodice. "The best plan I could come up with."

It was the last thing either of us said as we gave the touching and undressing our full attention. I think we were quiet about it all, really, and reasonably quick. If anyone had their suspicions, we never heard.

~ 25 ~

Raising My Goblet

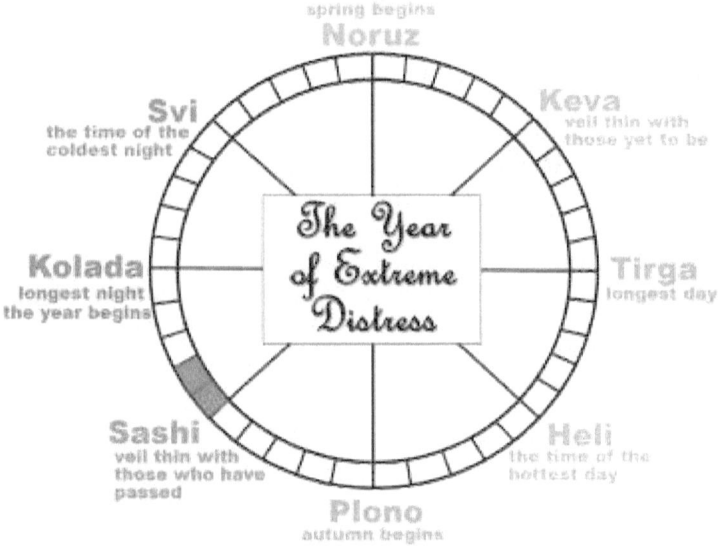

Sashi occurs half-way through autumn, when leaves fall, plants turn brown, and signs of death abound. We say we use the day to honor those who came before us, but in reality Ilarians celebrate Sashi by laughing at their own mortality and sometimes by challenging death to do its worst.

Most of us believe we're invincible, but of course we're not. Age and disease will someday do what battle and misfortune did not, and we all know it. We knew it then. Yet, our need to tell death to piss off was strong that year. I heard later that drunkenness and wild behavior abounded as adults of all ages partied into the night, ignoring the cold harsh wind beginning to blow through the land.

I've often thought if the Mongols had known us better, they'd have attacked us on Sashi and been done with it. But they didn't.

I spent the evening with Coral, so she wouldn't be alone for the night. Early on I played with Votto, now six eighths old and cuter than ever as he crawled around the cottage, pulling his little body up as he seriously considered learning to walk.

After Coral put him to bed, she and I kept drinking the rich red wine we'd had with our meal. When the jug was finished, I opened another. We were swept up in our country's collective denial of the dangers we'd soon face.

She told me more of her concerns that Hana could only be trusted so far, and then only under the best of circumstances. I'd already reached the same conclusion. Hana's plans themselves were sound, though, and both Coral and Celestine had come to terms with the risks they took. Our mother would be deep in the forest with Votto and Coral confessed she felt better knowing he'd be cared for if something happened to her.

"Did you know Hana has befriended Nevik's wife?" she asked once we were well into the second jug of wine.

I knew I tensed anytime anyone mentioned his wife, so I blew out a puff of air and tried to lighten my tone. "Hana is from Pilk so she has reason to go there and, given her family's status, she probably has ties to the royal court."

"Yeah, but I think she pushed those connections, hoping to learn something to hold over someone." Coral gave me a look and took another gulp. "I think she found what she wanted."

There was no sense pretending I didn't know what Coral meant. "So she knows about my affair with Nevik? So what. Plenty in the Velka do. Discretion regarding each other is part of our code. Hana wouldn't dare break that." I poured us both more wine.

"I agree. Not in a way anyone in the Velka would ever find out about, at least."

Okay, now I was curious. "What is it you worry she'll do?"

Coral shrugged. "Poison your arrangement. Fill the wife's head with how she shouldn't be putting up with Nevik's love for you. I think she wants to injure you in a way she can't be blamed for."

"Great." I slammed my hand onto the table in frustration. "You know what? I do not need this steaming pile of scump right now!"

Coral laughed, half liquor, half mirth. "That's an understatement. I shouldn't have brought it up. Tell you what, Ryalgar. Let's see whose dead by winter before we worry about any steaming pile of scump, okay?'"

She raised her goblet for a toast. It was a clear sign I'd had too much to drink when I responded by climbing all the way up onto her table, raising my goblet, and yelling as loud as I could "Pruck, yes! Here's to seeing which ones of us live through all this goat scump."

I think we both passed out on her bed not long after.

I woke up with a headache from consuming too much wine. I should have stuck with ale or mixed it with water. A little embarrassed by my juvenile behavior, I left Coral's place, doing my best not to wake her or the baby.

Things were quiet when I arrived at the lodge. I sought out my grandmother thinking she, at least, was unlikely to be suffering from too exuberant of a Sashi celebration. But she was still in her nightgown and after listening to her whisper and watching the way she held her head, I wasn't so sure. I suggested we meet for lunch and go over the status of our aspirations for moving fog off the lake.

No one else sat in the common dining area and not much food was being offered, so I guessed the cooks suffered from whatever ailed the potential diners.

"Something of a party here last night?" I asked

"Things got a bit out of hand."

"In an ugly way?"

"Oh no. At its best, I'd call it comradery building."

"And at its worst?"

"Headache inducing."

She'd made me laugh, which didn't feel all that good. "Should I have been here?"

"It's better you weren't. A lot of the motivation was fear, a fear many of the women don't want to show around you. It probably did them good to let it out."

"Well then. Tell me about the Water Snakes."

Happy to move on to another topic, she told me of how many mid- and low-level oomrushers she'd recruited.

"I didn't realize we had so many with this talent. More oomrushers won't help the Snakes because moving a single object like an arrow isn't improved with more people. They end up working against each other. But drops of water? Turns out the more people you turn loose on the problem, the better. I think we can dampen a lot of Bisu. It'll make the grass grow better too, and I've got the same group keeping warm air around the grass. You do still need a tempting grazing area, don't you?"

"Absolutely."

"Plus, your dad designed something with pumps he wants to run by you. He dug out the ground near the marsh and he thinks he can manage more sitting water to keep things damp. Once he's done with that, he wants to go around dousing houses and dead trees. He says if we can bring in the fog then, we can keep it all from drying out."

This was good news. "We don't have to make it impossible to start a fire, just difficult enough. The Mongols won't want to spend all day at it and will move on."

"So many unknowns," she said.

"Yes, and so many plans. I know it will come together in ways we can't predict."

Maybe her headache increased her honesty that morning.

"Most of me is scared to death about this day," she said. "But a little of me, a little of me is curious how this turns out."

"That sums up my feelings perfectly."

****

I'm not good at knowing when to give up, and I wanted to try again with the secluded Velka who lived in the northern part of the forest. My ability to find my way around had improved considerably, so several days later, after handling tens of minor things needing my attention, I took off alone to speak with the few women who hadn't threatened to hurt me if I came back.

I also went to inspect the poison arrows and learn more about them. We'd stored them along the border between the open forest and Zur, guarded on one side by leery Velka and on the other by distrustful Zurians. I greeted both and they all appeared to know who I was. As they showed me into the storage huts, I wondered if the whole realm recognized me now.

I studied the designs and inspected the batches for consistency and flaws. Whoever had made these had done an incredible job. The arrows differed from what I'd practiced with, but not by much. Probably not enough to matter to me, but perhaps enough to make them more efficient.

After I finished, I wandered off to find the hut of Yarnya, the strong oomrusher who'd hit Joli in the eye with a rock. I must have walked by it three or four times and probably never would have seen it, but as I retraced my steps one last time, a small rock hit me on the chin.

"There, my aim was better. The chin is good. Never the eyes."

Yarnya stood in between the trees surrounded by rocks of varying sizes floating off the ground.

"Don't worry. I won't hurl them all at you. At least not at once." She gave one of those hoarse, crackly laughs I remembered.

"You still think you're busy this coming Kolada?" I asked

"My social calendar is full."

"Yeah right. If anything opens up, would you like to know where to find me?"

"You are persistent. I'll give you that."

"I don't know yet where I'll be. Joli, the lady you hit, she's figuring out who goes where. But I could send word. That way, you could at least drop by and laugh at how pathetic my abilities are."

That earned me another cackle. "Could be entertaining. Tell you what, girly. Send word. If I get bored, maybe I'll come check out the show."

"Maybe even hurl a rock or two on our behalf?"

"Ah, I'd have to be real bored to do that."

"I'll let you know where to find me."

I wasn't going to hold my breath for this one showing up, but judging from all those rocks she had in the air, it'd be one Heli of a performance if she did.

****

Nevik and I managed to meet at the edge of the forest a few nights later, both realizing this could be the last time we'd see each other until after Kolada. Or the last time we'd see each other at all.

We held hands and stroked each other's hair, not exchanging even a kiss. Maybe it was fatigue, maybe it was fear. Or maybe we wanted to save the best part of the evening for later, after the conversation we both expected.

"I'm a father now," he said.

"I know." Word had spread fast after the birth, even in the forest. I'd asked no questions but learned anyway that Nevik had produced the necessary son.

"Your male child will earn you the throne."

"Yes, if he lives to the age of three, and if he remains in Ilari."

"Is the latter in question?"

"My wife left with him this morning for her homeland. They sent a boat to fetch her across The Wide River, to spend the upcoming holiday with her parents."

"It's nice to visit one's family. Is there some doubt she'll return?"

He shrugged. "I thought there was, as least before she boarded the ferry. She said she'd timed the visit to keep my son safe through Kolada. How could I object? Yet, I feared she'd refuse to return, even if we were victorious. Or worse, she'd agree to come back but place conditions upon it. Conditions I wouldn't like."

"I see." I did. I'd probably be one of those conditions.

"But the crew of the boat greeted us with sad news. Her people received an ultimatum from the Mongols just after Plono. They have until half-past Kolada to comply with the tribute."

"I'm sorry to hear it." I was. "What will they do?"

"I don't know. They're a much larger country, quite different than ours in many ways. They're more accustomed to battles, so I suppose they'll fight. They could prevail."

"I hope they do."

"The captain of the ferry thought perhaps my wife should change her mind and cancel her visit. She didn't, but the important thing is she promised me she'd return if Ilari succeeded at repelling our invasion. She said she'd rather be safe here when the Mongols attack her country."

"That's good then."

"Yes."

We lay on the bed together, but in the end, it's all we did. We held each other, and we fell asleep. Yet, I woke up calm and rested, thinking how a night of holding each other was exactly what I needed.

Our kiss good-bye was short and simple, a kiss between two people who had much to do. It was a kiss that said I'll kiss you again, much longer and harder, when the time is right.

~ 26 ~

Code Name Chimera

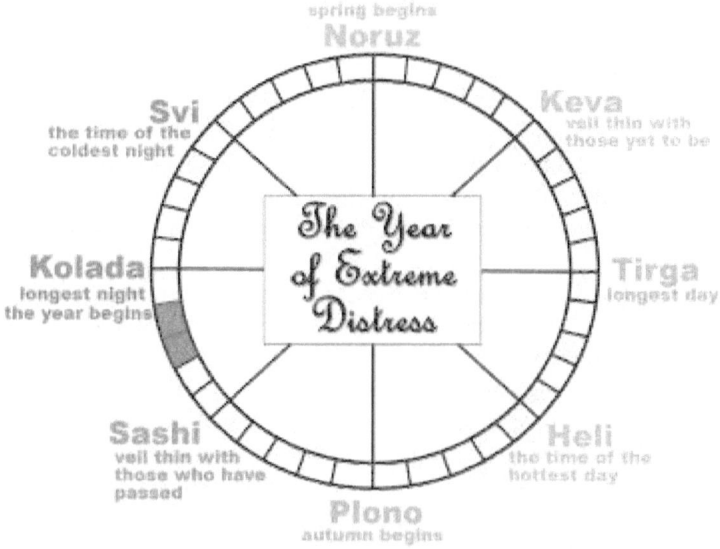

spring begins
Noruz

Svi
the time of the
coldest night

Keva
veil thin with
those yet to be

Kolada
longest night
the year begins

*The Year
of Extreme
Distress*

Tirga
longest day

Sashi
veil thin with
those who have
passed

Heli
the time of the
hottest day

Plono
autumn begins

Several days later I set off for my parents' farm. It wasn't all that far from the forest's edge, and I'd grown used to riding a donkey all the way so I didn't have to trouble someone to meet me with a horse. The donkey took longer but the ride gave me time to think, which I needed. It also gave me time to notice two tall poles in either direction as I came out of the trees.

They'd been placed along the forest's edge where they almost blended in, at least without a flag on them. I rode over to the closer one. It had to be five or six times as tall as me. Someone had inserted metal rods at intervals, so the pole could be climbed, and one rod stuck out enough for a small person to sit on it and reach a pulley system to raise and lower the flags. I had no doubt we'd found plenty of small limber people who could do things fast with their hands. This would work best if we had a breeze. What were the odds of getting attacked on a sunny, windy day?

I stopped at my parents' farm to pick up a horse, so I could ride out to the cliffs with more speed and comfort. My language teacher, Zirab, taught in Pilk now while his wife and child stayed in a cottage along The Little River, where they'd be safer on the day of the attack.

The lookouts we'd gathered lived in Zirab's cottage along with the astronomer Firuza, and they already took shifts watching the horizon through her moon glass. As I rode closer, I studied the pole erected next to the cottage. It looked like the one I'd already examined, but taller. Would its flag be visible to someone sitting high on the poles by the forest? The flat plain of Vinx made it possible, even though it took a good horse half a mornings' brisk walk to get from the forest to the cliffs.

Surely someone had checked. I'd make certain they had.

The lookouts greeted me with enthusiasm, putting out their best pink lunch wine and insisting I share in the soup and bread they prepared for their midday meal. As we ate, we talked through the various signals and how they'd handle situations not covered by any of our predesigned messages. We'd designed one flag, bright yellow on top and light blue below, to tell others to watch for flashing sunlight sending coded words. Without sunshine, putting one of them on a fast horse remained our best back up for messages we had no flag for. They had two such horses at the ready.

"Two anks to go," one of them said.

"We think," I replied.

Firuza nodded. "I confirmed that the Mongol envoy did describe the day they spoke to us as the day before the spring equinox. So I know our celestial calendars match or at least they did then. But of course, they could choose to come early."

"Or late," said another.

"It's why you're so important," I said. "We don't know what strategies they may employ to catch us off guard. Your vigilance will make all the difference."

They smiled, and I realized I'd become comfortable telling everyone how much they mattered.

I spent a bittersweet night in my old room at my parents' farm. Mom not only cooked, but she also made one of my favorite dishes, and then she and I worked mostly in silence as we cleaned the kitchen well. Dad and I would leave with her in the morning, escorting her as she headed into the forest. She had no idea when, or if, she'd return.

The day after tomorrow, all the smaller children in Eastern Ilari would move to safety, either inside the forest, high up in the hills of Lev, or into the mountains of Tolo. Our pregnant women would go, too, caring for everyone's children. The very elderly and those with conditions causing them to need protection would also take shelter and help with the little ones.

I'd picked tomorrow for our journey so I could get Mom and Votto to safety before this mass exodus began. As far as I knew, every able-bodied teenager, full-grown adult, and healthy older person in Eastern Ilari would remain, because each had been given a role to play on the day of the attack.

So, somewhere around twelve thousand people held their breaths, wondering if they could do what needed to be done. Wondering if their neighbors would come through. Wondering if this would work.

To be fair, thousands from Western Ilari had, or would soon, come over into our nichnas to help. Thousands more had already played a role from their homes, sewing flags for us or making mirrors and poles or doing things I might never hear of. This wasn't just Eastern Ilari fighting for her life. It was all of us.

The next morning Dad and I went over all he'd done. He showed me the apparatus for filling basins and carting water, and he explained how he and his crew would saturate everything flammable thing they could in Bisu. It was an ambitious plan and a labor-intensive one. I hoped the attack didn't come early and that Grandma's Water Snakes managed to keep everything damp so his efforts wouldn't be for nothing.

After they finished drenching our most vulnerable nichna, Dad and the core members of his road crew, as he called them, would spend Kolada barely inside the southeast corner of Zur. They'd be relatively safe there but could be mobilized if we needed unexpected adjustments in Gruen. I hoped we didn't.

The three of us left before noon. My mother kept her face turned away from me but Dad didn't. I saw the tears on his cheeks as we rode to Coral's cottage to fetch Votto.

Coral had told Mom she'd be teaching when we arrived. I'd wanted to see Coral, to wish her luck, but she'd asked the teenaged girl watching Votto to tell us not to come over to the school. She didn't want to say goodbye. It would be too difficult. We honored her wishes.

The young daughter of a nearby farmer played with Votto. Mom had agreed to bring this eight-year-old along to safety because the girl played with Votto often and Coral thought he'd be happier with someone he knew.

We put Mom on my donkey and set the little girl in front of her, then Dad handed Votto to Mom to put him into the carrier. She was awkward with it and he cried, the way children do when they sense something is wrong. The little girl tried to hush him and it helped. Once they began to move, he quieted down.

When we got to where the trees began, my dad dismounted and took my mother's hand in his. He kissed it and I saw the love in both of their eyes. Interesting. If it had been there when I was a child, I'd never noticed it. But perhaps it had.

I gave Dad the reins of my horse. Once I mounted the donkey we brought for me, he gave me a salute. It was an odd gesture, one I'd never seen him make before, but it made me feel stronger. I saluted him back and saw his smile.

He turned and rode away without a word. There was nothing left to say. We'd already said it all.

As we made our way through the thick underbrush, I remembered my mother had never made this journey.

"It thins out once we get further inside."

"I sure hope so."

"Uh, Mom? It can seem a little closed in if you're not used to it. Just take deep breaths if it bothers you. It won't take long to get to where you'll be staying, and there's a clearing there."

Mom handled her first trip in better than I had, but she sighed in relief when we got to the clearing. She'd be housed in the same little cottage where Coral had stayed. I helped her settle in and played with Votto to give her a short break. Then, it was back to work.

****

A few days later I traveled to Pilk for a final meeting with Davor and several other Mozdols. We intended to discuss specifics, ensuring they knew everything planned for Eastern Ilari and gaining their assurance that no well-intended soldiers of any rank would intervene.

As I entered, I saw Sulphur seated with them. She laughed when she saw the look of surprise on my face. "I've risen through the ranks."

"I guess."

"Sulphur is our official liaison to the Eastern Ilari operation," Davor said. "Code name Chimera, I understand."

I hadn't thought of it as a code name, but I guessed that worked.

Sulphur began to speak and gave a rather impressive review of the training given to the citizens in the outer nichnas. It was as thorough as I'd hoped. Maybe more so.

"Are they ready for what they need to do?" I asked.

"As ready as they can be, given the circumstances."

"You've done an amazing job."

"As have you," she replied.

Several of the Svadlu squirmed in their seats, uncomfortable with the sisterly show of affection or perhaps with hearing so many compliments in a military setting.

A man I hadn't met before took over the presentation and changed the topic to the flow of the battle. The Svadlu, of course, were mostly at the meeting to ensure I understood when and how the hand-off of operations would take place. They wanted to be sure all members of the Chimera would back off at the right time and let the army handle everything, irrespective of the circumstances.

"Kazimir, our chief commander," he pointed to an older Mozdol as he spoke, "will be prepared to negotiate as you requested if the circumstances warrant it. If they do, he will read the letter you've drafted, outlining terms and the process for the return of the prisoners. We plan to use the translator you found, as well as your sister Iolite."

"Oh, there's no need for Iolite to be involved," Sulphur and I said in unison. The man smiled.

"We'll have her on standby, and will only involve her if needed."

I turned to Kazimir. It bothered me he'd shown no curiosity about anything in my letter.

"You *will* do this negotiation, won't you?" I asked him.

"This highly irregular operation is so unprecedented. The Svadlu have no way of predicting what manner of foe we will face after you get done with them," he answered. "But yes, I agree to try if it seems reasonable. However, the uncertainty of your success makes it important we can trust all civilians to get out of the way and let us do our jobs."

"They will. You have my word."

"We accept your word," Davor said. "And we give you ours. We'll do our best to get those under our command to behave in the ways we've agreed. Now, is there anyone in this room who thinks we will have complete control over *anything* once this invasion starts?"

I held my tongue and so did everyone else.

"Good. At least we have a bunch of realists here. This is going to be chaos from beginning to end. Let's all hope when the confusion settles, we still have Ilari."

He stood, reached across the table, and offered me his hand. There was no smirk, no trace of condescension.

"Madam. I wish you every success."

I stood, wishing I'd been mentally prepared for this. Perhaps then, I'd have found a pithier reply. As it was, I only managed to say "Sir, I wish you the same."

~ 27 ~

Take Arrow, Nock Arrow, Aim

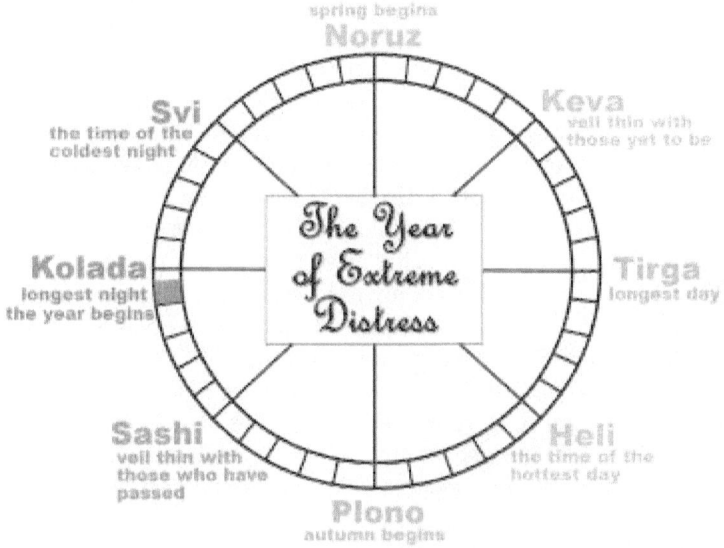

The Year of Extreme Distress

- spring begins — Noruz
- Keva — veil thin with those yet to be
- Svi — the time of the coldest night
- Tirga — longest day
- Kolada — longest night the year begins
- Heli — the time of the hottest day
- Sashi — veil thin with those who have passed
- Plono — autumn begins

As of one ank before Kolada, our lookouts hadn't seen anything suspicious enough to cause them to raise the something-of-concern-is-happening flag. The various people involved in the Snake met that day for individuals to receive their specific assignments. I knew Hana and the Lions held a similar meeting days ago. Gypsum and Idris would hold something similar for the Goats in a few more days. Each part of my plan had its own sense of timing, and I forced myself to be comfortable with that.

201

Joli had avoided me for many days, even declining to come with me to the final meeting with the Svadlu. I guessed she didn't want me involved in what we both agreed was her territory. She'd taken on all the logistical complications of placing our long-eyed archers and oomrushers, and I appreciated that she didn't want a second chef messing with her soup.

So I asked her no questions and took no offense. Once she began to hand out positions, though, I realized I'd misjudged the problem.

She spoke to us standing in front of a large map of Bisu, pointing to the flat ground and lush grass designed to attract the Mongols. Mid- and low-level oomrushers would be hidden on barges out in the marsh as they focused on maintaining the thick fog. We hoped the low visibility, along with the confusion caused by the missing fence and gate, would leave them inclined to let their horses enjoy the lush grass until the fog lifted. If our oomrushers were successful, it wouldn't lift until after dark.

Joli did a clever job of placing four teams to optimize the horses they could hit from a distance too far away to be suspected. She'd arranged smart hiding places for these teams once their work was done and allowed for ways they could move further to safety. It was brilliant, but it only used four teams and we had five.

Then she told us who was where and everyone realized Grandma, I, and Nikolo had no assignment.

"You need us *all*," my grandmother said. I could hear the fury in her voice. "We've trained for this, we can do it, and I will not be sidelined because of my age or my position. Nor will I allow you to waste the talents of Ryalgar and Nikolo because of me."

I had a different take on the problem. "If you're sidelining my team because of *me*, you should know I've set this up so I am not needed once the invasion starts. After the Mongols arrive, I'm as expendable as anyone. I'm a soldier ready to do my job."

"I agree," Joli said. "Completely. You have an assignment. I just haven't gotten to it yet."

She pulled up a second map, and I recognized the hills of Eds, with the small Eds Mountain complex and Mt. Eds in the middle.

"You told me to plan for everything. I did. We have a small but significant risk of more Mongols entering through northern

Eds. The only defense we will have against this is my second-best team, stationed on Mt. Eds watching. They will take down as many Mongols as possible should this occur."

"That's ridiculous. You know they probably won't come in that way. We'll be sitting there idle, while you handle everything without us. Come on, Joli. You need us in Bisu."

"I need you where I put you. Am I charge of this or not?"

Bat scump. Yes, she was, and I couldn't overrule her now, not in front of everyone. Why didn't she discuss this with me ahead of time? Dumb question. Because I'd have insisted she not do this. I knew Joli. She had Ilari's best interests at heart, nothing more, even if I thought she was wrong. Horribly wrong. Yet, she must have thought we had to do this.

"Yes. You're in charge of this."

"Very well. Then you three should prepare to go to Eds."

Nikolo blew out a long breath of air. He'd said nothing up until now.

"Not what I signed up for," he muttered. If Joli heard him, she ignored it.

My grandmother gave an exaggerated shrug. "Let's go pack."

I was so frustrated I couldn't even look at Joli as we left.

I spoke with Joli the next day before we finished our preparations to go. I begged her to reconsider and to let my team do our part.

"I gave this great thought," she said. "I can't let our friendship keep me from doing what I believe is best." She looked me in the eye now, and I could tell she wasn't going to change her mind.

I had two bad choices. I could override her decision, but I'd only lessen her considerable commitment and shake the morale of everyone involved. Two of the top Velka fighting. People being told they were in charge of things and then they weren't. Ryalgar having to have her way. Perhaps we'd have worked through such a shakeup if it'd been a few anks ago, but not now. Not mere days before the invasion.

So I opted for my other bad choice, and Grandma didn't argue with me. She'd probably reached the same conclusion. We sent to word to Nikolo and then plodded through our preparations with no enthusiasm.

Three days later, Velka guides helped Aliz and I fetch our team's arrows, and then helped us get our things to the extreme northern corner of the open forest where Nikolo met us with horses. We loaded the bulk of our supplies onto a two-horse wagon Grandma would drive. We needed camping gear, food, and water for over an ank. We couldn't afford to run out of supplies before the attack came.

We decided to camp on the near side of the Eds Mountains the first night, high enough above the surrounding hills for Nikolo to have a clear view of the flagpoles running along the northern edge of the forest. The wagon made the off-road journey difficult, but before nightfall we found an accessible spot partway up. The guide helped us set up our camp and stayed for the night.

The hard, cold ground made it difficult to fall asleep. Kolada was four days away. Firuza thought the Mongols knew what day the solstice was, but what if their astronomers weren't as good as ours and had gotten off by a few days since Noruz? The last thing we needed was a calendar mix up with this many people moving into place.

Every day we moved our campsite higher and further north. The better to stay hidden, and the better for Nikolo to see. Joli had told me all the evacuees in Eds went up into Tolo and most of the Edsers who could fight were moved to nichnas likely to see action. However, over a hundred had been left for us, clustered in small groups out of sight amongst peaks associated with Mt. Eds. They would keep watch and be there if we needed them.

****

Two days before Kolada, a red square flag went up. Nikolo could see it on the flagpole between K'ba and Scrud, and he watched as a second one went up closer to us, along the border between K'ba and Eds. We all knew the meaning. *They are coming. All of them.*

By afternoon Nikolo could make them out on the horizon.

"How many are there? Can you guess?"

He laughed. "Not really. I mean, it would take hundreds of riders to stir up that much dust. So … hundreds?"

He kept his eye on the horizon. After a while, I thought I could make out a faint blob of dust. He studied whatever he could see in the distance and gave a low whistle.

"A thousand isn't a bad guess. I'd say it's pretty close."

I don't know why, but being right about their numbers made me feel better.

Sunset comes early around Kolada and in dry windy Eds, the temperature drops fast. We huddled into our tents before dusk disappeared, bringing dried food with us to stave off hunger. Tonight there would be no fire, no cooking, and no candles. We didn't want to give the Mongols any clues to our whereabouts.

The day before Kolada we rose at dawn, moving in silence as we cared for our personal needs. Nikolo reported the pole at the edge of the forest still flew the red flag but we knew it would be brought down soon. We needed to look like the sleepy little country they expected.

As the sun climbed higher, the sky overhead flaunted its best bright blue, but fog began to fill the eastern horizon with growing mist of the Velka's making. I could imagine how hard the oomrushers worked to move it, and how much harder they'd work to hold it there until nightfall.

Nikolo stared into the fog. "Can't see a thing anymore."

If all was going as planned, a thousand riders picked their way through the open pasture, keeping their horses fresh for the attack by not rushing. By late morning they'd expect to find our border and possibly our tribute. But they'd find nothing. The passage leading in would be narrower due to hills they didn't remember and filled with gullies they didn't recall. More marsh than expected would slow them down as an unfortunate amount of fog obscured their visibility.

We hoped they'd have to make their way with such care that they wouldn't hit the lush grassland we'd provided until afternoon. There, the most logical decision would be to hunker down for the night and figure out their whereabouts the next day.

They'd arrived the day before Kolada. I wondered if the timing occurred by plan or by accident. Either way, we hoped their attack would be delayed until tomorrow, after they woke to discover two hundred of their horses apparently murdered in the night by unseen archers and unknown oomrushers.

Those archers wouldn't include Nikolo. Those oomrushers wouldn't include me. We'd be sitting up here on Mt. Eds picking dirt out of our fingernails.

We paced around for most of the day, snacking on cold food and trying to keep warm. Mid-afternoon, I kicked a rock in frustration and got sympathetic looks from both of my companions. Nikolo watched the rock roll down the mountain, then he muttered. "Scump."

He pointed off to the left. I couldn't see anything at first, then I could barely make out a line of something picking its way along the steep ridge leading into Ilari from the north. They were coming towards us.

"Archers on horses," he said. "They can't hit us from down there. Not yet."

"Can we hit them?" Grandma asked.

"I think so. Even more so because we're shooting down at them."

"Do you want to aim at the archers or the horses?" Grandma asked me.

"I say we hit anything we can," Nikolo answered.

"No." I knew that was a bad idea. "Horseless riders will use the animals of the men we've killed. We're half as effective that way. We need to go for one or the other."

"Then I say the riders," Nikolo said. "They're the ones who are going to start shooting at us."

He had a point, but I had a plan. "Our poison may only tranquilize the horses but will kill all the men. Hostages are valuable; let's stick to the strategy. The Edsers will grab prisoners as we kill the horses. Prisoners can't shoot us."

"Are you *sure* those Edsers will get out there and do that?"

I wasn't sure, but second-guessing our strategy now seemed like a worse idea.

"Your call," Grandma said. She grabbed a sheaf of arrows, ready to hand them to Nikolo. "Start shooting horses."

All our practice made a difference. We didn't need to talk, we didn't need to do anything but act as fast as we could. Nikolo picked up his bow and nocked his first arrow.

We all knew I was the strongest oomrusher. Although I would work to maintain the arrows speed, my most important task was to keep each one along the course Nikolo and his long eye had set.

"Now," Nikolo said and he fired.

I felt the crosswind on the arrow. It was stronger than we'd ever had while practicing and the effort it took to keep the arrow true to its path surprised me. The arrow hit a bush well in front of the lead horse.

The rider stopped, holding up his hand to halt those behind him. He looked around and saw nothing where he expected to see an enemy. He got off his horse and walked over to the bush, then he picked out the arrow and studied it. He shrugged, stuck it into a sheaf on his back, and got back on his horse.

"Can you *do* this, Ryalgar?" Nikolo asked

"Yes. Another one, please."

Grandma handed. Nikolo nocked. "Now."

This one flew more true. Grandma worked harder on the speed and I had a better feel for the wind. Odd as it seemed, I also had a better feel for the arrow. It almost listened to me, as if it sought instruction. I responded and it hit the lead horse where its throat met its chest. The horse stopped, shuddered, and sunk to the ground. I swallowed, hoping it would recover.

"Now." The next arrow barely missed the rider and hit the second horse in the flank. The horse stood confused before it fell to the ground.

I'd been counting horses. More than ten. Less than a thousand. Call it a hundred. The best Nikolo could do would be to shoot one horse in the time it took me to count to thirty. So count to three hundred for thirty horses. Count to three thousand to get them all. If we didn't miss.

By the time I counted to three thousand, they'd be shooting at us.

"Ryalgar?" Grandma looked concerned. "Now what?"

"We keep shooting until they get in range of us. We won't have time to get them all. Then we run like Heli for cover and hope the Edsers come out and gather up those on foot."

"What about those on horseback?!"

"We hope they ride on to whatever rendezvous they have. If they come for us, we shoot like crazy and do what we can."

Neither one of them said a word.

Take arrow, nock arrow, aim.

"Now." Nikolo fired.

Take arrow, nock arrow, aim.

"Now." Nikolo fired.

After twenty times, sixteen horses lay on the ground, dead as far as anyone could tell. A second arrow had missed. One had failed to release poison, barely wounding the horse. Another had hit a man on foot who stepped in front of it. One Mongol down. So much for my plan of killing none.

By now I could see them better. That would help.

Take arrow, nock arrow, aim.

"Now." Nikolo fired.

After forty shots, thirty-five horses were down. Our aim had improved but the line of horses moved faster as they closed the distance between us, leaving the horseless fighters behind without hesitation. There was no sign of anyone from Eds, and the fighters on foot were advancing as well, coming towards us with bows drawn. Of course, they thought we were nearer than we were, but the height the arrows flew from had them looking up suspiciously in our direction.

"Twenty more," Nikolo said.

Take arrow, nock arrow, aim.

"Now."

After sixty shots, fifty-five horses appeared dead, and the Mongols had spotted us up above them. It was time to take cover.

"Five more," Nikolo said. I noticed he was having trouble lifting his arms. Even with our help, he was going to be ineffective soon.

"Five," I agreed.

Take arrow, nock arrow, aim.

"Now."

As the last of the five went down, they began firing up at us. One of their first arrows hit Grandma in the arm. She cried out in surprise, and then yanked the arrow out without hesitating. I'm not sure I could have done that.

Nikolo and I grabbed her from either side, holding her between us. We lifted her off the ground, and we ran. Nikolo carried his bow in his tired arm, and I clutched the rest of the arrows Grandma had dropped. We rounded a hill and hurried down the backside to safety.

I gasped when a man stood up behind us.

"Shh. Thought you'd never get here. Why the Heli did you take those last shots?"

Huh?

"Joli put me out here. There are ten of us who are supposed to find you and get you to shelter if there's an attack from this direction. Come on." He turned to Grandma. "Can you walk by yourself?"

"It's my arm, not my leg." She stomped after him at a brisk pace.

He led us down a dried creek bed towards a small cave entrance half-hidden behind a lot of brush.

We were going in there? Into a small cave?

He saw me hesitate. "It's short," he said. "It'll be pitch dark inside but it's okay. My name is Salmo, you just follow my voice. Where we come out, they won't know where to look.

Nikolo tried to stay behind to be last, but I motioned him to keep up with Grandma. He was better equipped to help her, and I needed the extra breathing room I'd get from lagging behind.

Once it got completely dark, I had to duck down to walk, and I placed my hand along the wall of the cave to steady myself. I don't know how long we hiked but it seemed to go on forever; no one would call this journey short.

Then my foot hit a rock and I pitched forward into the darkness. Pruck. My arms reached out as I fell and a pain seared through my left hand. I brought it to my face. I could smell and feel the blood.

"You okay back there?"

"Just tripped. A little injury. Getting up now. How much further?" I could feel the panic closing in.

"Not much. Round three more corners and you'll see the light."

Three corners. I could do that.

Once we got out, Salmo bandaged up Grandma's arm with part of his jacket and then he bandaged up my hand with a kerchief.

"Look." He pointed to the trees not far away. "It's less than two thousand paces to the forest. That's Zur. They're expecting you and you'll get medical treatment there. Get going."

"Aren't you coming with us?"

"I've got work to do rounding up those Mongols on foot."

"Why didn't you people start on that sooner?" Nikolo asked.

"Because they also had forty guys on horseback looking for somebody to kill. We're hoping those riders have gone on by now. We weren't trained to deal with archers on foot, either, you know, but we'll figure out something."

~ 28 ~

Emerging From the Forest

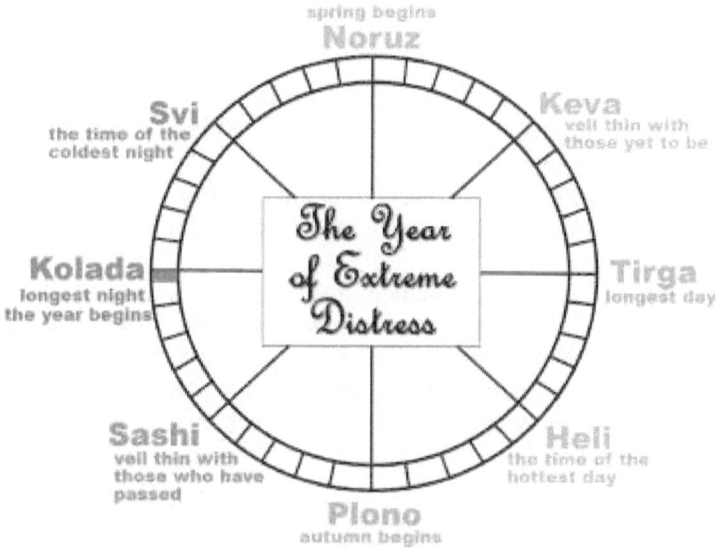

Zurians met us just inside the trees. I suppose they'd watched the three of us half run and half hobble our way across the open ground. Two of the larger people grabbed Grandma on either side, and they mostly carried her through the forest. My hand throbbed, but I had no problem following them.

We stopped at a good-sized cottage in a clearing, and two Velka I recognized as healers met us at the door. I never thought I'd see the day when Velka and Zurians shared a place, yet here they were. A young Zurian woman aided them as they got

Grandma settled onto a couch and examined her arm. After a bit, one turned to tend to my needs.

"Nasty gash," she said. "Let's get something on it."

Soon I had a warm poultice of herbs bandaged tight in my hand, and the pain subsided.

"You two rest," one said. "We've got wounded Edsers to tend to. Looks like some of those Mongol captures didn't go quite as planned."

They'd barely left the room when Grandma reached her good arm out towards me.

"Come closer, Ryalgar. I need to have a serious conversation with you. Now."

Really?

"Your wound doesn't look that serious, Grandma. You should be fine."

She laughed. "Yes, I probably will be. But, alas, I'm mortal, and this is a good reminder. I have something I need to ask you."

"Okay."

"Ryalgar. Will you consent to be my successor?"

"Do what? Wait. It's something one consents to? Could I get more information first?"

"Of course." She laughed again, and I wondered if the healers gave her something that made her giddy. "The Conclave handles governance of the Velka, as you know. But ultimate leadership is vested in a single woman, one who is obligated to pass her role on to a qualified other of her choice. An adopted daughter if you will.

"The Conclave must approve of her, of course, though custom encourages them to accept the leader's candidate. I was a second choice, by the way. Almost too old by the time she picked me, but her chosen one failed and I was a reasonable alternative. Given my age, I've been under a lot of pressure to get on with my own choosing but I've stalled ever since Hana became the most obvious candidate. I don't know, I never warmed to her. It is a personal decision."

"I'm honored." It seemed the right thing to say. "What do you mean the candidate before you failed?"

"It's a long process," she said. "And not an easy one. There are, well, tests. Tasks. Ceremonies. A lot of it is silly rituals, to be honest, but not everyone gets through it. You may not, either, though I think you will. If the Mongols are repelled, you'll have tremendous support in your favor."

"Speaking of Mongols, shouldn't this maybe wait until we're out of danger?"

"It's what I thought, but word of this wound will get back, causing concern. Many will rest easier if it's known I have a candidate. You see, the process of your initiation can happen with or without me."

"Should I be scared of this process?"

"I'd say yes, normally, but given everything you've been through, maybe not."

It was my turn to laugh. "I'd like to try. Now, sleep and heal. I prefer to go through whatever this is with you."

We must have been given something to help us sleep, for I didn't wake until the first light of dawn. I didn't know where I was, then I thought I camped in Eds. Then I remembered. Today was Kolada, the day I'd worked toward for over a year. On this day, what I set in motion would save everything I loved. Or not.

And I was in a forest in northern Zur, as far from the action as I could be.

I looked down at the bloody bandage around my hand. How had I managed to do so much damage with a simple fall? Yet, it was only my left hand. I could still ride and I could still use my head.

Grandma slept. Perhaps last night I'd given her some comfort by agreeing to whatever strange rituals she asked me to undergo. I hoped so. In the light of day, I had a few more questions, but that was a problem for later.

I needed to explore my options. It was obviously too late to help the archers and oomrushers shooting at horses in Bisu's dawn. Could I find a donkey and make my way to the south side of Zur and into Pilk? If so, perhaps I could be there as the last of the Mongols confronted the Svadlu. Perhaps I could help negotiate with the Mongols. When we planned this, it hadn't seemed possible for me to be present, but the idea of exchanging prisoners for our ongoing freedom *had* been my idea. Who better to articulate it?

I left my room, entering what must have been a main area. It held twelve cots and twelve sleeping men. How odd. Their accouterments spoke of wealth. Who were they?

I looked at each, hoping to see a face not buried in his blankets. One turned towards me.

"Are you a beautiful spirit sent to escort me to the netherworld?" he whispered.

"Don't be ridiculous, Nevik. I'm here because I hurt my hand. What in the Heli's name are you doing in Zur?"

He held a finger to his lips and motioned to the door. We crept out, making as little sound as possible. On the porch, he wrapped his arms around me and gave me a long, long kiss.

"I've been looking forward to that," I said.

"There are many more where it came from. I've had time to think since I saw you last and I swore I'd share those thoughts with you the next time we met."

I wasn't sure this was the best time or place to listen to Nevik's thoughts, but ...

"Sure. Tell me what you're thinking."

"Okay. I once made an agreement with a woman with whom I share an unfortunate situation. I've no reason to treat her poorly; in fact, I want to see her happy. But she has no claim over me beyond our original understanding. I promised her then I'd never encroach further into her life. Were circumstances different, she'd be furious with me for changing my mind. Well, she has no more right to change our agreement than I do. Ryalgar, I chose you. I choose you. I always will. She needs to accept that and find love elsewhere."

"Nice words, Nevik. Can you stick to them, no matter what comes?"

"I can. I will."

"Even if the woman you have chosen ends up as supreme leader of the Velka?"

"I don't think they have a supreme leader, but if you mean your grandmother's role, I'm not surprised."

"You know about my grandmother's role"

"Of course. The ruling princes of Ilari have always negotiated with the Velka, and generally with one woman. For years now, it's been this older woman with long white braids. My father says she's a tough lady, but reasonable. I didn't know she was your grandmother until recently. It'd be interesting to find ourselves across the negotiating table someday, wouldn't it?"

He kissed me again to imply negotiating with him could be fun.

"We'd have to start by learning to behave better in public," I said. I looked in through the window at all the sleeping men. "Who are these people?"

"Every one of the recently crowned or presumed soon-to-be crowned princes from Ilari's twelve nichnas," he said, gesturing to the sleeping men inside. "Our parents decided we all should be hidden here, for the safety and continuity of the realm. How foolish. Don't they realize we, of all people, should be out there today, leading the efforts?"

I understood his frustration, but his parents had a point as well.

"Instead of doing nothing, how about helping me find something to ride so I can get out of here and see what's happening?" I said.

"Only if I get to come with you."

"You're not going anywhere," another male voice said.

We both jerked around to see who'd found us.

"Not without me, that is." Nikolo grinned at us. "You love birds need my help. I got up first and I checked things out while you two played kissy face on the porch. These princes came in with *horses*."

Nevik nodded. "They brought us in along the river. Can't put a crown prince on a donkey, you know."

"Well, it's our good fortune; we need something with speed. Ryalgar, go get our arrows. Let's grab some horses and ride until we catch up with the action. Then, let's shoot at whatever makes sense."

"I like it. Let's do what we trained for."

The horses were tied up at the edge of the clearing. We made it that far when a voice in the trees said "Where do you think you're going?"

Not again.

Salmo got off his horse and came towards us. "I bring you all the way to safety and now you're leaving?"

I guessed he wanted to funny but the blood seeping out of a wound in his thigh obscured the comedy. He waved away my look of concern.

"I took an arrow; it's nothing. We got all those Mongols on foot taken care of, so I came in for medical care."

"I hope it's nothing," I said. "Did the Mongols on horseback move on?"

"The ones that were left did. Your friend has a Heli of a throwing arm. I've never seen anyone like her."

"What friend?"

Salmo gave me a puzzled look. "You know. The old lady who came out of the forest. After I sent you three here and went back to help take prisoners, she rode out of the trees on a donkey carrying a big sack of rocks. I figured you'd sent her, but what could she do?"

He had to be talking about Yarnya.

"She was nowhere near those remaining horsemen but she threw a rock at them anyway. It won't even get close, I thought. Then, bam. That first big rock not only travels the full distance but it hits one guy's horse in the head. Hard. It knocks the horse out! Then she does it again. And again. That old woman must have hit ten horses before they got mad enough to come after her. And she *still* kept throwing rocks. Probably hit another ten before they started shooting their arrows. Then she disappeared into the trees with this weird, cracking laugh. I never heard the likes of it."

"Did she get away?" I felt responsible for Yarnya's safety.

"Oh yeah. Those Mongols poked into the bushes to find her, but you could tell they didn't want to go into that forest. We hid and watched them take off, figuring they'd ride a little further then stop for the night."

I looked at Nevik and Nikolo. "Then they're still out there. These guys were our responsibility. Let's go get the rest of them."

"Are you sure we should bring him along?" Nikolo pointed to Nevik. "Important people put him here just so he wouldn't get hurt."

"I know, but he could be helpful."

"You want me to tell people where you've gone? Or not?" Salmo asked.

"If anyone asks, send them to my grandmother." I'd left her a quick note when I got the sheaf of arrows, asking her to keep anyone from coming after us. I knew she'd find a way.

We wasted no time getting out of sight, taking the horses along the bank of The Little River to the forest's edge. Once we got to the open part of Eds we rode faster, making our way towards K'ba. We saw them as we rounded the area where the Reczavy usually lived.

Nevik held up his hand for us to stop. There were about twenty riders. It appeared they'd spent the night in the abandoned Reczavy camp and now gathered their things to ride on.

"What's their game plan?" Nevik whispered.

Nikolo had no line of sight to anything helpful and he shrugged.

"Skunk scump!" I tapped the side of my head. "Why didn't I realize it sooner."

"Realize what?"

"It's a strategy. I read about it when I studied all those past wars. An army pretends to retreat and their adversaries, who think they've won, can't resist chasing them away. Except ...."

Nevik understood.

"Except once the other side has chased them far enough to be vulnerable, the army turns around and fights. It works because they get a small force to ride in from behind so they can surround their foe."

"Exactly," I said. "That's why these hundred horsemen came in through Eds. The Mongols gave us enough credit to have a backup plan. If we put up more of a fight than expected, this second smaller group makes that strategy work."

"They'll try to use the technique if we're even half as effective as we hope," Nikolo said. "Good thing there's only twenty of them left."

"Yeah, but twenty mounted archers can kill plenty of Svadlu, especially when they're unexpected and coming from behind," Nevik said.

"Wait. We can be unexpected and coming from behind, too," I said. "Come on. Let's follow them and take out as many as we can. We'll stay far enough away they can't shoot back and, if they turn around and ride towards us, we'll hide in the forest."

"You still want to shoot at their horses?" Nikolo asked.

"Yes. We stick with the plan."

He sighed loud enough for me to hear but didn't argue.

We took off, riding hard to get in range.

Once we closed the gap with them, my entire world reduced to my own galloping horse, a moving arrow, and another horse's hide.

And then another.

And another.

Once we begin hitting their horses, they didn't turn towards us. Instead, they galloped away harder, trying to get as many of them as possible to where they were needed. Their horses ran faster than ours so it was a good strategy, but my power as an oomrusher kept growing. I, and the little wooden arrows that listened to me, increased our range further as their lead grew. Because of that, we kept picking away at them as we all rode with a dangerous fury.

We didn't get them all and I have no idea what happened to the two who sped off out of our range. However, once we and our exhausted horses stopped, the eighteen horseless archers surrounded us on three sides. All of them moved towards us on foot with their arrows aimed.

The trees were at our backs.

"Into the forest," I said. There was no other direction to go, but I recognized this piece of land where the scraggly trees of Scrud came up against the northeastern-most Velka settlements. I knew it was the most difficult of the seven entrances, but we could get in. "I know this spot."

I gave my borrowed horse a gentle slap on the side, urging him to go. The others did the same. We didn't want to provide horses for these fighters. Then, we ran. Their arrows hit the shrubs around us as we dove into the bushes.

"You people go through this mess all the time?" Nikolo said as we pushed our way further into the thorny vines and thick growth.

"This is unduly difficult," Nevik agreed. "Do you have some sort of a plan?"

"I do. The entrance is off to our right. Not far. Once we get there, we'll make our way on foot through the forest. It won't be as slow as you think; it gets much clearer and I know the paths well."

"Shouldn't we be out there helping somehow?"

"We should and we will," I said. "The long-eyes and archers have already done what they could and the luskies and singers are out there now getting more riders thrown. We can't help any of them. If we cut through the forest, we'll come out in Gruen about the time the Reczavy start their thing, or maybe as they finish it. Either way, I promise you we'll be where the action is."

"Okay. It's better than sitting back at the cabin in Zur," Nevik said.

"Yes. Let's get there and find out how this battle is going."

We set off on foot, moving as fast as we could manage, pausing to rest only when we had to. Nikolo's bow slowed us down, but he wouldn't leave it behind. Luckily our path became wider as we wound our way along the donkey trails that kept us inside the tangled overgrowth on our left.

Morning had turned to afternoon by the time we neared the southern edge of the forest. I'd brought us to the mid-Gruen entrance. We made our way into the thick shrubbery and vines we needed to navigate to exit.

As we cleared the last of them and emerged from the forest, each of us held on to the desperate hope that we entered a world in which Ilari was winning.

Thank you for reading my story of
how I saved my entire world from oblivion
Ryalgar Renata Glenti

What's Next?

The War Stories of the Seven Troublesome Sisters consists of seven short companion novels. Each tells the personal story and perspective of one of seven radically different sisters in the 1200s as they prepare for an invasion of their realm.

Which sister saves Ilari? That will depend on whose story you are reading. For while each of these historical fantasy/alternate history books can be enjoyed as stand-alone novels, together they tell the full story of how Ilari survived. Each sister offers new information about why this didn't go as anyone expected.

Book 2, *She's the One Who Cares Too Much* became available in February 2021. Book 3, *She's the One Who Gets in Fights,* followed in May 2021. Book 4, *She's the One Who Can't Keep Quiet,* was released in August 2021.

Want to make sure you don't miss a release? Go to my landing page at *https://mailchi.mp/11db23804c68/tell-me-about-new-books* to be notified when each book is ready for purchase. I promise you'll only get notifications about the release of these books.

If you enjoyed this story, please leave a review somewhere. If you enjoyed it a lot, please leave a review in several places.

She's the One Who Cares Too Much

Coral, the second of the sisters, has been hiding her affair with the perfect man until her older sister can get her life together. But the perfect man is getting impatient, and now she's gotten pregnant. Coral decides it's time to consider her own happiness.

But what does she want? The perfect husband turns out to be less than ideal. She adores the small children she teaches but the idea of being a mother fills her with joy. Meanwhile, her homeland is gripped by fear of a Mongol invasion, and she can't stop crying about everything now that she's with child.

Then a friend suggests the ever-caring Coral possesses a power well beyond what she or anyone else imagines. Does she? And why is the idea so appealing?

When Coral's big sister loses faith in the army and decides to craft a way to use magic to save Ilari from the Mongols, she decides Coral's formidable talent is what the realm needs. Can Coral raise a baby, placate an absent military husband who thinks he's stopping the invasion, and help her sister save her homeland?

It makes no sense, but deep in her heart, she feels she can.

She's the One Who Gets in Fights

Sulphur, the third of seven sisters, is glad the older two have been slow to wed. It's given her the freedom to train as a fighter, in hopes of fulfilling her lifelong dream of joining Ilari's army. Then, within a matter of days, both sisters announce plans and now Sulphur is expected to find a man to marry.

Is it Sulphur's good fortune her homeland is gripped by fear of a pending Mongol invasion? And the army is going door to door encouraging recruits? Sulphur thinks it is. But once she's forced to kill in a small skirmish, she's ready to rethink her career decision.

Too bad it's too late. The invasion is coming, and Ilari needs every good soldier it has.

Once Sulphur learns Ilari's army has made the strategic decision to not defend certain parts of the realm, including the one where her family lives, she must re-evaluate her loyalty. Is it with the military she's always admired? Or is it with her sisters, who are hatching a plan to defend their homeland with magic?

Everywhere she turns, someone is counting on her to fight for what's right. But what is?

What About the Other Sisters?

Look for more information on the adventures of the remaining four sisters in the next book.

About the Author

Sherrie Cronin is the author of a collection of six speculative fiction novels known as 46. Ascending and is now publishing a historical fantasy series called The War Stories of the Seven Troublesome Sisters. A quick look at the synopses of her books makes it obvious she is fascinated by people achieving the astonishing by developing abilities they barely knew they had.

She's made a lot of stops along the way to writing these novels. She's lived in seven cities, visited forty-six countries, and worked as a waitress, technical writer, and geophysicist. Now she answers a hot-line. Along the way, she's lost several cats but acquired a husband who still loves her and three kids who've grown up fine, both despite how odd she is.

All her life she has wanted to either tell these kinds of stories or be Chief Science Officer on the Starship Enterprise. She now lives and writes in the mountains of Western North Carolina, where she admits to occasionally checking her phone for a message from Captain Picard, just in case.

Find her at:
Facebook: facebook.com/46Ascending
Goodreads: goodreads.com/author/show/5805814.Sherrie_Cronin
Amazon: amazon.com/Sherrie-Cronin/e/B007FRMO9Q
Twitter: twitter.com/cinnabar01
Author Blog: sherriecronin.xyz/
Book Series Blog: troublesome7sisters.xyz/

Information About Ilari

Words Used by Ilarians

Ank: A nine-day period. Business is conducted during the first six days while the last three are intended for family life and relaxation.
Heli: The hottest time of the year, but sometimes also used as a cussword.
Luski: A feared, possibly imaginary creature who can control others with her voice.
Mozdol: A member of the Svadlu who has been made into an honorary prince due to brave actions defending the realm.
Nichna: One of the twelve principalities of Ilari. Each has its own royal family and is ruled by a prince. All twelve coordinate as regards the Svadlu and other matters pertaining to the common good. There is no king, therefore Ilari is not a kingdom.
Oomrush: telekinesis.
Pruck: An extremely rude word sometimes referring to copulation and other times merely expressing disgust or dismay.
Pruska: An extremely rude word referring to a female possessing any number of undesirable qualities.
Rantallion: A man who is being disagreeable, dishonest, or disgusting.
Reczavy: a group of free-spirited people living in the open forest who choose to continue and extend the sexual freedom permitted to tidzys.
Scump: a rude word referring to excrement.
Svadlu: The Ilarian army and police force. A member of the Svadlu is called a Svadlu.
Tidzy: A young adult who is searching for a mate and is allowed a great deal of sexual freedom around holidays.
Velka: A group of women who live in the open forest, possibly performing magic. A member of the Velka is called a Velka.

The Ilarian Calendar

A year in Ilari is divided into eight parts based on the seasons. Each eighth lasts for 45 days and is named for the holiday at its start.

Each eighth is subdivided into five anks. An ank is nine days long. Businesses and schools are open during the first six days of an ank while the last three, called the ank-break, are intended for family life and relaxation.

Every year astronomers consult the stars to decide which of the holidays will be inside their eighth and which will be treated as extra days. Most years, five or six holidays are ruled to be extra days.

Holidays Marking the Beginning of Each Eighth

Kolada: The winter solstice, the shortest day of the year, and the start of a new year.

Svi: The coldest time of the year, halfway between the winter solstice and the spring equinox.

Noruz: The spring equinox, the start of spring.

Keva: A celebration of those yet to be, held halfway between the spring equinox and the summer solstice. More babies are conceived at Keva than at any other time of the year.

Tirga: The summer solstice, the longest day of the year, the halfway point of a year.

Heli: The hottest time of the year, halfway between the summer solstice and the autumn equinox. Ilarians are not fond of the heat and sometimes use "Heli" as a cussword.

Plono: The autumn equinox, the start of autumn.

Sashi: A celebration of those who have passed, held halfway between the fall equinox and the winter solstice.

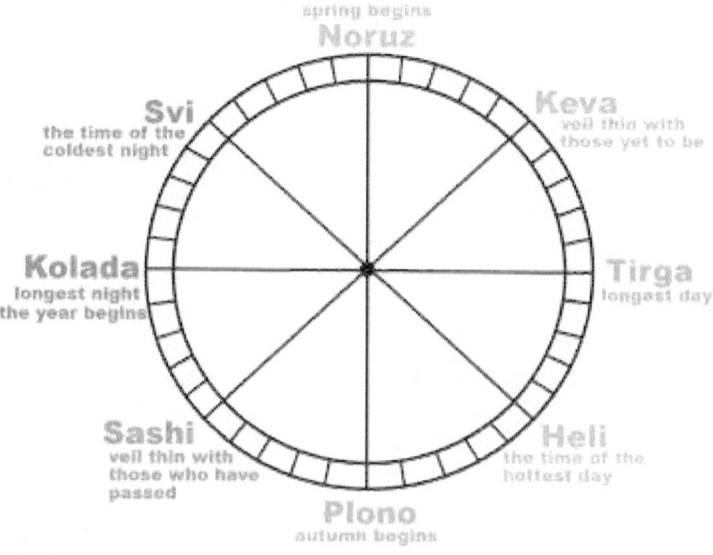

spring begins
Noruz

Svi
the time of the
coldest night

Keva
veil thin with
those yet to be

Kolada
longest night
the year begins

Tirga
longest day

Sashi
veil thin with
those who have
passed

Heli
the time of the
hottest day

Plono
autumn begins

The Twelve Nichnas

Bisu: These low grasslands at the eastern entrance to Ilari supply coveted beef and cows' milk to Ilarians.

Eds: These dry hills leading up to the mountains are sparsely populated with independent-minded goat herders.

Gruen: The fertile soil along the river makes for easy farming of fruits and vegetables and makes Gruen home to one of the two more densely populated areas outside of Pilk.

Faroo: This flood-prone nichna in the rivers bend struggles during heavy rains, but is known for fishing and the boating prowess of its residents.

K'ba: This drought-stricken nichna has survived by becoming home to artists, entertainers, and those seeking more freedom of choice. It is also a playground for the richest Ilarians and boasts a densely populated area known for its spectacular food and lodging.

Kir: Ilari's oldest farming region nestles between Pilk and Lev and grows specialty items for the connoisseurs in both of its neighboring nichnas.

Lev: This nichna is home to the realm's famed vineyards and supplies Ilarians with wine, their most important beverage. It also leads the fashion scene and sparks trends within the realm.

Pilk: As the informal capital of Ilari, Pilk is home to the Svadlu headquarters, most of the institutes of higher learning, and much of the commerce in the realm. The ruling prince of Pilk coordinates cooperation among the twelve ruling princes. The Pilk Palace outshines any other building in Ilari.

Scrud: Rain-deprived Scrud is the poorest and least populated of the nichnas and the most lacking in natural resources. Most Scrudites survive by taking menial jobs in adjoining Bisu or K'ba.

Tolo: Home to the highest mountains in Ilari, independent Tolovians mine for ore, produce lumber, and serve as a gateway to the even higher mountains to the north.

Vinx: With incredibly flat land sitting above cliffs, the high plains of Vinx provide the wheat, oats, rye, and barley that are the staples of an Ilarian's diet.

Zur: As the only nichna inside of Ilari's large central forest, Zur shares the woods with occupants of the Open Forest including the Velka, the reczavy, and scrounger Scrudites.

Map of Ilari

Meet the Ilarians in this Book

Aliz: Ryalgar's grandmother
Celestine: Ryalgar's sister
Coral: Ryalgar's sister
Davor: Coral's husband
Ewalina: an older luski who mentors Coral
Firuza: an astronomer
Gypsum: Ryalgar's sister
Hana: an ambitious Velka from Pilk
Idris: a Velka from Eds, Hana's friend
Iolite: Ryalgar's sister
Joli: a Velka oomrusher, Ryalgar's friend
Kazimir: chief commander of the Svadlu
Markita: Ryalgar's mother
Natia: a Velka from Lev, Hana's friend
Nevik: a Prince of Pilk, Ryalgar's secret lover
Nikolo: a long-eye from Gruen
Olivine: Ryalgar's sister
Ryalgar: (Ree-al-gar) the oldest of seven sisters, named for the mineral we call Realgar
Salmo: a helpful Edser
Sulphur: Ryalgar's sister
Votto: Coral and Davor's son
Yasen: Ryalgar's father
Yarnya: an ancient Velka oomrusher
Zirab: a former Mongolian captive

www.ingramcontent.com/pod-product-compliance
Lightning Source LLC
Chambersburg PA
CBHW022012170626
46808CB00001B/367